LIAR LIAR

Recent Titles by Deborah Nicholson from Severn Hous

The Kate Carpenter Series

HOUSE REPORT
EVENING THE SCORE
SINS OF THE MOTHER
FLIRTING WITH DISASTER

Books should be returned or renewed by the
last date stamped above

LIAR LIAR

Deborah Nicholson

This first world edition published in Great Britain 2006 by
SEVERN HOUSE PUBLISHERS LTD of
9–15 High Street, Sutton, Surrey SM1 1DF.
This first world edition published in the USA 2006 by
SEVERN HOUSE PUBLISHERS INC of
595 Madison Avenue, New York, N.Y. 10022.

British Library Cataloguing in Publication Data

Nicholson, Deborah, 1961-
    Liar, liar
    1.   Women theatrical managers - Fiction
    2.   Arson investigation - Fiction
    3.   Detective and mystery stories
    I.   Title
    813.6 [F]

    ISBN-13: 9780-7278-6360-7
    ISBN-10: 0-7278-6360-6

*This book is dedicated to a few of the people who give so freely of their time;
I am in awe of their generosity.*

*Joe Grassi, my favourite fire captain and arson advisor,
Daryl Penner, my favourite dentist and medical advisor,
Allan Radke, my favourite lawyer and legal advisor.*

And in loving memory of my favourite former smoker, my uncle Brian Warren.

*A charitable donation has been made in the name of this novel to the
Calgary Firefighters Museum.*

Typeset by Palimpsest Book Production Ltd.,
Polmont, Stirlingshire, Scotland.
Printed and bound in Great Britain by
MPG Books Ltd., Bodmin, Cornwall.

JUNE

The Beginning

*I*t had been dark and quiet. The sun had set and the construction site had been empty for a couple of hours now. Another
cardboard condominium complex. All the same, like Christmas
cookies cut from the same cutter. No imagination, no design
and no quality. And no matter where they were built, they were
bought up in record time. In ten years, when the construction
flaws all came to the fore, windows were leaking and prices
plummeting, people's lives would be ruined. And it didn't
matter what city it was, there were more and more of these
going up. It was almost like a public service, wiping a couple
of these off the face of the earth. And it would pay off in so
many ways. Another ugly architectural nightmare gone, another
useless human being gone with it. The news would be popping
tomorrow, lighting up this little berg like it hadn't been lit up
in years. Nothing like this every happened here. A public service
and a self service all rolled up into one nice package.

So here they had been, the fire-starter and the unconscious
body on the floor. The mesh netting that had been wrapped
around the unconscious man to move him onto the site was
untangled from his heavy limbs and put in the backpack, and
a hammer and a couple of nails were taken out. The circuit
box was turned off and then a couple of nails were pounded
into the electrical wiring running to the first outlet beside the
box. Then, just to make sure there had been enough of a fire
load, a bunch of newspaper was stuffed around the wire. The
body was dragged to where the fire should start and for good
measure a couple of paint cans were pulled over too, and the
lids popped off. This was the first time, the first fire, and every-

1

*thing had to work, everything had to be just right. So every-
thing was moved close by to take the most advantage of the
heat and flames that would be created. When everything was
satisfactory, the circuits had been turned back on and the fire-
starter left the site. But not too far away. Part of the pay-off
would be to watch what happened next.*

*This had been the first. But it would not be the last. It had
been exciting. More exciting than anyone could ever imagine.
And the pay-off would be very rewarding, in so many ways.
Yes, there would be more.*

*It had become like an addiction. An addiction to the flame
and an addiction to the fame. Until it had brought the fire-
starter to this place, here and now, sipping coffee and fondly
reminiscing about that first job while waiting to see the first
signs of flame from this latest one.*

*The flames broke through the roof of the building and leapt
toward the stars. That was when the alarm was called in. Nobody
had noticed it before that; the security guard was sleeping in
his truck and there was no one else on the site at this time of
night. The Fire Department was there within three minutes, but
by that time the flames were tearing through the wooden building
and climbing over sixty feet into the air. The Fire Captain had
talked to the District Chief and he in turn had called in a second
alarm and three more engines were on their way. The firefighters
in attendance were hosing down nearby buildings, trying to keep
the flames from leaping across the street and starting the houses
on the north side of the street on fire. An emergency-response
unit unloaded more gear, bottles of water for the firemen, extra
oxygen bottles, first aid until the paramedics arrived.*

*It was a beautiful sight to watch. Standing with the rest of
the crowds, held back by a barrier of police officers. The crowd
jumped as little mini-explosions went off, sending flames
shooting even higher into the air. It could have been chemi-
cals, or electrical, but it was thrilling. The hair on the back
of the neck stood up, hands were clenched into fists and nails
dug into palms, but the face remained calm and didn't break
out into a huge grin, like it wanted to. The fire was beautiful,
if you could ignore the devastation the flames were leaving in
their wake, and not wanting to be noticed, the fire-starter had
to maintain that horrified look the other onlookers shared. But*

2

fire was enthralling, like a campfire when you were a kid, or a fireplace on a cold winter's afternoon. You couldn't help but sit and watch it. Stare at it. Lose yourself in it. The other fire trucks were approaching and it was time to go. The police and the arson investigators did like to search the crowds on the scene, just in case the fire-starter was hanging around to watch the results. The fire was out of control and the job was done well. The fire-starter turned and walked away, just another passer-by who had stopped to check out all the excitement and was now going home. A normal person that no one would even remember seeing in an hour or so. One day it would be nice to stay, nice to see it burn to the ground, see the job through.

We were in the kitchen, which is where we always spent our time at Sam's place, either in the kitchen or sitting around the dining-room table. She was a caterer and food was at the heart of her house. I was at the breakfast bar, sitting on one of the stools with a cup of coffee. Cam and Sam were chopping up vegetables for a salad. We were just waiting for Ryan to get home so we could start the barbecue. The TV was on in the background, with the sound muted, but something caught my attention. I grabbed for the remote when one of the local stations broke into the afternoon talk show with one of those 'live and on the scene' updates. I turned the volume up and everyone stopped talking and turned to watch the television.

'We interrupt our regularly scheduled program to bring you this breaking news.'

The station logo flashed on and I noticed the kitchen grew silent as my friends had stopped chopping and were staring up at the TV.

'City fire crews are responding to a two-alarm fire at the MacKay Corner Condo units. This station's Geneva Arnold is on the scene with the story.'

The camera angle switched to the scene, where a young woman stood facing the camera, looking energized by the action at the scene.

'Good evening, and thanks, Jim. We were here for what is supposed to be the grand opening of this first stage of re-development of this area. Instead, it has turned into what could be the largest fire Calgary has ever seen . . .'

3

'Wow, look at those flames,' I said, not realizing Sam was staring up at the television still.

'That's Ryan's truck,' she said. 'I can't watch this.'

'I'll turn it off.'

'No, don't. You watch it for me. Come get me if anything happens.'

She took her coffee cup and went and sat on the deck outside the kitchen.

I turned to Cam. 'I didn't even think . . .'

'I know,' he said. 'Katie, we can't really ever understand what she goes through every time he's late getting home or when there's a big fire.'

'He'll be OK.'

'Yes, he will.'

And then we both turned back to the television and we watched the fire all night long, as it slowly burned out. I took a sweater out for Sam when the sun set and tried to get her to eat dinner, but she just stared into the river well into the early hours of the next morning.

The next morning, we went out to restock the milk and coffee we had been up all night drinking, and we decided to take a quick walk past the site of the fire. There were still firefighters there, and news crews from all the local stations. I looked across the street and thought I noticed a familiar face. He held his head low to avoid being accidentally seen, but was watching the scene out of the corner of his eye, as a pretty auburn-haired woman with smart-looking glasses ran her fingers through her hair before her cameraman gave her the count-down and she was on the air reporting today's events. There were arson investigators in the background, trying to track down where the fire had come from, looking for any obvious signs that would point them in the right direction. But they wouldn't find any and it would take them weeks to sift through everything and finally track it down, she was telling her viewers. Just like all the other fires. Some of the other fire-fighters were doing a safety check, looking for hot spots. It was one of them, using a crowbar to flip over a pile of shingles, who found the body. Even from across the street we could tell it was a body because of the shape, two arms, two legs, a torso and a head, but that was all that distinguished it as ever being human.

'Over here,' the firefighter yelled, and his captain came running.

The police chased all the news crews away, and then started moving the barricades back further. This fire had just turned into something much more serious. This would definitely speed up the work the investigators were doing. And it would bring the police detectives down here too. Things were about to get very exciting and the red-headed reporter was busy arguing with the police officer who was trying to move her off the scene.

I turned to Cam, squeezing his hand, overwhelmed by the emotion.

'Cam, isn't that . . .' I turned to point to where I had seen the familiar thatch of blonde hair, but it was gone.

'Who?' Cam asked.

'Never mind.'

'Do you see Ryan anywhere?'

'No, we'd better get back in case he's on his way home.'

But we stood and watched as the female reporter raced by the police officers, trying to get to where the commotion was, disregarding what the ash and soot was doing to her tan suede boots and lovely floral skirt. Her eyes were ablaze as she waved at her cameraman to start recording and she tried to continue her on-air narrative.

There's a woman who loves her job, I thought, as the police tried to pull her back behind the barricades.

Tuesday

'Sam's Catering,' I said, picking up the phone while Sam was upstairs with her screaming, temper-tantrum-throwing child.

'I want my daddy!!' the petulant voice screamed from upstairs.

'Is Sam available?' the voice said.

'Sorry, she's busy at the moment. Can I take a message?'

'Yes, I'm returning her call. About an event scheduled for next month.'

I grabbed the pen and notepad beside the phone. 'Your name, please?'

'Jones.'

'First name?'

'Mister.'

'Sorry?'

'That's M-I-S-T-E-R.' He laughed. I wasn't sure if he was laughing at his joke or my incompetence.

'I hear you can abbreviate it too,' I teased, forgetting for a moment I was on Sam's business line. But I was rewarded with a soft chuckle.

'Sam has my number. Thank you very much for your time.'

I heard a door slam upstairs just as I hung up the phone. I wrote down the name and slid the notepad back in its place just as Sam came storming down the stairs.

'Never have children. Especially stubborn ones.'

'Oh, right, and should we talk about where she got that from?'

'Excuse me?' Sam asked, eyebrow raised, ready for a fight.

'I mean, would you like some coffee?' I asked, quickly turning around and grabbing the pot. Cam had gone to work but I didn't have to be anywhere for another few hours and I had opted to stay with my friend. Sam's husband Ryan had been fighting the big condo fire all day yesterday and crashed for a few hours at the fire hall last night, before returning to the scene today. Sam didn't say anything out loud, but she didn't have to, I knew she was worried sick about him. The fire might be out, but the clean-up could be just as dangerous and she was going to be on edge until he finally walked through the front door. And I was going to stay with her until he did. No matter how grumpy she got. After all, she put up with my moods and dramas.

'Who called?' Sam asked. She was still sounding grumpy, but at least her aim was turned away from me at the moment.

'Mr Jones,' I said. 'No first name given.'

Sam laughed. Thank God for that.

'We think that mister is his first name.'

'Huh?'

'I first ran into Mr Jones back about fifteen years ago when I was working at Benny's downtown. His company had an account with us and he would call to book all the catered events and stuff like that. He kept telling us he worked in the mailroom at an oil company and that he drove a Volkswagen Beetle. And then one day he came in with a client. Let's just say his office was considerably higher up than the mailroom and had a great view. His Volkswagen turned out to be a BMW. I can see the confusion, though, they're both European cars.'

'And the mister part?' I asked.

'That's what he liked to say to the girls that answered the phones. They were instructed to take a thorough message, first name and last name, telephone, company name, all that stuff; and he knew it threw them off and made me laugh.'

'So what is his first name?'

'Oh, I have no idea,' she admitted. 'I guess I just never thought to ask.'

'Or you know and just won't tell me.'

'Well, there is that whole caterer–client confidentiality, you know.'

'And he still uses you for catering?' I asked.

'Yes, he does.'

'You must have quite a reputation with that oil company by now.'

'He doesn't work for the oil company any longer, Kate.'

'Oh, what's he do now?'

She hesitated for a moment, looking me in the eyes and taking a deep breath before she answered.

'What?' I asked.

'He's in real estate with his wife.'

'Mr Jones? Rob Jones? You traitor!'

'What do you mean?' she asked.

'Our real-estate agent is your client? You referred Cam to him, didn't you? You went behind my back and set up my boyfriend with a real-estate agent. Do you know what a living hell this has made my life?'

'Kate, Mr Jones is not the only real-estate agent in town.

If I hadn't recommended him, don't you think Cam might have found someone else?'

'You're supposed to be my friend,' I said. 'Why didn't you give me his name?'

'Because you didn't ask. And yet your building is falling down around you and you still didn't ask if I knew anyone,' she said. 'And if I had suggested him, given you his card, you would have misplaced it or forgotten about it or something.'

'Well, we've got a few months still, before we have to get out of the building.'

'Do you know how long it takes to close a sale?' she asked. 'You're going to be camping in our backyard because you don't have a place to live.'

'We are not.'

'Besides, instead of looking at this as a big and dramatic ending, why not look at it as a beginning? You and Cam get to start your life for real, in a brand-new place . . . together.'

I really didn't have a good answer to that one, but luckily I was saved by a weepy four-year-old, calling down from her bedroom.

'Mommy?'

'Yes?'

'I just wanted to tell you I love you,' Bonnie called down.

'That's nice, dear, now keep cleaning up your toys.'

'How do you resist that tearful little voice?' I asked, wanting to run upstairs and hug her.

'I resist it because she is the world's greatest little faker. She was hoping that if she said she loved me that I would forgive her and let her out of there before she was finished cleaning up and then she could go next door and play with her friend.'

'Sam, she's only four. She's not old enough to think all that up.'

'Hah! Talk to me when you've had kids,' she said. 'You have no idea what they are capable of.'

Just then the front door opened and a very smoky-smelling Ryan walked through. Sam got up and poured him a coffee, as he came into the kitchen.

'Hi, honey,' she said, handing him the coffee. 'Tough day at the office?'

'Woman, I need food, I need a bath and I need clean sheets to sleep on,' he joked.

'I'll get right on that,' she said sarcastically, but rushed to the fridge and started pulling out leftovers.

But Ryan stopped her, setting his coffee cup on the counter and grabbing her arm, pulling her into his arms.

'But first of all, I need you,' he said.

They kissed as if they hadn't seen each other in ten years, and didn't show any signs of breaking apart soon. I felt my cheeks grow hot and definitely felt like I was no longer needed in this room.

'That's OK,' I said, getting my backpack and tossing it over my shoulder. 'I have to get to work anyway.'

I let myself out quietly, as he was leading her up the stairs, still locked in a tight embrace.

It was a beautiful day outside, a sneak preview of what I hoped summer would be, and since it was still early I decided to walk down to the Plex, rather than take a cab or a bus. And I certainly didn't want to break up this big reunion and ask Sam or Ryan to drive me in. I work at the Calgary Arts Complex's Centenary Theatre, Calgary's largest live-theatre company. I love the backwards lifestyle, working nights, sleeping days, as it fits my late-night personality. I also love the excitement of live theatre and the interesting personalities it brought into my life. I'd been at the Centenary Theatre for about three years and my entire circle of friends seemed to stem from there now, my boyfriend Cam was an HVAC technician in the mainte-nance department, my friend Sam ran a catering business and was frequently catering events at the Plex, and her husband Ryan was just a few short blocks away at fire hall number one. Like Robin Hood, I had a loyal band of thieves working for me, and we tried not to get in trouble as much as be a merry band and have a good time. They were as quirky and diverse a group as could be imagined. And Cam and I were trying to find a new home, a place to start our lives together. Which was amazing because less than a year ago I had broken up with him and thought he was gone from my life forever. I always thought his greatest feature was the fact that he would never let me push him away, no matter how hard I tried.

So I pulled my backpack on and cut down to the pathway along the river and followed it down to 4th Avenue. I stopped at the Starbucks and filled up my go-cup with a hazelnut latte and then wandered slowly down the street, looking in all my favourite windows as I went. It was funny how much I loved looking at furniture and dreamed of how I was going to set up my first house, but I couldn't get past the mental block I seemed to have about buying that first house. Urban Barn had a wonderful big overstuffed leather sofa in the window that was exactly what I'd been dreaming of. I made a quick detour inside the store to write down the model number, so Cam and I could look it up on the Internet later. I knew he loved that butter-soft distressed leather look, and as long as I could get a big over-sized armchair in some sort of coordinating print, I decided I could live with the leather. Actually, that look was kind of growing on me but I wasn't ready to admit that to him yet.

I stopped in and bought two Donairs to go at Ouzo, the new Greek restaurant, and tucked them in my backpack, hoping the sauce didn't leak out like last time. I would smell like garlic and onions for a week if it did. I made it down to 8th Avenue and then headed up into the Plus 15 to get to the Plex. My arms were pink from the sun and I didn't have any sunscreen in my backpack. I stopped at the drug store in TD Square and picked up a small tube to carry with me, and then finished my trek fifteen feet above street level, to the Performing Arts Complex. The Plus 15 system was wonderful in the winter, closed-in corridors built fifteen feet above the street, heated and enclosed to protect us from the cold and winter bluster. But they were nice to escape the summer heat too, being air-conditioned and several degrees cooler than the streets outside.

I crossed over MacLeod Trail and into the Plex. I pulled out my keys and let myself into one of the stairwells, cutting from the front of the building to the back of the building and let myself out at the stage door.

'Hi, Nick,' I greeted the security supervisor. 'Do you know where Cam is?'

'I'm pretty sure he's in his office,' Nick said. 'You want to go down?'

'I brought lunch.'

'I'll page him and let him know you're on your way,' Nick

said, while I let myself onto the freight elevator and pulled the door closed.

My keys were only good for certain public areas and the theatre I managed. Cam was way down in a sub-sub-basement somewhere and I couldn't even get halfway to where he was, so I had to have him paged to meet me at the freight elevator and take me the rest of the way. I reached the bottom floor and pulled the door open, to find my very own personal knight in shining armour waiting for me. I was overcome by the sight of him, and the emotional reunion that I had witnessed between Sam and Ryan, and I jumped into his arms, wrapping my arms tightly around him.

'Is everything OK?' he asked, concerned about my exuberance.

'Everything is fine. Ryan made it home safe and sound and I just realized I hadn't told you I loved you yet today.'

'Katie, I know you love me and I love you too,' he said, setting me down gently, as I finally loosened my grip. He pulled the elevator door closed and turned back to me. 'Is that the only reason you're here?'

'Nope, I have a surprise for you,' I said, following him to what we jokingly called his office. It was a beat-up desk and several filing cabinets, surrounding by chests and a couple of chairs with more duct tape than upholstery on them. The powers that be didn't waste a bunch of money on the maintenance department until you went upstairs and saw the director's office. But Cam didn't seem to mind, since he spent most of his time responding to calls anyway.

'A surprise? Should I lock the door?'

I rolled my eyes at him and set my backpack on his desk.

'I made lunch,' I said, pulling out the takeout containers.

'Oh, that smells so good,' he said, clearing a spot on his desk for us to eat.

'Ouzo's special Donair,' I said. 'Extra garlic sauce today, I think, from the aroma.'

'That's OK, the only one I'm planning on kissing today is you,' he said, opening up his container and tucking a napkin in his lap.

'Well, I still haven't heard back from George Clooney, so I might want to keep my options open.' But I couldn't resist

11

the smell, my mouth was watering. I peeled back the foil and bit into the sandwich.

Cam laughed at me and handed me a napkin, as sauce and tomatoes dribbled all over his desk.

'Well, thanks for working so hard on lunch, it's really good. Your cooking talents have definitely improved since you've met me,' he teased.

'Why, because I don't always stop at Subway now?' I laughed. 'I did know there were other takeout restaurants out there, you know, it's just that Subway was the closest.'

'Yeah? I counted a hundred and fifty Subway bags when I was cleaning out the kitchen.'

'You counted them?'

'A hundred and fifty, Katie,' he repeated.

'Cam, I'm not shocked that there were a hundred and fifty, I'm shocked that you counted them.'

'Well, if I didn't count them how could I tease you about them later? But a hundred and fifty?'

'I've lived there for six years now, things pile up.'

'It's no wonder you had no room to keep food, between the takeout bags, the disposable chopsticks, the plastic forks and the plum-sauce and soy-sauce packages!'

'You didn't throw those out, did you?' I asked, feigning shock.

'I donated them to charity. Some other poor person who can't cook and hasn't found a boyfriend like me yet will benefit from your years of hoarding.'

'You are a smart-ass, you know?' I asked.

'It's the price you pay for making me clean out that kitchen and then having the building go condo two weeks later.'

'Yeah, about that . . .'

'Katie, I didn't mean to bring that up,' he said. 'Honestly, it was just a joke.'

'No, but I did mean to bring it up,' I said. 'Eventually.'

'It's OK.'

'No, it's not. Look, I know I'm having a really hard time giving up my old life. And I know I'm being fairly childish about looking at houses. And I'm trying so hard not to be, but it just seems to happen.'

'So this isn't the big conversation about how you're going to become a changed woman?'

'God, no,' I laughed. 'I was just going to tell you how much I appreciate you putting up with me.'

'Oh, well, you're welcome.'

'Are you disappointed that I'm not going to reform my wicked ways?'

'A little. But on the other hand, I would probably be more suspicious if you just started behaving and getting along with our realtor.'

'I wish I could promise you that I will be better,' I said. 'But something just comes over me when we're looking at those bungalows.' An involuntary shudder ran down my spine as I said those words.

'Yeah, if I wanted boring I'd be dating someone else, wouldn't I?'

'Yes, you would. But you wouldn't be bored for long because I'd kill you if you were dating someone else!'

'All right, I understand the rules now.'

I took the last bite of my Donair and crumpled up the foil, putting it inside the takeout container with my pile of soiled napkins. I slid it across the desk for Cam to dispose of.

'I guess I should get upstairs and check out my office. I haven't been there in three weeks, after all. Who knows what is awaiting me.'

'Well, I'm sure you'll muddle through. I'm betting Graham is up there already, halfway through whatever you have to do.'

'It's a nice thought,' I said, remembering my overachieving assistant. 'But Graham's auditioning today. I'm going to actually have to do most of the work myself.'

'My goodness, do you remember how?'

'To talk so disrespectfully to me when I've just brought you a nice home-made lunch.'

'Home-made?'

'Well, I'm sure whoever made it had a home.' I laughed, standing up and pulling my backpack on. 'Can you see me back out of this maze?'

'I need to go do rounds anyways. Might as well now as later.'

He tidied up his desk and grabbed his keys, opening the door and leading me to the stairwell.

'Stairs?' I asked. 'What's wrong with the elevators?'

'Stairs are better for you, especially after that big lunch.'

13

'It's a good thing you're so darned cute,' I said, heading through the door he had opened for me and starting up the first flight of stairs. Three flights later we were at the stage door and I gave him a quick kiss as he headed west and I east.

As predicted, I was alone in my office, no youthful exuberant assistant to brighten up a couple of hours of paperwork. I didn't realize how much I had grown used to having him around until he wasn't there and I heard my voice echo through the empty office. And then I realized I was talking out loud to myself. I turned on the speaker that piped in whatever was happening on the stage. I was rewarded by the sound of a rehearsal pianist running through some warm-ups for a lovely soprano voice. There, a little noise helped me get more focused. I made a pot of coffee, lit a cigarette, watered my plants and sat down to a list of memos from production about show schedules, rehearsal times and upcoming summer events.

I heard the door open in the hallway and turned to see who was coming – since Graham was on stage and I had just left Cam, I couldn't imagine who else was around at this time of day. I was surprised that it was a face I had never seen before.

'Hi,' he greeted me, coming into the office.

'Hi, can I help you?' I asked, looking up at the pleasant-looking middle-aged man standing in front of me.

'I'm Frank Kotkas. I'm going to be working around here for the next couple of months. We're re-keying all the doors with the new electronic system.'

'Nice to meet you, Frank. I'm Kate Carpenter, house manager here,' I said, shaking his hand. 'Just like usual, though, no one mentioned you would be around.'

'Yeah, well, memos get lost. Look, I'm just starting out by recording the door codes and making sure they match up to my plans. Do you mind if I poke around the theatre a bit?'

'Not at all. The only thing to avoid is the auditorium until the auditions are over.'

'No problem,' he said, turning to go. 'Well, I'll probably see you around, then.'

'Stop in for coffee any time,' I said. 'We're open practically twenty-four hours a day around here.'

'Thanks,' he said, stopping to write down the code on my door before moving on down the hallway.

I pulled out my calendar and wrote in the shows that were scheduled and pencilled in the tentative dates. Then I pushed that aside, as I heard Graham's voice on stage, laughing with one of the other actors. Their voices grew louder, as I pictured them walking closer to the stage.

Graham had started working for me when he was still in high school. He had approached me after attending a student matinee and asked how he could become an usher. I could never remember if he had always wanted to be an actor and thought this would be a good first step, or fell in love with the theatre that day and just wanted to be closer to the action – and it didn't matter. Graham was now a high-school graduate and determined to become the greatest actor the world had ever known. He was serious in his goals and took any job he could, professional or non-, just to get the experience and make contacts. So far, he had mostly done some minor children's theatre and a few community productions, but he was one professional credit away from getting his Equity card. I was more proud of him than I would ever let on, knowing how hard he worked on his singing, dancing and acting, and even at the gym, to present the best package he could. And now he was auditioning for Rolfe in *The Sound of Music* and I had to be there.

I locked up the office and climbed another flight of stairs, up to the second balcony. I let myself in the door, patiently waiting for the first to close behind me until I opened the second. I didn't want a big beam of light shining down on the stage because Graham would know I was sneaking in to watch him, and I didn't want to distract him from his performance. Once I was secretly and safely in, I pulled an usher chair as far forward as I dared, and sat down, waiting patiently to see my protégé.

I paid the price for my subterfuge too, listening to an endless parade of six- to twelve-year-olds audition for the von Trapp children. I swear if I heard the song 'Tomorrow' from *Annie* one more time I was going to scream. And then finally they moved on from the children to the older characters, hearing several singers for what I assumed to be the roll of Captain von Trapp before finally Graham's group of potential Rolfes was called. Graham was third in line and the first two singers were quite good. I held my breath as Graham handed his music

15

to the pianist, planted himself centre stage and opened his mouth to sing.

I snuck out afterward, finished my preliminary schedule layout and then closed up shop for the day. I didn't want to stress myself unduly after the time off I'd had and I was hoping that tomorrow Graham would be able to help me out, not so much with the work but with the company and some distraction. Plus I knew Cam was home and my mouth was watering at the thought of a night at home alone with him, a good home-cooked meal, and hopefully no outside distractions afterwards. I hopped the C-train and hurried home, letting myself in and being rewarded with the sights and sounds of my man in the kitchen.

'Hi, honey,' I said, kissing his cheek and dropping my backpack off in the closet.

'You're home early.'

'Yeah, I wasn't into working as much as I thought I was. Besides, the thought of you at home was an irresistible siren's call.'

'Oh, the power I wield.'

'Well, don't get all cocky about it.'

He poured a glass of wine and handed it to me. 'Well, I'm afraid I'm going to bring your mood down a bit.'

'Oh, what now?'

'Graham just called. He didn't get the part.'

'Oh no!'

'Yeah, he sounded pretty broken up by it. But he said not to worry, he'd be in like usual tomorrow.'

'Oh, the poor kid,' I said. 'He did such a good job, too.'

'You watched him?' Cam asked.

'Yeah, I kind of snuck in and watched his audition.'

'Well, it's the life of an actor,' Cam said. 'He knows what he's in for.'

'And he's young. I imagine by tomorrow he'll have bounced right back. Or at least I hope he will.'

Cam held up his glass, waiting for me to join him. 'Here's to Graham, and the next audition,' he said.

I clinked glasses with him and then took a sip of the wine. 'Hey, did you know they were re-keying all the locks at the Plex?' I asked.

16

'Yep.'

'Did I know?'

'I don't know, I might have mentioned it. They're switching to an electronic system, so you'll just have a little fob that is programmed to allow you access to the doors you have authorization for. I think there's an electrician coming around that they've contracted to do the work.'

'I met him today. Frank something.'

'Frank Kotkas,' Cam told me. 'He's from Moose Jaw. My dad knew his family and recommended him.'

'Not enough electricians in Calgary?'

'It's booming here. You can't hire a tradesman to save your life.'

'Oh, well that was nice of your dad to recommend your friend.'

'More like my family's friend. I probably haven't seen him since we were eight years old. But I'll have to make sure I say hi to him tomorrow or Dad will be all over me.'

'We could have him over or something,' I offered.

'Here? At construction central? I think our entertaining days are over until we get set up in a new place.'

'You're not nagging, are you?'

'Mentioning, Katie, not nagging.'

'Okay.'

'Well, I imagine we'll be seeing a lot of Frank this summer. This project is going to take some time. We'll have lots of opportunity to get together. Are you hungry?'

'Tired. Can we just order in and sit out on the deck tonight?'

'Your wish is my command,' he said, opening the oven and revealing a pizza box, nice and toasty warm.

'How do you do that?' I laughed.

Wednesday

'Do you love me, Katie?'
'You know I love you.'

'If you really love me, then just get out of the car.'

'I don't need to get out of the car. This isn't the one.'

'How do you know?' he asked, his voice showing his exasperation.

'I can just tell. I mean, look at it.'

'I'm looking at it.'

'Don't you see?'

'What, Katie? What don't I see?'

'It's a freaking bungalow in the suburbs.'

'Yes?'

'Cam, I'm not a freaking-bungalow-in-the-suburbs kind of girl.'

'No, you're a freaking-insane kind of girl.'

'It's just not what I want.'

'Neither were any of the last ten we've seen. Ranchers, bungalows, split-levels, condos, town houses, duplexes and even a penthouse. But come on, the realtor is waiting, he's booked an appointment, we're going to be grown-ups and go see this house.'

'I don't want to.'

'Do it for me.'

I stared up at him for a minute or two and finally heaved a deep sigh and opened the car door. How could I not do it for him? And he knew it.

'I'll make you pay for this,' I whispered, as I stormed past him and up the walk.

'Oh, I am fully aware of that fact,' he said, following me.

I put on my fake smile, which I'm pretty sure our realtor was already on to, and shook his hand.

'Hi, Rob, how are you doing today?' I smiled.

Robert Jones was a middle-aged and very patient realtor who had built a great business with his wife. She had started out with us, taking us around to five houses the first week we had contacted them. She had then turned us over to her husband after I had been through those first five houses. According to Cam I had a bit of an attitude problem when it came to buying a house. According to Mrs Jones her husband was much better with selective customers such as myself. Luckily, Rob seemed to be an endless fount of patience, because to the best of my knowledge, I hadn't adjusted my attitude at all.

'I'm doing very well, Kate,' he smiled at me. 'Looking forward to showing you the house. I'm pretty sure Cam will quite like it and you'll be able to find at least thirty things you hate about it.'

'Only thirty? Well, you're doing better at selection now. Didn't I get up to fifty on the last house we viewed?'

'I stopped you at thirty-five,' he laughed. 'But I'm sure you could have got to fifty if we'd let you go.'

'Katie!' Cam hissed at me.

'It's OK,' Rob assured him. 'I've dealt with thousands of new homeowners and a lot of them have this kind of trepidation. It's become a challenge for me to put Kate together with something she likes.'

'Good luck with that. I'm thinking we're going to be living in boxes on the street corner soon.'

'No, honey, Sam said she's put up a tent in her backyard for us, so there's nothing to worry about.'

'We'll get it taken care of,' Rob assured Cam.

'Yeah,' I said. 'We've got an extension on the move out.'

'We've got two months, Kate. Two months while there is construction going on all around us. I have to say I'm hoping we're not going to have to stay there the whole two months.'

'Well, yeah, but we want to find exactly the right kind of place,' I said, my halo slipping.

'We'll find it,' Rob assured us. 'Shall we check this one out?'

Mr Jones opened the door and led us through the house. And he was wrong; there were only twenty things I could find wrong with the house. And I know that for sure because I was writing them down in my little notebook. I had a full record of everything I hated about every house we had looked at.

After we'd been all through the house, Cam walked me back to our car in stony silence and we drove back downtown.

'I'm going straight to the Plex.'

'That's fine with me.'

He finally pulled into his parking spot and got out of the car. I knew better than to wait for him to come around and open my door for me when he was in this kind of mood.

'Let's go have a coffee?' I suggested.

'I've got to get to work.'

'Cam, you've got half an hour,' I said. 'Please?'

He stared at me for a minute and then gave in, turning to walk to Grounds Zero, the little coffee shop at the end of the block. I scurried along behind him, trying to keep up. At least he stopped and held the door open for me, rather than letting it slam in my face, as I had been afraid he might do.

'Latte?' I asked him, as he headed for an empty table.

'Double.'

I went to the counter and Gus, the owner, came over.

'Kate, how goes the house-hunting?'

'Two double lattes, please.'

'That good, huh?'

'Yeah, we just don't seem to have the same vision. Cam wants a house in the suburbs and I don't want to leave my loft.'

'You do realize that they are tearing your building down around you?'

'I had noticed the jackhammers at six o'clock this morning,' I admitted.

'So what are you going to do?'

'Close my eyes and pretend it's not happening?' I tried.

Gus chuckled and went off to make our coffee. I crossed the restaurant and joined Cam at the table. He was still uncharacteristically silent.

'Cam?'

'Katie, I know this is hard for you.'

'It is. I don't want to move, they're making me.'

'Yes, they are. Calgary is going condo-crazy and we're the latest victims. But we have to deal with that.'

'I know.'

'But you do know we're never going to find anything if you don't start going in with a better attitude?'

'I don't have an attitude.'

'You go in expecting to hate the house.'

'Oh, that attitude.'

'Yes.'

'Well, Cam, you guys keep taking me to see the same house. Aluminium siding, bungalow, suburbs. That's not me.'

'Well, I'd love a mansion in Mount Royal too, but I don't think we can get pre-approved for a million-dollar mort-gage.'

'I know. I just wanted something different. Something with some character.'

'But you said you didn't want to look at any more condos. If you did, we could find a two-bedroom loft, maybe?'

'No, I don't want another loft, I want my loft. And if we're spending that type of money we need to get a real house, don't you think? Something with a yard and some space to grow?' I said. 'Oh my God, listen to me . . . room to grow? What am I saying? I want my loft and I want all those construc-tion workers to get out.'

'Yes, I agree,' he said. 'But that's not going to happen and you might just have to compromise a little bit on your dream home, unless we win a lottery in the next two weeks.'

'Yeah, I'm not real good at that.'

'Compromise or the lottery?'

'Cam, this is not a time to be light-hearted. This is the time for a nervous breakdown.'

'I know. But you know, I'm a pretty handy kind of guy. I can probably do some renovations and turn these houses into something cute. You just have to have some vision.'

'This is so hard,' I sighed.

'Not as hard as living in a hotel after we get kicked out of the apartment and still don't have a house to live in.'

'That's not going to happen!'

'At this rate, Katie, that is exactly what's going to happen.

We don't just buy a house and then move in. It all takes time and we are running out of time.'

'I know—'

But I was interrupted by the screeching of the fire alarm. Cam and I both looked up into the air, for what I don't know. It was like we expected the alarm to start speaking English and tell us what was going on.

'OK, everyone, please take your stuff and exit the building. Please gather across the street in the parking lot until the fire trucks have cleared the building,' Gus hollered. He was rapidly turning off his machines, while instructing the customers. I grabbed my purse and Cam grabbed our lattes, which Gus had set on the counter just as the alarms started ringing, and we crossed the street with everyone else. I found a seat on the fence of the parking lot. I sipped my coffee and lit a cigarette, then watched two fire trucks pull up to the stage door and several firemen run into the building. I was pretty sure things were OK when I saw several of them walking out of the building, instead of running, and then had it confirmed when one of the firefighters crossed the street and came over toward us. He took off his helmet and I recognized Ryan, who I was surprised to see. I didn't think Sam would let him leave the house for at least a month.

'Hey,' Cam greeted him.

'Hey,' Ryan answered.

A news van came screeching to a stop right in front of us and parked. The reporter got out while the cameraman raised the antennas and loaded up his equipment.

'Hi, guys, I'm Geneva Arnold from E-News,' she smiled.

She was a beautiful woman, auburn hair falling to her shoulders, sparkling green eyes peeking out from behind the glasses she obviously wore to make herself look more intelligent, and that hundred-watt smile that would put Julia Roberts to shame. I noticed both Cam and Ryan stood a little straighter as she made eye contact with both of them.

'Can any of you tell me what's going on here?' she said, still smiling.

'The captain's across the street,' Ryan said. 'You know updates come from him. I'm just a no-comment hoseman.'

The smile immediately left her face and she raced across

the street with her cameraman racing to keep up. I noticed she stopped long enough to fluff her hair before talking to the fire captain.

'You allowed to be here fraternizing with us?' I asked him jokingly.

'The captain said I could give you an update,' he said, wiping the sweat off his brow.

'So what's going on over there? Do I get the night off or not?'

'Just a little fire near the Heritage Theatre,' he said. 'We got it put out with a fire extinguisher. Didn't even have to unroll the hoses.'

'Well, that'll save some clean-up later,' Cam laughed.

Ryan opened his jacket against the heat of the July day and leaned against the fence beside Cam.

'Was the fire in the theatre?'

'In that back hallway that leads down to your theatre.'

'Tin Pan Alley?'

'Yep, that's it. There was a pile of rags that had been used to clean up some gasoline or something and they ignited. It's careless but it happens.'

'What? Nobody around there would leave stuff like that laying around.'

'It's nothing, Kate, somebody was probably taking them outside and got distracted and then almost anything will set them off.'

'But these technicians are all licensed in safety and pyro and stuff. They wouldn't leave anything like that lying around.'

'Well, maybe one of the janitors did. No big deal. We put out the fire and we'll write up a little report and that'll be the end of it.'

'I just think this sounds a little fishy,' I insisted.

'How's the house-hunting going?' Ryan asked, changing the subject.

'Can I go up to my office now?' I asked, ignoring that one altogether.

'Yeah, you can.'

'Say hi to Sam for me,' I said, giving Cam a quick kiss and then racing across the middle of the street before the light changed and the traffic started.

'I can write you up for jaywalking,' Ryan called after me.

I held up my middle finger as a sign of my respect for his nagging, and I raced into the building and up the stairs. I ran down the hall and into my office, surprised to find Graham sitting behind the desk.

'What are you doing in here?' I asked. 'Didn't you hear the fire alarm?'

'Yeah, but it's always a false alarm,' he said. 'No point in leaving.'

'Now that's the kind of attitude that will get you fired.'

'There's nobody in the theatre,' he insisted. 'Just me.'

I stared at him, eyebrow raised in a high arch.

'Really, I checked.'

'Don't let it happen again, Graham,' I said.

'You mean there was a real fire?'

'Yes, there was a real fire.'

'Holy shit. And I missed all the excitement.'

'Not much excitement. It's out and no damage. What are you doing here so early, anyway?'

'Well, I'm not sure if you noticed, Kate, but we've suddenly got a very busy summer ahead of us.'

'Yeah, I've noticed.'

'I mean we've got *The Sound of Music* this week, then we've got that Jann Arden concert and then it's Stampede Week and we've got the lunchtime concerts and two weeks of dance festivals after that. And then rehearsals start for *Fire*, which opens right after Labour Day.'

'I know, Graham. I'm the one who's trying to work out vacation time with Cam. I am reminded every day how busy we have gotten this summer.'

'Well, there's lots of work to be done,' he said. 'So I'm here to do it.'

'Graham, you want to tell me why you're really here this early?'

'You just won't leave it alone, will you?'

'No.'

'I just wanted to get away from home for a while. Mom is just acting all freaky these days. I think it's menopause.'

'Well, that's really supportive of you. You sure she's not just trying to get you to move out? You are the last one left.

24

She might be getting a little anxious to be alone with your dad again . . . all those mid-afternoon romantic interludes?'

'Oh, don't even go there. Yuck. That is my mother you're talking about.'

'Have you thought about finding a place?'

'I did ask her. But she just hugged me and cried and said she never wanted me to leave her.'

'I guess you're still welcome, then.'

'I'm thinking so.'

'Well, if you want my advice, don't ever leave home. Moving is just too stressful.'

'Out with the realtor again this morning?'

'Ugh, yes. Graham, I don't know what comes over me. I get up, I'm in a good mood, I get in the car, have a lovely drive and then I see the house we're supposed to look at and something inside me just goes psycho. I just seem to have this huge block about buying a house.'

'It's just that you're known for having a cute and quirky little place. If you buy a house then you're just like everyone else.'

'I know. But it's the next logical step for Cam and me. I mean, someday we might want to raise a family and things, so we need a house and a yard and all that.'

'Kate, Cam knows you really well. He'll find something you can live with.'

'Cam was barely speaking to me when we left the viewing this morning.'

'It'll all work out,' he insisted. 'Look, after everything else you've been through, how hard is this, really?'

'You try it.'

'No, I like the whole living-at-home thing, thanks. It's cheaper.'

'OK, well I'm going to go and sit in on the rehearsal and see how it's going. You want to come and watch with me?'

'Kate, I'm still a little bitter about all of it, if you don't mind I'll just sit it out.'

I looked at Graham. He was my assistant at the theatre, newly turned nineteen and still wanting to become an actor, as he had been for years. I had thought that once he had finished high school he might find a new dream and head for college. But I should have known better. That's why he was working here, to be around that kind of life, the auditions, the directors, the rehearsals. He had soaked it up and worked any extra shift I had offered him, even coming in on his own time like he had today. Graham used to joke that he was so serious about that that he had a dermatologist on call throughout his teenage years. Though with Graham's incredibly healthy lifestyle, the doctor would not have been needed very often if it had actually been true. Graham worked out and had his hair highlighted monthly, he had a great wardrobe for auditions, he could become almost anyone with an hour's notice. Which is why it surprised me so that he was sitting here, bitter that he hadn't got a part with our latest production. He'd been turned down a million times, like every other actor. What was one more?

'Graham, you auditioned, you lost out. It's the life of an actor. I thought you were OK with this part of it?'

'I know, it's never bothered me before. But then, normally after an audition, I leave the building and never have to see any of these people again. This is different. I run into them every day and I will for the next few weeks.'

'And it bothers you?'

'Yeah, it bothers me. I never thought it would, but it bothers me.'

'OK. You work out your angst and I'll be in the theatre if you need me, OK?'

'OK,' he agreed, as I grabbed my little notebook and headed for the theatre.

I was happily ensconced in one of the back rows, watching the fitful stops and starts of the show. Summer times were usually really slow for us, but with the Jubilee auditorium closed for the year for renovations we were turning out to be much busier than originally anticipated. Cam and I had planned a long, languorous summer of long weekends and perhaps a holiday involving a beach somewhere. But between me working the festival last month and the way the summer schedule here was filling up we were going to be lucky if we got a week of camping in. And then there was the whole house-hunting issue that I was trying to work in around everything else. Something that I was sure I was making more of than need be, but I just couldn't seem to help myself.

26

So I fought this inward battle while Maria taught the children how to sing their Do-Re-Mi's on stage. *The Sound of Music* was being put on by a local company that normally used one of the theatres at the Jubilee Auditorium, but since that venue was closed for renovations, they were forced to use our stage. Graham had auditioned for the part of Rolfe, the young German boy that Liesl was in love with. I was very surprised that my young blond, talented assistant didn't get chosen for the part of the young blond Aryan love interest but who knew what went on in a director's mind. After what seemed like hours, the children knew how to sing their Do-Re-Mi's and we moved on to 'Sixteen Going on Seventeen'. I pictured Graham turning down the speaker in my office so he wouldn't have to sit through it again, and I felt my heart ache for him. That is until Rolfe tried a pirouette on a bench top, lost his balance and fell. Liesl jumped out of the way, not believing that everyone should go down with the ship, and I could hear the snap of the bone in his leg when he hit the stage, even from where I sat. For a moment, there was silence, as if we had all turned to stone. And then a sound rang out from the stage.

'Holy fuck will somebody get out here and help me?' the actor formerly known as Rolfe cried out.

Trevor and Scott, our technical director and stage carpenter, ran out from the wings, Trevor already had a first-aid kit in his hands. They looked at the angle of the leg, though, and Scott ran back to the office to call an ambulance. There was much fuss and great histrionics, as the actors congregated on the stage and in the front row while the paramedics struggled to get that badly broken leg into a splint and then transport the poor actor to the hospital.

I was excited, though. I fought down the sensation, but I knew this opportunity had happened for a reason. Because Graham was meant for this role. And I was just waiting for the right moment to approach the director and tell him that his new Rolfe was sitting right upstairs just waiting for the opportunity. When the stage was finally clear, the director called a lunch break and I waited for the actors to dissipate. Then I made my way over to the director.

'Excuse me, I'm Kate Carpenter, I'm house manager—'

'Yes, yes, I don't have time for this right now. We preview

in less than twenty-four hours and I am suddenly one lead character short.'

'But that's what I wanted—'

'Look, we can talk about your front-of-house concerns later, when we figure out if we have a show or not.'

He stormed past me and I felt my stomach sink. Poor Graham, I had failed him. I slowly climbed back up the aisle, the opposite direction as the director was going. He was climbing up on the stage, barking at anyone who came too near him.

'I need a phone,' he screamed at no one in particular. 'I need to call my second choice from the auditions.'

I sighed and closed the door behind me, slowly walking back up to the office. Graham sat in blissful innocence, having turned the speakers off and missed the entire event.

'Hey, you missed the excitement, Kate,' Graham greeted me when I went back into my office.

'Oh?'

'Yeah, there was an ambulance out at stage door. I wonder what happened?'

'It was one of the *Sound of Music* actors,' I told him. 'He fell and broke his leg.'

'Which one was it?' he asked.

'The one who plays Rolfe,' I said quietly.

'Oh, no, that's tough for him.'

'Poetic justice, I would think.' I was jumping to Graham's defence, even if he wasn't as excited about it.

'No, I wanted the part but I didn't want anything bad to happen to any of them, Kate.'

'Well, I tried to talk to the director about you, but he was having a little freak-out. I'm so sorry, Graham.'

'You did that?' he asked. 'You tried to put a good word in for me?'

'Yeah, despite the fact that it means I'd be without you for the week that the show is running, I did try to put a good word in for you,' I said. 'But don't they have understudies?'

'Production is too small. They couldn't afford understudies.'

'That part should have been yours.'

'Well, thanks. They'll find someone. The city is filled with good actors.'

'It should have been you,' I insisted, smiling at him. I was so proud of the way he was handling all this. Graham was going to make a good man, I thought.

And then the phone rang before I could get any more mushy.

'House manager's office,' Graham answered, having been the closest one to the phone. 'Speaking.'

There was silence as he listened to the caller and I dug through my backpack for a cigarette. I lit up my smoke as his face broke up, a great smile suddenly appearing, splitting him from ear to ear.

'What?' I asked in a stage whisper.

He held up a finger to silence me.

'Great, I'll be there in five minutes,' he said enthusiastically and hung up the phone.

'What is it?' I asked. 'Where are you going?'

'That was the director of *Sound of Music*. I was his second choice. If I can learn the role by the end of this afternoon, the part is mine.'

I jumped up off my chair, screaming and yelling, and grabbed him in a huge bear hug.

'Oh, wait,' I said, reining myself in. 'Can you learn the part this afternoon?'

'I already know it. I've been watching rehearsals from the second balcony where no one could see me.'

'Yippee!' I started yelling some more. 'Well, what are you still doing here?'

'I thought I should help you get this stuff all in order before I left,' he said.

I picked up his bottled water and put it in his hand, turning him around and pushing him out the door.

'Graham, go. This is real paid Equity work and you are not going to make them wait another second. Go!'

'Are you sure?'

'You just have to call me when you're done and tell me absolutely everything.'

'I promise.'

'Good. Now go break a leg!' I said and then realized what I had just said.

He laughed anyway and then raced off down the hall. I tied things up in the office and then turned things off, wondering how hard I was going to have to work this summer. I'd already lost ten pounds and worn through a good pair of sandals working the Dandelion Festival. Now, running a show without Graham as my assistant was going to put a whole new slant on things. Oh well, I had done it before Graham had appeared and I was sure I could manage it again, although it was nice that he took over all the stuff that I didn't really enjoy doing. I turned out the lights and locked up the office. Cam had instructed me to meet him at the stage door and we were going to go out to an early movie and maybe grab a bite to eat. I hurried through the theatre and down Tin Pan Alley to the stage door.

'Hey, Kate,' Nick said. 'You done for the day? Should I shut everything down in the lobby?'

'I'm done but Frank was still in there looking frustrated about something.'

'OK, I'll send someone down and see how long he's going to be.'

'Night, Nick,' I called over my shoulder, as I pushed through the doors and escaped the building.

He was waiting when I got down there and we headed off in his beautiful old car, a gleaming white 1971 Hemi Barracuda that he had painstakingly restored and maintained in the most pristine condition. I was proud to ride in this car, with all the boys staring at us, and feeling so special. But I loved to tease him about it and I always referred to it as the Fish. Besides he really did spend more money on it than he did on me. I buckled up and he pulled carefully out into the traffic on 9th Avenue and made his way around the block.

'Hi, Cam,' I leaned over and kissed him. 'Hey, I just saw Frank in the lobby again. Did you two ever get together?'

'No, we said a quick hi in the hallways a couple of times but that's it.'

'Maybe we should invite him out for dinner sometime.'

'We could do that I suppose. Do we have any spare time coming up soon?'

'We're awfully early for the movie tonight,' I mentioned.

'I just have one quick stop I wanted to make before the movie.'

'A big secret?' I asked and then realized what he was up to. 'Oh, no, please, not another one.'

'Katie, it'll be quick.'

'Couldn't you just rip my heart out with a rusty knife?'

'Oh God, the melodrama queen. It's a house, Katie, we're just looking at a house. It really won't kill you.'

'But it may kill *you*,' I warned him.

He turned off 9th Avenue and headed up MacLeod Trail.

'Where are we going?' I asked.

'Up into Mission. Apparently it's a nice little house.'

'I didn't think we could afford anything in Mission.'

'Well, it's a fixer-upper, so consider yourself warned.'

'How bad a fixer-upper?'

'That's what we're going to check out. So I'll check the amount of work needed while you decide how much you hate it and why.'

'I'm not that bad.'

He looked at me as we sat at a red light, but amazingly restrained himself and didn't say a word.

'Am I?' I asked after I couldn't stand the silence any longer.

He pulled the car forward from the light and after a couple more turns parked next to Mr Jones' gleaming BMW.

'I see you've got the silver one out today,' I said. 'Didn't feel like being flashy in the red one.'

'Good afternoon, Kate. I would have brought the red car if I knew you liked it. You know my main mission in life is to make you happy.'

'You're not doing a very good job of that yet.'

'I haven't been at it very long yet. Miracles take time,' he smiled. 'You ready to do this again?'

'Lead the way, Rob,' I laughed.

It was definitely a fixer-upper that we now stood in front of. An old Victorian with an addition on the back that didn't match any form of architecture that I could name. Windowsills hung crookedly, paint peeled off the siding and the numbers hung upside down. It was a house that needed someone to love it. We walked up to the front door and Mr Jones rang the doorbell. There was no answer so he took the key out of the lock box and opened the door.

'Hello,' he called. 'Rob Jones. I'm here to show the house.'

There was no answer so he held the door open for us and followed us in. Some lights were on and some were off and

31

we weren't quite sure if anyone was expecting us or not. The place had the look of a flophouse, with a couple of beds in the front parlour and dining room. The kitchen was a mass of dishes piled in several precarious mounds and the smells were equally as off-putting. Cam had a quick look at the wiring and then we headed upstairs. The stairs creaked and groaned but Cam made some sort of comment about good bones. We opened the door to the first bedroom and had a quick look inside. It was as messy as the rest of the house, but it did have a great bay window looking out onto the river. We crossed the hall to the second bedroom and Mr Jones opened the door. Cam and I both followed him in but stopped about two steps into the room. There, on the bed, lay a man and a woman, totally naked, her hand playing half-heartedly with his penis while he inhaled deeply off a large joint. The sickly sweet smell took me straight back to those illicit teenage years and the afternoons spent behind the junior high school. I didn't know where to look but seemed unable to avert my eyes anyway.

'Rob Jones, CTS Real Estate,' Rob said, not offering his hand in greeting for once. 'I had an appointment to show the house.'

'No worries,' the man said. 'Just poke around anywhere you want.'

'We'll stay out of your way,' the girl giggled, taking a toke off the joint and then holding it out for me.

'No thanks,' I smiled, wondering why I was being so polite.

'Whatever,' she said, handing it back to the man beside her.

'Well, thanks for your time,' Mr Jones said, leading us out of the room and closing the door behind us.

We made our way down the stairs and out of the house before we uttered another word. Once safely back at our car, with the key back in the lock box, we all turned to each other.

'No,' the three of us said at the same time, and then started giggling.

'I think the fumes may have gotten to us,' I laughed.

'I'm feeling a little light-headed myself,' said Mr Jones. 'OK, well I'm going to go put a warning on that one on the computer network and see if I can find something a little more suitable for you to look at.'

'Well, at least you've accomplished one thing,' I said.

'What's that?'

'You've made me happy.' I compulsively gave Mr Jones a hug.

Back in the car, Cam turned back for downtown. We were headed for the Globe Theatre and one of the foreign films sure to be nominated for an Oscar next year. You couldn't very well call yourself a film buff if you didn't see all the Oscar nominees. Besides, it was fun to see a film in French every once in a while and see how much I still actually remembered. And Cam didn't seem to mind a foreign film or the occasional subtitle, another good reason to keep him around.

The film was good and we sat in the car, trying to decide where to go to eat. We always ended up at one of a handful of places, in or around the Plex. A big downside of living and working downtown, you tended not to expand your horizons very effectively. So on impulse, Cam put the car in gear and we pointed it south, driving until we found something new and interesting to try.

Our hunger overtook us before we found something new, so we stopped at Smuggler's, where we hadn't been for a long time, instead. It was dark and quiet, like a cocoon, and they made a great steak. Cam ordered a beer and a twelve-ounce New York steak, I settled for wine and something slightly smaller. We sipped our drinks, sitting beside each other in the booth, like newlyweds or high-school sweethearts. I didn't really care what we looked like, I was so happy to be feeling good about my relationship with Cam again that nothing else mattered.

'Do you know who that is?' Cam asked, pointing over to a table of ten or twelve very large men.

'Should I? I don't think I've dated any of them.'

'They're with the Saskatchewan Roughriders,' he said, smiling broadly.

'The hockey team?' I asked.

He just about spit his beer across the table.

'It's summer, Katie.'

'Yeah, so there's no hockey?'

'Football.'

'Oh, sorry.'

'It's my team, you know, you could show a little more respect.'

'Your team? You live in Alberta.'

'Yeah, but once a Saskatchewan fan, forever a Saskatchewan fan. They make us take a blood oath as we're leaving the province.'

'Funny.'

'So that's the quarterback, and that's most of the defensive line sitting on his left.'

'Wow, that's really exciting,' I tried.

'OK, no more football.'

'No, really. If they're in town, there must be a game, right?'

'Saturday.'

'OK, if you can get tickets I'll go with you.'

'Really?'

'Really,' I told him. 'Besides, I hear they make great hamburgers there.'

He laughed.

'I really mean it about the tickets, though. I'll go to the game this weekend if you don't get pissed off at my dumb questions.'

'OK, I'll see what's available,' he said, and kissed me.

'Oh my God, look at that,' I said, turning back to the football players.

Several waiters were approaching the table of football players, loaded down with platters filled with roasted potatoes, vegetables and what looked like an entire roast beef on each plate.

'That's the prime rib,' Cam said. 'I think they call it the King's cut or something like that. It's thirty-two ounces.'

'Two pounds of beef? Wow, that's amazing.'

'Well, they burn off a bunch of calories in a game, you know.'

'Wow again. Well, I'm sorry, dear, but I was planning on being impressed by your twelve-ounce steak, but now it's just going to seem like table scraps.'

He laughed. 'No problem. I'll impress you later tonight with my manliness. You'll forget all about those football players.'

Stomach full and warm from the wine I had enjoyed, we got back in the car and followed Macleod Trail back downtown. We passed the Plex and I reflexively looked up to my office window.

34

'Oh, shit, I left a light on in my office,' I said.

'Security will get it.'

'No, I'd like to check it out and make sure everything is all right up there, if you don't mind.'

'Well, I sort of do mind, but I'll sleep better tonight if I just pull in and let you do this right?'

'Pretty much.'

Cam pulled into the loading dock and turned off the car. We climbed up the stairs and entered through the stage door. Nick the security supervisor had a football game on his radio, so Cam sat with him while I raced down the hallway and then cut through the theatre up to my office. I put my key in the door and turned it, expecting to find an empty office and just a light that I had forgotten to turn off. That's not what was awaiting me.

'Graham?' I asked.

He sat at my desk, in his jeans and T-shirt. His jacket was thrown on the floor and his backpack was lying spilled across the bench. In front of him he had a Mickey of Scotch that was almost empty. Now a Mickey might not be much for most people, but I had never seen Graham drink more than a beer. He didn't look very well.

'Graham?' I asked again.

'Oh, hi, Kate,' he finally turned to look at me.

'Graham, what is going on here?'

'I'm having a little drink.'

I crossed over to the desk and grabbed the Scotch before he could continue to fulfil that prophecy.

'Why are you having a little drink in my office?'

'I still live at home, and there isn't really any place for me to be alone there. So I came here because I knew it would be private and I could just drink and be all morose and no one would bother me.'

'Why, Graham, do you want to be alone and drunk?'

'Why are you here, Kate?' he asked. 'It's still night-time outside, isn't it?'

'Yes, Graham, it's still night-time. Now how about if you answer my question?'

'It's my mom,' he said.

'Aw, Graham, don't tell me she wants you to get your own

place after all?' I asked, remembering our conversation from this afternoon. 'But you know, we all have to leave home at some time.'

'No, she's leaving me.'

'What? She and your dad are splitting up? That's not possible. They're like the best couple in the world.'

'No, Kate,' he said, tears streaming down his eyes. 'She's got cancer. She's leaving me. She's leaving all of us.'

'Graham?' I was shocked. 'Are you sure?'

'Yes, they just told us tonight. She's going into the hospital tomorrow for surgery.'

'Tomorrow? Is it that urgent?

'Well, it's serious. But apparently she's known about it for weeks and just didn't want to worry us. She was going to tell us she was going to the spa for a week but Dad made her confess.'

'Well, Graham, if she's having surgery, it should be OK then.' At least I hoped it would. 'They wouldn't operate if they didn't think they could help her.'

'Kate, it's not OK. It's *cancer*. In her throat.'

'Graham,' I began, overwhelmed by the rawness in his voice.

'They might have to take her tongue out.'

'What?'

'The surgery could take eight hours.'

'Oh my God.'

'She says she has cancer from smoking. My mother might never be able to talk again. She might never be able to swallow properly and might have to be tube-fed. There is huge chance they can't get it all and a big chance she won't make it off the operating table. That's why Dad made her talk to us. He didn't want to risk that we wouldn't have a chance to say goodbye to her.'

I stared at him, not knowing what to say, not knowing what to do. I wished I was a doctor, so I could actually argue with him about the odds he had just quoted me and tell him everything was going to be all right. But there was only one thing I knew how to do for sure. I walked behind the desk and wrapped my arms around him. I pulled him close to me, hugging him tightly and rubbing his back. I felt him start to crumble and then the sobs came. He almost pulled me over with the weight of his pain, but I held him tightly and let him cry.

I heard the door open behind me and Cam poked his head through.

'Katie, what's taking you so long . . .'

'Cam, can you grab Graham's stuff, please. I think he's coming home with us. He needs some coffee and I don't want him to be alone.'

'Sure,' Cam said, diving into action and not waiting for an explanation.

We walked Graham to the car and got him up to our place. He was a little unsteady on his feet but we had him out numbered. I pulled open the sofa bed in the living room and got the comforter out for him. I wrapped him in the comforter and sat beside him, my arm still around his shoulder and tears still dripping down his face. Cam made coffee in the kitchen and brought some out for all of us. He sat on the other side of the bed, a hand on Graham's shoulder as he choked down his coffee.

'I'm sorry,' Graham said, wiping at his eyes and trying to be all manly about this.

'Don't be sorry,' I said. 'Graham, we're always here for you.'

'You don't need me here. I really am feeling better. I think I should go home now and you guys can get on with your lives.'

'Graham, what is going on?' Cam asked, finally not able to contain his curiosity.

Graham took a deep breath, but I noticed several hitches in his sigh and I took over.

'Graham's mom has cancer,' I said. 'Apparently, it's serious. She's having surgery tomorrow.'

Cam squeezed Graham's shoulder and they both took a sip of coffee.

'You are staying here tonight.' Cam reaffirmed what I had been trying to tell him. 'And we'll go to the hospital with you tomorrow if you want us to.'

'Do I want you to come? Of course I do. You guys are always welcome, my mom thinks you're her fifth daughter.

37

She loves you guys. She said she was going to fight this so she could dance at your wedding. And then she said she might die of old age before that ever happened so she'd better find a new goal.'

I couldn't help myself and I laughed.

'I'm sorry, Graham,' I said, stifling myself.

'No, I should apologize too, we laughed like crazy when she said that.'

'Well, I guess there is a certain amount of humour in our relationship,' Cam admitted.

'OK, enough laughing about me and my lack of commitment,' I scolded them. 'What time do we need to be at the hospital tomorrow?'

'But I can't go to the hospital,' Graham sniffed, new tears filling his eyes.

'Of course you can, Graham,' Cam said. 'We'll be right there with you.'

'No, you don't understand. Mom doesn't want me there. She told me that if I missed my rehearsal she would never speak to me again.' And then he started crying again. 'Although she may just never speak to anyone again.'

'Graham, your mother was speaking nonsense. We are going to the hospital and seeing her. We will go bright and early so that you can see your mom and then go to rehearsal. And then we can take you back to the hospital after you're done. She'll probably not even be back from recovery by the time we're back in the afternoon, so the timing will be good, right?'

'Mom will kill me,' he repeated.

'Graham, I will talk with your mother, don't you worry about that. So, how about if we all try and get some shuteye and we'll set the alarm for six in the morning?'

'Sounds good to me,' Cam agreed.

'And Graham, we're not giving you a vote in this,' I told him, taking the coffee cup out of his hand and tussling his blond hair. 'Try and get some sleep, kiddo.'

'I will. Who knew that Scotch was so sedating?' he asked, snuggling down onto the sofa bed. He was snoring softly by the time Cam had locked the place up and I had preset the coffee for the morning.

Upstairs, I changed out of my clothes and into a T-shirt,

climbing into bed. I felt a chill and I was anxious for Cam to be there, beside me. I couldn't tell if the chill was in the air or in my soul. I loved Graham and his mother was one of my favourite people. This was all too scary and too real all of a sudden. Cam hung his clothes up and finally climbed in beside me. I rolled over and wrapped my arms around him, thinking I was ready for sleep. Until the tears started.

Thursday

S ix o'clock came way too early for me – although most days, nine seemed way too early. Cam had shut the alarm off seconds after the music began, shaking me gently, and I lay there for a moment, quiet in the morning peace. Until the rumbling of Graham snoring from downstairs broke through my reverie. I got up, not really happy to face any part of this day, but tried to keep my grumbling to myself, and Cam and I got ready before we woke Graham. I snuck out onto the deck to have a smoke, not wanting Graham to see me smoking today. While Graham was in the shower, Cam made up some breakfast for us and I managed the coffee. Pouring it in mugs was well within my culinary scope. Graham joined us but just stared silently at his plate.

'You know there's no point in arguing with me,' I said, looking him in the eyes. But I had a little compassion because I opened the bottle of aspirin and handed him a couple.

'But I'm not really hungry . . .' he insisted after swallowing the pills.

'What did I just say?'

'Kate?'

'Graham, you're not going to do us any good today if your blood sugar is low and you pass out or something.'

He picked up his fork and started pushing eggs into his

mouth. I did the same, feeling almost as inappetent as Graham, but I knew if I didn't eat I was going to have the same argument with Cam and be on the losing end. I tried valiantly to do my crossword puzzle, but that wasn't working for me either, as six down was a six-letter word for malignant disease. I wrote in cancer and then pushed the paper away. We finished our meal in silence and I tossed the dishes in the dishwasher while Cam pulled the car around front for us. Graham and I gathered up our backpacks and then I wrapped my arm through his, giving him a squeeze for support and a smile that I hoped was reassuring and led him downstairs.

We drove to the Foothills Hospital in silence, none of us ready to fill the void with small talk. Cam parked and we stopped at reception to find out which room Graham's mother was in. Then, directions in hand, we made our way through the maze of wards and floors and finally found her room. Graham was losing courage, worried that his mom would be angry with him. I left him with Cam in the hallway and decided to go in first and take the heat.

Rose was a lovely woman, just approaching sixty. She had a shock of white hair cut into a fashionable layered bob and sparkling green eyes. She was dressed in a hospital gown and her husband sat at the bed beside her, holding her hand and whispering into her ear. I'm guessing his words were related to how he felt about her, due to the blush on her cheeks.

'Kate?' she said, surprised to see me.

'Rose, how are you doing?'

'Kate, what are you doing here?' she asked and then her eyes narrowed. 'Graham talked, didn't he? He's such a little blabbermouth. I warned him . . .'

'Rose, Graham is very upset about this. I found him drunk in the theatre last night and took him home.'

'See, Nathan, I told you we shouldn't have told him. Kate, when he came home yesterday, so excited about getting that role in the play, I was going to cancel my surgery.'

'I wouldn't let her do that,' Nathan jumped in, squeezing her hand.

'Well, I said we shouldn't have told him and I was right.'

'No, you weren't,' I said softly. 'He needed to know and he needs to see you before your surgery.'

'I do not want him missing his rehearsal.'

'We'll get him back to the theatre in time,' I promised. 'But please let your son be with you. Rose, if anything were to happen to you, he would never forgive himself.'

She sighed and turned to her husband. He nodded slowly and she turned back to me.

'All right, Nathan, you were right again. Send him in. But, Kate . . .'

'Yes?'

'You warn him. No tears.'

'I'll warn him,' I said, going back out into the corridor. 'You can go in, Graham.'

'Thanks, Kate,' he smiled at me, his lip quivering.

'But no tears. She doesn't want everyone being morose.'

'Hey, I'm an actor. I think I can manage that.'

He took a deep breath and shook out his arms, before setting his face into a warm smile and pushing through the door into the room.

Cam and I grabbed some really bad coffee from one of those machines and had a seat in the waiting area by the nurses' station, not wanting to intrude any further on this family moment. We could see down the hall and were pretty sure Graham could see us if he came out. In about a half an hour, a stretcher was wheeled into Rose's room and then shortly afterward, Rose came out on the stretcher. They stopped for a minute so Graham could say his goodbyes and then Nathan followed them as they headed for the elevator and the surgical waiting room, where he would spend his day. Graham watched until the elevator doors closed and then turned and came down the hall to us.

'Is your dad going to be OK alone?' Cam asked. 'I could wait with him.'

'Thanks, Cam,' Graham said. 'But we successfully talked that stubborn woman into telling my sisters that it was OK for them to come down, so they're on their way and they'll sit up there with Dad.'

I rubbed his back, but somehow he seemed much more at peace having seen his mother this morning.

'So, shall we get you to rehearsal, then?' I asked.

'I guess there's nothing else I can do here,' he admitted.

41

'Besides, she said she'd kill me if I missed it and even from a hospital bed she scares me.'

'OK, then, off we go.'

At the theatre, I sat in my office, going slowly through my work, not wanting to be finished too quickly. I had my speaker turned up full blast and was listening to Graham's rehearsal like a proud mother. Well, older sister, since I refused to admit I was old enough to be his mother. He was doing brilliantly, letter-perfect on his lines and lyrics, and just needing a little help on the choreography. At about noon the director called an hour for lunch and then the full dress rehearsal would proceed at one o'clock. I raced down to the green room to congratulate Graham on the amazing job he had done. I poked my head around the corner, only to see a bunch of actors I didn't know, but Scott, our stage carpenter, was there too, sitting on the sofa, eating a sandwich.

'Have you seen Graham?'

'Hi, Kate,' Scott said, between bites. 'I think he took off with that girl he's been seeing.'

'Mandi?' I asked.

'Cute, blonde, nurse's uniform?' Scott said, obviously one of those visual males.

'Her name is Mandi,' I laughed. 'Can you say Mandi?'

'Nope. But I can say to let me know if she gets tired of that boy and is ready for a real man.'

'I will. I just hope you can find a real man for her!'

'Funny girl,' he yelled after me. But I was safe, he was engrossed in his sandwich. Otherwise, I might find myself tied in a bosun's chair and swinging from the auditorium ceiling.

I found Cam and we wandered across the street for a quick sandwich, and then I snuck into the back of the theatre, just as the lights were going down. I had my notepad, as I liked to mark cues for intermissions and end of the show, but I have to admit I was paying much less attention to my work and feeling very nervous for Graham. The overture started and the rehearsal began. Three hours later I was resisting the urge to stand up and cheer when he came out for his curtain call, but I knew the girls in the audience tomorrow night probably would make up for my silence.

I raced up to my office and called Cam to let him know Graham was almost finished at the theatre, so Cam could finish up his work and drive us back to the hospital. I listened nervously, as the director gave notes to each actor for the opening-night performance. Graham's name finally came up and he was praised for how he had jumped right in and fit in with everyone so well. Beaming with pride, I shut things down and grabbed my pack, then went to the green room to wait for him. I tried to wipe the grin off my face, as I didn't want to seem too effusive before opening night. These actors all have a lot of weird superstitions and 'good dress rehearsal, bad opening' was a big one. So I just smiled the normal smile when he poked his head around the corner a few minutes later.

'Kate, I just need a minute to wash up and change,' he said.

'I'll be here.'

And true to his word, he was just a minute or two. Frank was working on the door from backstage to Tin Pan Alley, but he kindly moved out of the way and held it open for us as we passed.

'Thanks, Frank, see you later,' I called, as we headed to the stage door. It just wasn't a day at work any more unless you tripped over Frank and his tools somewhere.

'Did you have a nice lunch with Mandi?' I asked Graham, ready to tease him.

'No.'

'No?'

'She broke up with me.'

'What?'

'Yeah.'

'Graham, what happened?'

'I don't know. She started to talk about wanting someone with a stable job and everything and then I asked her to stop talking. I just realized I had so many other things I had to deal with right now, I didn't need to know about why she didn't want to see me. So I paid for lunch and I left her there.'

'Oh, Graham,' I tried to console him, my arm going around his waist.

'Don't, Kate,' he said.

'What do you mean?'

'I've got everything held together right now. But with a

43

very thin wire. Let's just not talk about Mandi until Mom's home safe and sound.'

'I can do that. However, if I see her, I cannot promise I won't give her a black eye.'

'I'm not sure I would ask you to restrain yourself right now anyway.'

Laughing, we climbed into the car and made our way to the hospital. We parked and were still laughing as we made our way through the lobby. Graham stopped laughing though when he saw Mandi crossing the lobby, anger in her eyes.

'What are you doing here?' she asked. 'I thought I made myself perfectly clear this afternoon?'

'Oh, believe me you did,' Graham said.

'Look, don't make me call security on you. Let's just do this like adults, please.'

I saw Graham struggling with his emotions and stepped in between them quickly, pushing Graham toward Cam and the elevators.

'Graham, why don't you and Cam go on up and I'll just have a quick word with Mandi?'

'Katie?' Cam asked, a warning carried in that one word.

'I'm OK, I'll see you in a minute.'

I watched them walk toward the elevator and then grabbed Mandi's arm and pulled her roughly over against the wall, out of the way of the crowds.

'Look, I don't know what your gripe is with Graham and I really don't care.'

'Good, because I am going to call security and have you thrown out of here.'

I ignored her warning, I was on a roll right now.

'And I know you're not a total bitch, you've just had a little bit of fun with Graham and he's had fun too.'

'And what business is any of this of yours?' Mandi asked indignantly.

'And I know you didn't know that Graham's mom is upstairs right now, after having undergone eight hours of surgery today for cancer.'

'Oh my God, he never told me.'

'He didn't know, Mandi. His mom just told him last night.'

'Oh my God,' she whispered. 'I wish I had known that. I

would have never chosen today to break up with him.'

'I know.'

'Oh my God,' she said again. 'What can I do?'

'Just leave him be. He's going to be at the hospital a lot for the next little while, just leave him be.'

'I'll do that. And if there is anything I can do, please call me.'

She hurried off, dabbing at her eyes, and I headed back for the elevators to follow my men upstairs. I was stopped halfway there when someone grabbed my arm.

'Excuse me.'

I turned around to see who wanted me. It was that reporter.

'Sorry to bother you,' she smiled. 'I'm Geneva Arnold from E-News. Didn't we meet at the Calgary Arts Complex fire?'

'We didn't actually meet,' I said.

'Well, I'm Geneva,' she said, holding out her hand.

I took it so not to be rude but really wanted to be upstairs right now. 'Kate Carpenter.'

'I'm sorry, I wasn't spying or anything, but I noticed you were arguing with that girl and I just wondered if it were anything to do with the fire at the Arts Complex.'

'No.' I turned to go.

'I'm just wondering if you would really tell me if it did have something to do with it?' She turned up the wattage on her smile but it just wasn't working on me.

'Probably not.' I smiled back at her and got in the elevator.

Cam and Graham were waiting for me at the nurse's station.

'What's wrong?' I asked, my heart sinking, as I wondered why Graham wasn't in with his mom.

'She's in ICU,' Cam said.

'What?'

'Apparently it was expected. If they were worried about her breathing they were going to move her to intensive care.'

'Just something else she forgot to mention,' Graham added.

Cam took my hand and led us back to the elevator.

'They gave her a tracheotomy and a breathing tube because the swelling was really bad. And because of that, she has to be in ICU until the tube comes out. And that won't happen until they have ensured the swelling is on its way down and that she can swallow OK and breathe OK.' Graham's voice was wavering but the look in his face said he was determined to keep himself together. 'So there's nothing for us to worry about, according to the nurses.'

'Speaking of nurses,' Graham said, 'did you hurt Mandi very badly?'

'Nah, I only grazed her. I couldn't hurt her too bad because there was a reporter in the lobby. Mandi's really sorry though, Graham, and she said to just call her if there was anything she could do.'

'I appreciate you talking to her for me,' Graham said.

The elevator opened and we made our way down the hall. We buzzed the doors to the ICU and a nurse came out.

'Hi, who are you here to see?' she asked.

'Rose Becker,' Graham said.

'And are you all family?'

'I am,' Graham answered. 'These are close family friends.'

'I'm really sorry, folks, but ICU is a family-only area. And with all your sisters here, we're pretty much full to the brim right now.'

'Kate, I'm sorry . . .' Graham started.

'No worries, kiddo. You go see your mom and give her our best wishes.'

'Do you want us to wait for you?' Cam asked.

'I can get a ride home with one of my sisters,' he said. 'You guys head on home.'

I kissed him on the cheek and gave him a quick hug. 'No stopping for a drink on the way home tonight, OK?'

'I'm sworn off alcohol for a while, I promise.'

'We'll see you tomorrow night, then?' I asked.

'I'll be the young German boy on the stage,' he promised. 'Mom made me promise that one for sure.'

Graham turned and followed the nurse through the ICU doors. I took Cam's hand and let him lead me back toward the car. As we crossed the parking lot, I heard sirens and turned to see a fire truck pull into the driveway and speed around the back of the hospital.

'Man, I've seen one too many of those this week,' I said.

'It's not Ryan's company, at least,' Cam said.

'Yeah, I like Ryan's job much better when I don't actually think about what he does all day long.'

46

'You're right about that,' Cam agreed. 'I don't know how Sam can stand sending him to work every day.'

'It takes a special person to do the job and a special person to marry into it,' I said. 'Now take me home and tell me how your job is never dangerous and I never have to worry about you.'

Cam did take me home. He parked that car of his and I went upstairs to make dinner while he stayed in the parkade and polished the road dust off the car. I watched him for a minute, lovingly inspecting and rubbing it down, and I detected a momentary stab of jealousy, thinking he'd better inspect me that closely later tonight or he was in big trouble. I shook my head to try and clear these idiotic thoughts out of it and went up to the apartment.

The hallway was a disaster; they had ripped out the carpet while we were gone today, obviously planning to start construction on our floor shortly. Soon walls would be tumbling down and hardwood would be laid and I could no longer tell people I lived in a cute but tiny loft downtown. But like Scarlett O'Hara, I pushed that thought out of my mind to deal with it tomorrow, and let myself into the apartment.

By the time Cam got upstairs, I was changed into sloppy shorts, big wool socks and an oversized sweatshirt, not one of my sexier looks but definitely one of the comfier ones. I had the *Sound of Music* DVD in the machine, awaiting Cam's return, as I had a sudden urge to be able to compare the performance tomorrow night to the movie.

'Supper ready?' Cam asked, locking us in for the night.

'Another ten minutes,' I called back.

'What did you make?' he asked, from the bathroom where I could hear him washing up.

'Chinese. Hope that's OK?'

'That's fine,' he said, sounding disappointed.

'Well, you didn't think I was actually going to cook, did you?'

'Did you order mu shu?'

'Mu shu chicken, hot and sour soup, bok choy in oyster sauce and . . . '

'Ginger beef?' he winked at me, thinking he knew me so well.

'And ginger beef,' I admitted. 'I put some steamed rice from the freezer into the microwave.'

'Wow, I am impressed,' he laughed. 'What movie have you got in?'

'*Sound of Music.*'

'Really? You don't think you're going to get sick of that over the next week or so?'

'I haven't gotten sick of it in the last twenty-five years, have I?'

'Good point. I'm just going to go change. Do you need some cash for the delivery guy?'

'Nope, I've got money.'

'Wow, using the microwave and carrying cash. What has come over you?' he asked sarcastically, running up the stairs before I could throw something at him.

I chased him up the stairs, feeling playful, and threw myself at him, tackling him and landing on the bed. I had his shirt off and belt undone when the door buzzer rang.

'Damn,' I said. 'I forgot that was coming.'

I gave him one last long lingering kiss, which ended rather abruptly with the second and much harsher ring of the door buzzer. I raced down the stairs and buzzed the deliveryman in.

'If you set the oven to 200 degrees, everything will stay nice and warm,' Cam called down from the bedroom.

'The bok choy will get soggy and the mu shu pancakes will stick together,' I whined, waiting by the door to pay the man.

'You sure?'

'Cam, you'll still be here in an hour or so after we eat,' I said. 'I'm pretty sure I'll still be in the mood and you being a man, how hard is it going to be for me to get you turned on again?'

'I don't know, I may feel all bloated and just not in the mood to get naked in front of you,' he laughed, coming downstairs in his bathrobe.

Suddenly, soggy bok choy wasn't sounding so bad. But then the doorbell rang and I took the bag, paid the delivery guy and brought the food into the kitchen. And it smelled really good. Cam was getting out plates and chopsticks without even asking what I wanted to do. Food over sex, I never thought I would be old enough or boring enough to make that choice. But then again, it was really good Chinese food.

Friday

Iset the alarm for 9:00 a.m. It really does kill me to get up in the morning to the sound of the alarm. I just can't get into the habit of going to bed early, whether I have a show the night before or not. And I always feel I have to apologize for that. I was pretty sure that with Graham being an actor that week instead of my assistant it would take me considerably longer than usual. Graham joked that I made him do all the work, which I was loath to admit, but he did do a lot of the legwork while I did a lot of the paperwork. We were like a finely balanced machine and could get the place closed down in pretty good time most nights, which was a bonus now that I had someone to go home to. I had noticed that since he had been dating Mandi, he had even been less likely to sit around and chat and more motivated to get home. Or wherever it was that those sexually charged nineteen-year-olds went to party.

I wanted to try to get a hold of Graham before he went to the hospital and see if there was any news on his mom. There was no answer at his number. I guessed he and his dad had headed in at the crack of dawn, so I was going to work on the assumption that no news was good news.

Cam was out running or at work, I couldn't remember what shift he was on right now, at least not without my morning coffee in hand, so since I had no enticement to remain in bed, I got up and stumbled downstairs to get said coffee. I also got the newspaper and a croissant and jam from the fridge. Sam kept me well supplied with jams and syrups and other seasonal canning products, a definite treat in a winter province where fresh fruit could be an impossibility.

I took my breakfast out to the deck and sat out there, enjoying the light breeze and morning sunshine while I ate and did the crossword puzzle. I realized I was really going to miss my little apartment. I know I was supposed to be focusing on the fact that I was starting this wonderful new life with Cam, and in my heart that did make me very happy. But I was definitely mourning my first home, where I had spent the last six years of my life. We were never going to find a place with a location this perfect or this cute, no matter how many houses or condos Mr Jones found for us. And then I got stumped on the crossword puzzle and knew it was an omen of worse things to come. I put everything away and had a shower.

'I'm going to wash that thought right out of my hair,' I sang loudly, hoping to lighten my mood before I headed to the theatre.

It was opening night and I certainly didn't want to jinx that with my mood. Final dress rehearsal at one, show at seven thirty and Graham on stage instead of assisting me. It was going to be a long day. I found some jeans and a tank top, dried my hair quickly and slipped my feet into some sneakers. I grabbed a light jacket, never trusting the weather in this city, and headed out to the theatre. The walk to the Plex through the heart of downtown was beautiful this morning, doing more to lighten my mood than the shower Broadway musical had. It was mid-morning on a Friday and there were people everywhere. I always marvelled at how I could sit on my balcony in my nineteenth-floor loft and feel like I was totally alone in the world, and then when I got off the elevator, I was surrounded by people. I walked quickly, feeling muscles that were getting used to riding in a car stretch out a little. I looked into all the windows, spending thousands of dollars of imaginary money as I totally revamped my wardrobe and picked out several rooms of furniture. I stopped at the Glenbow Museum and grabbed a brochure of upcoming events, determined to expand my artistic education a little before I convinced Cam to take me to Paris for a holiday. The cobbled street finally turned into the paved plaza surrounding the Calgary Arts Complex. The plaza was bursting with beautiful flowers, as the summer had been warm and kind to our gardens this year. They were setting up the main stage for some sort of outdoor concert or event that would happen this evening. The plaza was alive from the time the Dandelion Festival hit, celebrating our first flowers of the year, right throughout the year, culminating with the Winter Festival. There was everything from summer-solstice drumming to ice carving, from the Calgary International Children's Festival to jazz and folk festivals with performers from around the world. It was an exciting place to be. And it was only a five-dollar cab ride home. I felt myself start to grow melancholy over the impending move again, and shook it off, entering the marble-floored Plex and pulling my jacket on, finding it several degrees cooler inside. I hurried through the corridors, fumbling for my keys. I had a big heavy ring, with all the different keys I required to navigate my way around the building, and it always sank to the very bottom of my backpack. I opened the front door and left it unlocked. The actors were supposed to use the stage door, but a couple of stragglers would come in this way, and I just never saw the point in arguing about it.

Once in my office, I made sure I had clean dress clothes for the performance that evening and when satisfied, lit a cigarette and did the next most important thing and got the coffee started. It just wasn't a day at the theatre until I had gone through my first pot of coffee. Not bad timing. It was 11:00 a.m. and all I had to do was a liquor inventory and set up the floats for tonight. Then I could watch the dress rehearsal and get a feel for the show. Well, that's what I was telling myself. Really, I just had to see how well Graham was going to do today. I had a meeting scheduled later with the theatre company presenting the show, to take the T-shirts and coffee mugs that they wanted us to sell, and one of the ushers would come in early to help me set up a nice sales table for them. After that, we just opened the doors and prayed for no major problems. Of course, with a nice, well-known show like *The Sound of Music*, you didn't have to worry about the crowds complaining, they knew what to expect. But there were always the double-sold tickets, the people unhappy with the price of our drinks, the occasional drunk and a few lost items. We never got through a night without something, however minor, coming up.

I pulled my cigarettes out of my backpack and tossed them into the desk drawer, then locked my backpack up in my file-cabinet drawer. I traded my jacket for a lighter sweater, and poured myself a coffee. There was a piece of paper on my desk and after I lit another cigarette, I flipped it over and found a note from Graham.

> Kate, I hope you don't mind, but I feel so guilty about leaving you this week, so I came in early this morning and I restocked all the bars and did the liquor inventory sheets for you. I moved the programs up from the loading dock to the storage room. And I pulled up a couple of tables from storage for the merchandise. I wish I could do more but my presence is actually required on stage during the running of the show! Hope this helps, though . . . Graham. PS – please put that cigarette out.

Bonus points for Graham and all that hard work, I thought, but I'd thank him later. I didn't want him doing this every day, while he was trying to focus on the show and worry about his mom. I really could manage running the theatre myself for a couple of weeks. And in deference to Rose and Graham's feelings, I did put my cigarette out. I didn't say I was going to quit, but I could make this one offering to him. I picked up the phone and dialled maintenance.

'Maintenance, Cam speaking.'

'Hello there, you are at work,' I said, smiling at the sound of his voice.

'Where did you think I was?'

'Honestly, this morning, I wasn't sure. I seem to be a little preoccupied. But do you know what would help me?'

'Yes.'

'You do?'

'I can meet you at Gus's for a coffee in fifteen minutes.'

'You are such an insufferable smart-ass,' I said. 'So therefore you're buying.'

'Love ya.'

'Yeah, me too,' I joked, and then hung up.

I looked around the office, making sure there was nothing that had to be done urgently: my voicemail was empty, Graham had given me a head start on the day, so I locked up and trotted down the stairs. I cut through the theatre, looking official. They discouraged us from the backstage areas when rehearsals were underway and there were actors there, warming up and running scenes already, not to mention the wardrobe and hair people, doing all their last-minute adjustments, but I pretended I had business and never bothered them, so rarely did anyone complain about my presence. I hurried down the concrete passageway at the back of the theatre that we all called Tin Pan Alley and waved to the security guard on duty as I let myself out the stage door and climbed down the two stairs that led into Gus's little coffee shop.

Grounds Zero was situated in a spot directly below the stage of the concert hall. It zigged and zagged a bit, as it had been built to fit the space, not planned as part of the original construction. But Gus had counter space for a half-dozen people, and enough tables for another twenty or so, and room for outdoor tables, weather permitting. And he used those too, even if it was January; if the thermometer climbed high enough from one of our winter Chinook winds, Gus had the outdoor tables set up and ready for use.

I sat at the counter and dropped my backpack beside me on the floor. I was about to greet Gus and order my coffee when I noticed a new sign hanging behind him.

'Gus?' I asked. The look in my eyes must have given me away.

He hurriedly slid a café mocha in front of me, which I grabbed but still felt empty handed.

'Just calm down, Kate,' he tried to reassure me.

'Are you serious?' I asked.

'It's the way of the world, Kate, there's nothing I can do about it.'

'But no smoking? Here of all places?'

'Sorry, Kate. But you do know that smoking is bad for you, don't you?'

'Well yes, and I am trying to quit, but I don't want to be forced to quit.'

'With the new by-laws I would have had to put in a separate smoking room and a whole new ventilation system, Kate. I just can't see doing that here.'

'I understand,' I said, but I was still shocked. 'I just don't know if I've ever had a coffee without a cigarette.'

'Maybe you'll finally taste the coffee,' Cam said, sneaking up behind me and kissing me on the forehead.

'You knew about this?' I asked.

'I've been hanging signs up all over the Plex this morning,' he said. 'You knew this was coming. City council's been debating it for months.'

'Yeah, but it's kind of never been real before. So no more smoking in the theatre lobbies?'

'No more. We're moving all the ashtrays outside the door as of Monday.'

'OK, well I'm not even going to ask about my office until I get a memo. I can't imagine after all these years not being able to smoke up there.'

'You could finally quit.'

'So could you.'

'I just smoke to keep you company.'

'Hah! Easy thing to say.'

Cam took the coffee Gus had made for him and grabbed mine for me. 'Shall we get a table?'

'Sure,' I said, wondering what he wanted the privacy for, but I followed him over obediently. We sat down with our coffee and he smiled across the table at me.

'So, how was your morning?' he asked.

'Fine.'

'Did you sleep OK?'

'Are we down to small talk right now?' I asked. 'Did we have a fight or something?'

The door to Grounds Zero opened and Cam waved to the person walking in. Normally, that wouldn't have meant a thing, since between us we knew pretty much everyone in this building, but today he had my spider sense tingling, so I turned around to see Mr Jones crossing the room and coming toward us.

'You didn't?' I hissed at him.

'We're not going out looking,' Cam said. 'I know you have to work. He's just bringing some printouts of some new listings. He thought it might help you sort the ones you don't like out first, and then we could just see the ones you're interested in.'

'That's all?'

'Katie, it's not like I'm torturing you or stealing all your money or drugging you and selling you to my friends. I'm just trying to help us find a place to live.'

'God, would you quit making it all sound so valiant. I feel petty when you do that.'

'Well, you are being slightly petty about it,' he began, and finished quickly before I could get angry, 'but I totally understand why this is hard for you. So I'm OK with it.'

'You are?'

'I am, if you can learn and grow through it. If we're going to be stuck here for the next six months, I'm going to get less and less understanding.'

'OK, that is duly noted.'

Mr Jones crossed over to us, steaming coffee in hand, and stood beside me.

'May I join you?' he asked.

Reluctantly, I slid over and he sat beside me, pulling a large file folder out of his briefcase and setting it in front of us on the table.

'I see you got a large coffee,' I said.

'I know it's never easy with you, Kate, so I thought I best get my caffeine boost in.'

'And that's a very large file there.'

'Well, aren't you going to summarily dismiss at least half of them?' he asked sardonically.

I matched his wry grin. 'At least.'

'Good, well let's get started.' He opened the file and slid it in front of me.

I took a big sip of coffee and looked at the picture of the first house.

'This is beautiful,' I said, shocked and almost choking on my coffee.

The house was an older home, but obviously recently renovated. It had a huge front porch, covered with lovely wooden Adirondack-style chairs and tables. It was three storeys high and looked like it had a basement too. I read through the sheet and was astounded. Three thousand square feet, four bedrooms, industrial-style kitchen, two-car garage, double-size lot, fully fenced yard, home theatre in the basement, fully wired for cable and Internet in all rooms, security system, formal front parlour, family room off the kitchen, four working fireplaces, fire pit and built-in barbecue in the backyard.

'This is totally amazing,' I said, turning the paper toward Cam who just smiled sweetly at me.

'It's beautiful, isn't it?' Mr Jones agreed.

'Where is it located?'

'It's a block off the river in Roxborough.'

'That's a great location for us,' I said.

'Terrific,' he said. 'We can go have a look at it anytime.'

'Well, I've got the afternoon tomorrow,' I said, excited we might have finally found something we all agreed upon.

'Any time that you can show you've been pre-approved for a $1.2 million mortgage,' he finished.

'Oh.'

Cam giggled as he slid the paper back across the table to me.

'This is your reality-check house, Kate,' Mr Jones continued. 'This listing has absolutely everything you told me you wanted in a house, and is also located in one of your top-five locations. However, you probably won't be able to afford it for at least ten years.'

'Oh,' I repeated myself.

'Now, I don't want you to be depressed about this, that's not my point. My point is I want you to realize that you will have to compromise a little with what you want in order to find what you can afford. I think if you can keep that in mind, this process might be a little easier for you.'

'Mr Jones, you know I'm not doing this on purpose.'

'I know that.'

'We all know that, Katie,' Cam said, taking my hand in his. But I noticed he hadn't wiped that stupid grin off his face yet. 'But you have to know that our current residence is being torn down around us and our time is running out.'

'You're both right,' I admitted, knowing it probably wasn't going to change my attitude much once we were actually out looking at the next house. I just had a real problem picturing myself living anywhere else than I did right now. I was just totally blocked and not sure what to do about it. But I sat there and went through the listings, picking out five we could look at the following afternoon. And then I went back to my office, feeling slightly hopeful about the five we were going to go and see. At least trying to, since hopeful was better than feeling defeated.

I breezed through the rest of the afternoon, delighting in the terrible dress rehearsal, knowing it would mean a great opening performance, superstition overtaking me as well. I met with

56

the theatre company and accepted their stock and got the ushers setting things up in the lobby. I had three new ushers coming in, to replace some old staff that had left, and I ran them through a quick orientation and assigned to them quiet spots with experienced volunteers. I put a couple of the senior staff in key positions on each floor, trying to make up for the fact that Graham was in the back of the house tonight, rather than the front of house, and declared us ready to go. I changed quickly into a skirt and sweater and Cam turned up just after I'd changed, looking handsome in his dress pants and black T-shirt. He also had two Subway sandwiches in his hand, bringing me dinner, and we ate quickly in my office while the ushers opened the doors and the bars. As predicted, things were quiet and ran smoothly. I sent Cam to his seat, choosing not to sit with him tonight, as I thought I might be needed by my staff. So I waited until after I made my announcements and we closed the house before I snuck in the theatre, standing just by the rear doors. No way in the world was I going to miss Graham's opening night. And I stood there and watched him until he took his final bow, tears filling my eyes.

As was typical on an opening night for a local theatre company, the lobby didn't empty immediately after the performance, with so many of the audience being related to the people who'd been on stage. We all stood around, waiting as the actors slowly changed, washed the stage make-up off and headed out to meet the fans. Afterwards, most of them were heading to Vaudeville's, where the bar had been closed off for a little opening-night party. Cam and I had other plans, though, we had promised Graham we would take him to the hospital as soon as we got the lobby cleared. Actors started to come out and people were hugging and squealing with delight. The performance had been letter-perfect and everyone was ecstatic about the evening. Graham finally appeared, and I couldn't help myself. I ran over to him and wrapped my arms around him.

'Well?' Graham asked.

'You were amazing!'

'You have to say that, you're like my sister,' Graham protested. 'Cam, what did you think?'

'It was great, Graham,' he beamed at him, pulling him into a huge embrace when I finally released him.

'Well, there were a couple of places . . .' he began to argue.

'Graham, you learned that entire part in two days under incredible personal pressure. I don't care if you missed a little step somewhere. You were brilliant and the whole show was fun. You should be proud.'

'I have to say I am,' he said. 'At risk of sounding vain.'

'OK, let's get these people out of here and get you over to your mom.'

'Want me to pull the fire alarm?' Graham asked, jokingly.

'No!' Cam and I both screamed at the same time.

'OK, well let me take care of it,' he said, and let himself into the booth where the lobby microphone was. 'Good evening, ladies and gentlemen, and we would like to thank you for coming to the Centenary Theatre for tonight's perform-ance of *The Sound of Music*, starring Graham Becker.'

A ripple of laughter rang through the crowd.

'However, we need you all now to get the hell out of the lobby so that Graham can go see his mom and regale her with stories of how he stole the show this evening. Besides, the bars here are closed and Vaudeville's is ready and waiting. So to all of you – "Farewell, adieu, to yieu and yieu and yieu," ' he began singing, before I pulled him out of the booth.

But the rest of the actors turned and waved and sang a beautiful *goodnight* in perfect harmony, before leading all their guests down the stairs, everyone laughing. Cam and Graham went to pull the car around to the stage door while I signed the ushers out and locked the doors. I raced down to the green room to pick up the little surprise that Scott had arranged for me, and then out to the waiting car.

It was a beautiful night and we drove with our windows wide open, enjoying the warm sweet summer air. I had tried some small talk, but Graham's euphoric mood became considerably dampened as we got closer to the hospital, so I gave up on it and just enjoyed the ride. We pulled up to the main doors and Graham jumped out. I opened the door and quickly stopped him.

'Graham?'

'Oh sorry, Kate, I'm distracted. But thanks for the ride.'

'No, not that. I have something for you.' I dug into the bottom of my backpack and pulled out a videotape.

'What's that?'

'It's a tape of your opening-night performance,' I said. 'Scott and the director and I arranged to do this so your mom could see it.'

'That's nice. I'll make sure she gets a TV when she moves into a regular hospital room.'

'Graham, you underestimate my powers of persuasion,' I laughed. 'And the guilt that Mandi felt about all of this. There's a TV and VCR in your mom's room already and she is awake and waiting for you.' I smiled.

'What?'

'I thought it would be nice if she got to see your opening-night performance on your opening night. And the doctors and nurses have been just great about helping us out. So, do you want it?'

He took the tape and I saw his eyes fill.

'This is the most amazing thing that anyone has ever done for me,' he sniffed, swiping at a stray tear, which I pretended I didn't see.

'Go enjoy the show.' I smiled again, and turned to get back in the car.

'I love you, Kate,' he called out to me, as he raced into the hospital.

'That was a good thing you did.' Cam said, kissing me on the cheek as I got back into the car.

'I'm really glad you suggested it,' I said, kissing him back.

'So what do you want to do?'

'Really? I want to go home and go to bed. I'm exhausted.'

'Me too.'

I woke, hearing a noise from under my pillow and confused about what it was.

'Phone,' Cam called out from the dark.

'I know,' I said, as the second ring pierced my consciousness and my brain registered what it was.

'Where is it?' he asked.

I felt around under my pillow and grabbed the receiver. I had no idea how the phone had gotten under my pillow but I had stopped questioning things like that, since I was terrible at putting things away.

'What time is it?' I asked.

'Three o'clock.'

'Hello?' I said, finally finding the talk button and answering the call.

'Kate, it's Graham.'

My heart skipped a beat. 'What's wrong?'

'Mom's gone,' he whispered.

'We'll be right there.'

'No, it's OK, I'm just going to take Dad home. I just wanted to let you know.'

'Graham, we'll meet you at your place, then. No arguments.'

'Thanks,' he said, his voice finally cracking as he hung up the phone.

Cam was already out of bed and pulling on some jeans.

'You don't have to go,' I said, turning on the bedside lamp.

'No argument,' he said, pulling on a sweatshirt.

I got out of bed and looked at the bedside table. I felt totally disgusted with myself and I walked across the room and picked up the little garbage can that sat beside the armchair. I grabbed the ashtray, cigarettes and matches that were sitting on the table and tossed them in. Then I headed downstairs and searched out every ashtray in the house and every package of cigarettes I could find, tossing them all into the trash and then I headed out into the hall and emptied the garbage can down the trash chute. I came back in, returned the garbage can and grabbed a pair of jeans and a sweatshirt for myself.

'Feel better?' Cam asked.

'No, but I'm sure I will in a couple of days. Everyone always says how much better you feel when you quit smoking.'

The Next Week

I sat at my desk. I listened to the third Rolfe singing 'Sixteen Going on Seventeen' and imagined him and Liesl dancing across the stage. It was such a shame Graham wasn't closing this play, as he should have been, but I knew he had one too many things on his mind to continue on, even for just a couple more nights. He needed to spend time at home with his family right now, as they were all having a hard time with the loss of their mom. I heard a noise in the hallway and turned to see if it was Cam, who was supposed to be on his way up to have a coffee with me. It wasn't Cam, it was Graham. He stood there, in the doorway, wearing jeans and a T-shirt with the *Sound of Music* logo on it. He held his coat in his hand and it dragged on the floor behind him. His shoulders were slumped and his eyes vacant.

'Graham?' I asked but I didn't really know what to say to him.

'I just thought I'd stop by and see if you needed any help?'

I stood up and took a step toward him.

'I can't believe she's gone,' he choked.

I raced over and grabbed onto him. It was all I could do to hold him upright as he fell into me, sobs wracking his body. His pain was palpable and it cut me like a knife as I held him to me. My eyes filled with tears as the gravity of his statement weighed upon my shoulders.

'I'm so sorry, baby,' I said into his ear, holding him as tightly as I could.

I heard the door at the end of the hallway open and Cam rounded the corner.

'Katie?' he asked.

'It's OK,' I mouthed over Graham's shoulder. 'I think he just needed to get out of the house for a while.'

Cam pulled us both into his strong arms and held us tightly, his hand rubbing Graham's back, his lips kissing the top of my head. This was one of those clarifying moments in my life. It was the moment that I realized what it really meant to have someone in my life who loved me like Cam did. Someone that I loved as much in return and could share the pain that was in my heart, just as he shared the weight that rested on my shoulders, both literally and figuratively.

I had learned a lot this week. I learned that musicals are fun but not the most important thing in life. I knew I loved my job but how little it mattered when tragedy struck. I knew that despite the fact that you wonder how you will ever get through these kind of events in life, somehow you do. I knew that I was surrounded by amazing friends who were ready to do anything for me or Graham or his family, just for the asking. I also learned all there was to know about funeral arrangements and writing obituaries and filling out insurance forms and engraving headstones. The Becker family had been distraught and Cam and I had done everything we could to help them through this first week and make all the arrangements. We had been at their place all morning and had just come home to change and then were back to their house, to take them to the church for the funeral service. The family had waited several days until *The Sound of Music* had closed, not wanting to put a further pall on the cast and production. I stood in the bathroom, brushing my hair and staring pointlessly into the mirror. I had on my plain black dress, which I had bought for the final concert of the piano competition, a much happier occasion than this. I put on a simple strand of pearls and I had a black sweater in case it got cool. Cam came up behind me and put his hands on my shoulders. He wore a plain black suit with a white shirt and black tie and the sight of him brought tears to my eyes.

'Your hair is fine,' he whispered, taking the brush from my hand and setting it on the counter. 'We have to go.'

I nodded and took a deep breath, realizing he was right and I couldn't avoid it any longer. Cam draped my sweater over my shoulders and handed me my purse. I hated death and I hated funerals and I hated cancer. I also hated the way I felt from not smoking, but I popped some nicotine gum into my mouth and followed Cam to the car. We drove in silence to the Becker household. There were four black limousines parked in front of the house, silently waiting to be filled. We went up to the front door, feeling there had to be something we could do to help them face this day.

Graham must have seen us coming up the walk, as the door opened just as we made it up the steps. I gave him a big hug.

'We're almost ready, I think,' he said. 'It's hard to tell with all these kids running around.'

We followed Graham into the living room, where children

ranging from a couple of babes in arms up to the very mature-looking ten-year-old in his little suit and bow tie amused themselves with cards and games and toys. Graham's sisters were all married and had managed to produce ten grandchildren thus far. As soon as the older ones saw Cam they pulled him into their game. He was definitely their new favourite playmate. I sat down on the couch beside Simone and her new baby.

'She's so beautiful,' I said, pulling the blankets away and revealing that perfect little porcelain-doll face.

'Do you mind holding her?' Simone asked. 'I promise she's got a clean diaper and has already been burped. But I just need to finish my make-up.'

'I'm not very good with babies,' I protested.

'Kate, I'll be right down the hallway, just call me if you need me,' she said, as she draped a towel across my shoulder and laid the baby in my arms.

This was the first time I had held a baby since my miscarriage. I thought I would be overwhelmed with emotion, as I had been initially. And I was, but not in the way I had expected. I cradled the tiny little girl in my arm protectively, and one of her tiny hands found my finger and grasped onto it. She smelled like baby powder and I couldn't help but feel a smile break out on my face, just a little one, but it was there. Her name was Angel and I suddenly knew why, she brought great comfort to all those who held her. Well, maybe I was being a little melodramatic, but it wouldn't be the first time. I looked up as one of the kids screamed, 'Bingo!' and noticed Cam watching me.

'You OK?' he mouthed.

'Fine.' I smiled back at him, and then turned my attention back to that beautiful little face.

My peace lasted only a minute, as several women from the Beckers' church turned up to babysit the younger children and prepare the house for the reception after the funeral. Simone and her sisters introduced the children to them and they left their various instructions for their various children. Numerous others started to arrive at the house to join us in our procession to the church – aunts, uncles and cousins. When the kids were settled, we formed a loose line and marched out to the waiting limousines. The drivers helped us sort ourselves out. Simone and her sisters Danielle, Amelia and Beatrice were heralded into one car, with the various husbands. The aunts, uncles and cousins were sent to another couple of cars and Graham, his father, Cam and I were in the first one. Graham sat beside his dad, ramrod-straight and ready to be the man of the family for the day. Nathan Becker looked ten years older than he had a week ago. His shoulders were slumped and his eyes were red and sunken. Graham had his arm linked through his dad's, offering what strength he could. The limousines pulled out slowly, heading downtown to the Knox United Church. When we arrived, the casket had been set up at the front and there were flowers everywhere. We followed the Becker family in and sat in the second row, beside some cousins I hadn't met yet.

'I always wanted to get married in this church,' I whispered into Cam's ear.

His eyebrow raised, not ever expecting me to bring up the subject of marriage.

'When I was little,' I added. 'And dreaming of what my wedding would be like. My friends and I did a lot of research and this church had the longest aisle in the city. I always thought if I was going to spend all that money on a dress, I wanted a really long aisle to walk down, so I could get my money's worth.'

Cam stifled a laugh. 'Well, I'll remember that whenever you decide you are finally ready to do it.'

People filtered into the church for the next twenty minutes or so. Rose had a large circle of friends. There was a large contingent from the Cancer Society, where she had volunteered for over ten years, since the day she had quit smoking, as a matter of fact. Lots of her former students arrived, having read of her passing in the newspaper. I was pleased to see almost all the ushers from our theatre there, including two of the new ones I had hired for the summer, who barely knew Graham. There were also several of the backstage crew and all the cast from *The Sound of Music*. The church was nearly filled when the attendants closed the doors in the back and the minister made his way down the aisle, stopping to whisper a few words to Mr Becker and then making his way up to the altar. I listened to the words, as he read several Bible passages and spoke to us about life and death and suffering and faith. I really did listen, but my thoughts were on Graham as I saw his arm go around his dad's shoulders. Beatrice sat on the other side of her father and passed him a handkerchief.

The minister's sermon was followed by several eulogies, led by a former student from Rose's teaching days, then a close friend, a fellow volunteer and then Nathan Becker's younger brother, who spoke for the family, summing up their joy at having Rose in their lives and their sorrow at losing her so soon. He paused to clear his throat.

'One of the great sorrows Rose had was that she missed her son Graham's big theatre debut last week. The family has asked Graham if he would sing one of the songs from the show for her today and Graham has agreed.'

He stepped down and took his seat. I could see Graham steeling himself, almost like he was getting into character, and then he stood and walked to the front of the church. He was joined by another young man from the cast, with a guitar, who sat on a stool beside him. Graham and I had talked about this moment in the last couple of days. He didn't know if he could do it. I had told him it didn't matter if he couldn't get through it, only that he tried. I looked down and saw my fingers were crossed. That was probably bad in a church, so I uncrossed them, took Cam's hand in mine and then we both looked skyward and said a quick prayer for Graham.

A few chords were strummed and Graham began the opening words of 'Edelweiss'. We had talked about what to sing as well, considering Rolfe's only song in the musical was 'Sixteen Going on Seventeen', and he chose 'Edelweiss' instead. It was a melancholy plea for things to return to the way they had been, and he thought it was appropriate for the occasion.

His voice was strong and clear and I was proud of him. The guitar played a few notes in between the verses. That was when Graham made the mistake of looking at his dad and that was the moment his voice broke just as he started the second verse. I saw his eyes fill with tears and I knew he wasn't going to make it. I just didn't know what to do about it. This wasn't my theatre, after all.

But I didn't have to rescue Graham this time, someone else took care of that for me. A sweet soprano rang out from the back of the church. I turned and saw the actress who played Liesl stand up and walk down the aisle to the front of the church, singing the words that Graham couldn't get out. She joined him, took his hand in hers and smiled at him, never missing a beat. And then another voice joined in and then another and before the second verse was over, the entire cast had surrounded Graham, singing strongly. And he found the strength to join in with them. The song ended and there was total silence except for the rustling of tissue. Cam handed me his handkerchief and I realized I had tears streaming down my face.

The pall-bearers moved to the front of the church, and took their places at the coffin. One of the actors stepped forward and began to sing 'Amazing Grace'. The coffin was lifted off its stand and the men began to move slowly down the centre aisle, toward the waiting hearse. Graham walked over to his family, took his father's arm and they followed the casket down the aisle, his sisters close behind. The rest of us slowly filed out after them, all to the strains of 'Amazing Grace' echoing off the roof of the near empty church.

We climbed into the limo, and began the slow drive to Queen's Park Cemetery and the ground that waited to accept Rose. I couldn't speak, but I reached over and took Graham's hand, holding it tightly and not letting go until we arrived.

I used to think there was no image sadder than that of a freshly dug grave. I was wrong. The saddest thing in the world is watching a young boy and his sisters lower their mother into that awaiting grave, years and years before it ever should have happened.

Graham's house was filled to capacity. The ladies from the church had laid out a beautiful spread, covering the kitchen table, the dining table and several small folding tables that had been set up throughout the house. They had apparently been baking for days and more food was arriving with each guest. There was coffee and tea laid out, juice for the kids, and a few bottles of wine opened up later in the afternoon. I was trying to help and be the dutiful almost-daughter, greeting all the guests, ensuring everyone had food and was happy. Then I noticed Graham and Leonard and one of the other ushers were in the living room moving coffee tables off to the side. Graham moved to the karaoke machine and put a disc inside.

'Ladies and gentlemen, I have already sung a song for my mother,' Graham said. 'Now my father has asked if I would sing a song for him. This was one of my mother's all-time favourite songs. She and Dad would sing it at every party, no matter how much we begged them not to.'

Everyone laughed.

'To help me with the song, may I introduce the lovely Jackie Manson, my Liesl from *The Sound of Music*.'

She joined him by the karaoke machine, and a couple of people clapped for her.

'So, ladies and gentlemen, in honour of my mother and to please my father, may we present Meatloaf's "Paradise by the Dashboard Lights".'

The music started, a rock guitar screamed through the living room and Graham took his cue.

'I remember every little thing as if it happened only yesterday . . .' he began.

Some toes were tapping but some faces looked like they didn't know what to make of this sudden outburst of rock and roll on this solemn occasion. Well, I knew what to do. I grabbed Cam's hand and pulled him out into the middle of the room, and we jived while Graham and Jackie sang.

' . . . so now I'm praying for the end of time . . .'

Soon, people were dancing all through the house.

'I don't know what my favourite was,' I laughed, as Cam and I were driving home. 'However, I really liked your version of "Muskrat Love". And I must say after all this time together I never knew you could sing like that.'

'Oh, you liked my voice?'

'I never said that.'

'I have to say the church ladies singing "Bat Out of Hell" was something I wish I had a videotape of,' Cam laughed back.

'That's how I want to go out,' I said. 'I want people to sing and dance and laugh.'

'Me too,' Cam said. 'And drink lots of wine.'

'I agree. However, we're going to have to have a rule,' I said.

'Another one?' he asked.

'Oh yeah. A big one.'

'OK, what's this rule?'

'If you die before me, I'll kill you.'

He laughed. 'Katie, I promise we'll go together. In a screaming blaze of glory, like Butch and Sundance or Thelma and Louise.'

'Or Bonnie and Clyde?' I asked, offering a male–female duo for him.

'I suppose that would be a little more appropriate.'

'Can we wait until we're very, very old, though? And we can skip the whole part about robbing a bank, too, if you don't mind?'

'I'd prefer that myself.'

'Or falling screaming off a cliff.'

'Fine.'

'Or in a hail of bullets?'

'You're taking all the drama out of our big dramatic ending,' he protested.

But I didn't answer him. Instead I reached over and turned up the radio, pretty sure I recognized the opening strains of the next song. And then we both laughed as 'Paradise by the Dashboard Lights' came on the radio. Cam cranked the volume up even higher and we sang all the way home.

JULY

A heat wave had hit the city, just like it did every year in time for Stampede. Everyone joked that the First Nations did some sort of mystical ceremony to maintain the good weather while they were camped out at the Stampede grounds.

Thought it was late at night the heat still radiated off the concrete. The fire-starter felt it when leaning down to wrap the nylon webbing around the body so it could be easily pulled inside. Those firefighters came up with some very clever time-saving ideas. The body was pulled into the condominium and the door was closed so as not to draw attention. The body was dragged to the centre of the room and a tool belt placed around its waist, just as a diversion. Then, the contractual work done, the fire-starter moved to the part of the job that made it all worthwhile. The part that got the adrenaline flowing. The condominium was only roughed in and the electrical panel sat out, open and unfinished, accessible to the world. The wires were inspected, the correct one chosen and the connection reworked. When finally satisfied with the work there, it was time for the coffee pot that sat in the corner of the room to supply the workmen. A couple of adjustments to the wires and then it was plugged into the wall. As the finale, a couple of cans of paint and paint thinner were placed next to the coffee pot and the pot itself was filled with turpentine. A second can of paint thinner was set beside the first, then knocked over, making it seem as if it had been kicked by a construction worker, carelessly hurrying home at the end of the day.

A final inspection showed everything in its place. A final distasteful look at the body showed that it wouldn't wake up and escape before the fire or heat or smoke overtook it.

'I am sorry about this but you just have to be careful who you piss off in this world,' the fire-starter stated matter-of-factly. 'They say it's a very peaceful way to die. The smoke will be harsh at first, but then you'll just go to sleep.'

And then it was time to leave, and go find the perfect spot to wait.

Tim Horton's was busy at this time of night and that was a surprise. But it provided a very good alibi. It wasn't until after three coffees and two donuts that the sound of the first sirens could be heard a couple of blocks away. Soon the acrid smell of smoke pierced everyone's nostrils, even this far away from the fire, and that was a good thing. The fire had taken good hold before they had found it. An inward smile was all the reward that could be offered at this time, while slowly finishing the word-search puzzle in yesterday's newspaper before ordering a coffee to go and driving slowly in the direction of the sirens. The car edged closer and closer to the fire. The sun was breaking the sky to the east, but to the west he could see the jagged line of flames as they shot up past the line of trees. A half-block away the road was blocked by a line of police cars. The line of early morning commuters were waiting impatiently, but the fire-starter turned the car off without complaint and sipped from the coffee cup. The entire condominium complex was ablaze, and the field across the street had caught fire from errant sparks blown across the street on the breeze. There was a loud popping sound and then the streetlights went dark as a power pole crackled and toppled, exploding a transformer just down the line. Another sip of coffee was followed by another inward smile, pleased at how well this was working out. A thrill running up the spine as more sirens were approaching, and yet another fire truck arrived on the scene. Then the reporter came into view, the pleasant-looking one with the glasses, standing at the side of the road, her brown hair seemingly set ablaze by the fire in the background. She looked like Medusa, her hair alive and writhing for a moment. And then, as she finished her report and her microphone fell to her side, she looked in toward the car and their eyes made contact. The fire-starter couldn't help it, but raised the coffee cup to her in a silent toast and smiled.

Friday

'Katie.' I heard the voice but tried to ignore it. 'Katie!' It was much more insistent and now someone was shaking my shoulder.

'Go away,' I mumbled, curling up and trying to find my

pillow to put over my head and drown out the voice. But I couldn't find it. I opened my eyes and suddenly realized I was in the car with Cam, parked outside the Plex.

He smiled and gave me one last shake, just because he could, before I could push him away.

'I hate you morning people.'

'Yeah, yeah, yeah, that's old news. Come on, we're here, get out.'

I slowly dragged my mind from its unconscious state and tried to remember what I was doing here. Then I looked around and noticed there were people up and down the street, setting up lawn chairs, carrying coolers, wearing cowboy hats. It was obviously the first Friday in July and we were here for the Stampede Parade. At six thirty in the morning. I opened the car door and got out when I noticed Cam was already at the trunk, unloading lawn chairs and picnic coolers. We picked a spot just west of the stage door, easy access to the washrooms, and close to Gus's. Gus's Grounds Zero coffee shop, which wouldn't be open for another thirty minutes.

I helped Cam with the chairs and we set up a double row, with enough for all our friends and family, and the two coolers filled with pop and juice and water. Cam tossed out a couple of blankets and kissed my forehead.

'I'm just going to go park the car,' he told me.

I pulled one of the blankets around me, chilled in the morning air, and plopped down in one of the chairs. Cam parked across the street and then hurried back across to me. He reached into one of the coolers and pulled out a thermos.

'How much would you love me if I told you this was coffee?' he asked.

'Honey, I couldn't possibly love you more than I do right at this very moment.'

He laughed, opened the thermos and poured me a steaming cup. I greedily took a sip, burning my tongue, and set it on the sidewalk to cool a bit.

'I'm cold,' I whined.

'I told you not to wear shorts.'

'But it's going to be blazing hot later.'

'So, you could change. Your office is just two floors up.'

'Why do we have to come this early?'

71

'Because the roads close at seven thirty, Katie. How long have you lived in Calgary and why don't you know this?'

'But it's six thirty, not seven thirty.'

'But you promised thirty people you would save seats for them, so we had to get here early,' he explained slowly to my caffeine-deprived brain.

'But weren't you supposed to offer to come down and set up for us and then I would wander down later and meet you here?'

'You don't think I'm catching on to this yet?' Cam said. 'We've been living together for almost a year now, Katie. I'm on to your tricks.'

'Damn, then I guess I'll have to find some new ways.'

'I look forward to having you try those new ways out on me,' he laughed.

The clock moved slowly and at seven I rushed into Grounds Zero and came back with lattes for Cam and me. I sat back down and wrapped myself in my blanket again, happy to have a little espresso in my system. The crowds started to get thicker and the curb was rapidly filling up with lawn chairs. At seven twenty-five Sam and Ryan's car went racing by, trying to get to the fire hall, where he was going to park, before the roads closed. I waved as they passed, hoping they made it or they were going to pay a fortune for parking today, if they could find a spot. I ran back to Grounds Zero and got a couple of lattes for them and a hot chocolate for Bonnie. They had just arrived along with Ken Lincoln and his wife Rebecca.

'Detective Lincoln.' I smiled, having not seen Ken for a while. 'I don't see a single dead body around here, so to what do we owe this pleasure?'

'We found him at the fire station,' Ryan said.

'And invited him along.'

'Switching to the Fire Department, are you?' I asked.

'No, there was another fire last night,' Ken said. 'I was just talking with the captain about some of the details.'

'Yeah, he forgot to tell me that part,' his wife Rebecca teased him. 'We were just going to the parade he said, but I should have known with police headquarters right here it would never be just the parade. That somehow he'd sneak some work in.'

'Well, we rescued her,' Sam said. 'We figured we could find space for a couple of extra chairs.'

'There's always extra room. And coffee. What would you guys like?'

'Ryan and I will get the next round,' Cam said, wrapping the blanket around me when he saw me shiver.

'Morning, Cam, Kate.'

I turned and smiled at Frank as he strolled past.

'Morning,' Cam answered.

'Hey Cam, I was talking to my folks last night and they said to be sure to say hi.'

'How are they doing?'

'Good. Hoping I've met a nice girl and settled down since I got out here. I think they're anxious for grandchildren.'

'What is that about?' Cam laughed.

'I don't know. But Mom says she and your mom were both talking about weddings and grandchildren when they went out for coffee the other day. So I guess you better get ready for the phone calls to start coming.'

'They already have,' Cam said. 'They want me to bring Katie home to meet them.'

'They do?' I asked.

'Frank, would you like to join us?' he asked, ignoring me for the moment.

'Thanks for the offer, but I'm over there in the single guys, beer-drinking, swearing and no-children zone. I have to enjoy it while I can. Nothing personal, ma'am,' he laughed, doffing his cowboy hat in Sam's direction.

'No worries,' Sam laughed back. 'I wish I could join you there.'

The roads had closed and Sam had laid a blanket out curb-side for Bonnie, who was happily playing with her cowboy Barbie. Sam left Rebecca to watch her, as Rebecca was saddling Barbie's palomino pony, and started to unpack her cooler. She had bacon-and-egg burritos, a whole selection of fresh fruit, yogurt, granola, and fresh muffins. We all chipped in ten bucks every year and she came up with a wonderful breakfast and snack assortment for the parade. The most amazing thing was that her coolers always seemed bottom-less and I don't know how she did it. I fixed a plate for Cam and me as he came back with a tray of assorted coffees, and soon we were joined by a herd of ushers, led by Graham. I hadn't seen him for a week, but he was looking pretty good. I heard they had all gone to the Stampede sneak-a-peak last night and stayed until the park closed. From the looks of the group they had found some beer afterward and stayed up most of the night. They all had that hung-over kind of look as they descended upon the food. Oh, to be nineteen again, I sighed.

I sat down in my chair again, noticing the sun was finally on the far side of the street and should be over our way within another half an hour or so. Ken sat down with his plate in the empty chair beside me.

'Do you guys do this every year?'

'Yeah, it's kind of been a tradition since I've been working at the Plex.'

'And this feast?'

'Pretty good, huh? It started out humble but it's grown over the years.'

'It's amazing. I heard Graham say that you all chip in for it?'

'You can be my guest this year,' I said. 'Next year we'll hit you up for your share.'

'Well, thanks.'

'So, another fire last night and you're talking about it with Ryan's captain. I guess that means you found another body.'

'I think it's going to be a great day for the parade, don't you?' he asked.

'So, was the body dead first or killed in the fire?'

'Has it ever rained on the Stampede parade?'

'Ken, you're not going to tell me anything about this, are you?'

'That's right.'

'But it's kind of scary. I just wanted to know if we should be worried.'

'Honestly, Kate, I don't know. We don't know what these fires are about except that someone is lighting them and someone always dies in them. And that's all I can tell you.'

'There was a fire in Victoria like this, wasn't there? And some in Saskatchewan too? Same type of thing at condo complexes with bodies being found at the scene?'

'Have you ever ridden a horse?' Ken asked, misdirecting me again.

'And wasn't there one in Winnipeg a while ago? Same MO?'

'Kate, you know we are not going to discuss this case, don't you?'

'Even for a free breakfast?'

'Yes, even for a free breakfast.' Ken laughed, taking the last bite of his burrito. And then he looked up at me. 'There isn't anything you know about this, is there?'

'What do you mean?'

'Well, every time you and I get together here, there seems to be some sort of crime committed that you seem to know a lot about. Is this one of those times?'

'No,' I laughed. 'No. I was asking because we're worried about Ryan. It's bad enough that he has all the normal fires and rescues. We were all at Sam's house when that first big fire happened last month and it scared me. I suddenly realized what Ryan actually did at work, you know?'

'Well, I don't but I bet my wife does.'

'I'm sure she does. Anyway, remember I turned over a new leaf and I now tell you everything I might know or suspect or even had a dream about.'

'Well, I know you say that, but I'm just never sure if you actually mean it.'

'Trust me.' I crossed my heart. 'I mean it. I realized I'm just not really into the whole adrenaline lifestyle you guys seem so hooked on.'

'Yeah, well trust me, I'm not really hooked on the adrenal part myself, I'd rather investigate and arrest quietly.'

'Well, I swear to God, Ken, that if I even see anyone playing with matches, I will tell you about it.'

'While running away from the scene, right?'

'While running quickly away from the scene!' I seconded.

'The parade!' Bonnie squealed from her blanket.

We turned en masse, looking westward down 9th Avenue, looking for a sign. But it was just the pre-parade, friendly volunteers who felt sorry for us folks who had to get up this early in the morning and then wait three hours for the parade to start. There were clowns and some musicians, a barbershop quartet and a large Sweet Adeline's choir sang some Boot Scootin' Boogies, and a trick roper followed with his lasso, all spaced just far enough apart to give us something to look at every few minutes. And then there were the police with their navy-blue police-issued cowboy hats, handing out their trading cards and posing for pictures, walking up and down the block; the paramedics, the parade marshals. We got free balloons, free newspapers, free paper hats. And I noticed Frank left the single-guys contingent long enough to get a date with a pretty police officer. We spent a fortune on coffee and ate our way through breakfast. Sam cleaned up the entrée and then laid out the rest of the snacks. Cam and I moved the drink coolers to the middle to use as tables, where everyone could reach then. I checked my watch and we had about twenty minutes to go.

'OK everyone, it's charity time,' I announced. 'And this year the proceeds are going to the Kate Carpenter needs a house fund, a newly registered charitable organization.'

'It should be going to the Cam needs a beer fund,' Ryan laughed. 'Since you're driving him to drink.'

'Nobody likes a smart . . .'

'Children present,' Sam reminded me.

' . . . aleck!' I pulled the sidewalk chalk out of my backpack. 'Who's in?'

'Here's one for Ryan, one for me and three for Bonnie's college fund,' Sam laughed, handing me a five-dollar bill.

'I'm down for two,' Graham called, tossing a toonie to Cam.

'Me too,' Leonard called, digging into his wallet.

'What are we betting on and is it legal?' Ken asked.

'Don't go ruining my fun and asking me if it's legal betting,' I said. 'You know I don't stop to check these things out!"

'We call it Parade Bingo,' Cam said.

'What do we do?' he asked.

'You give me a dollar for every chance you want in the game. And then we wait for the parade to start.' I smiled at him.

Ken pulled a couple of dollars out of his pocket and handed it over.

'Winner takes all,' I said. 'And we let Cam keep the pot

because everyone thinks he's more trustworthy than I am.'

Ken laughed out loud at that one, but turned and pretended he was having a coughing fit when I shot him a dirty look. Bonnie and I headed out to the street with the sidewalk chalk. She was drawing pretty pink flowers with her piece of chalk, but I drew a bunch of random circles, a couple of feet in diameter, up and down and across the street. I put a name inside each circle to correspond to the money people had bet. When I was done, Sam came out to verify my work and drag Bonnie in off the street. We all got settled with a beverage as we heard the first strains of the Stampede Show Band marching toward us. The sun had just touched our side of the street and I finally got brave enough to unwrap myself from the blanket. Sam passed the sunscreen to me after she had finished slathering it on her daughter and herself.

'So how does this game work?' Ken asked, settling back in his chair and letting his guard down long enough to link his arm through his wife's.

'You weren't born in Calgary, were you, Ken?' I laughed.

'Vancouver,' he admitted. 'We've only been here since I started with the Calgary Police Department.'

'You don't know much about livestock, do you?'

'I can't say that I do.'

'Well, then basically what we do is sit here and wait and see whose circle gets filled first. And that's the winner.'

'Filled with what?' he yelled, as the band approached us, playing one of the old standard marches.

'You'll see.'

The band was here now and the parade officially started. The Stampede Show Band was the opening act every year, the official band of the Calgary Stampede and Exhibition, or Greatest Outdoor Show on Earth, as they liked to call it. They consisted of a marching band followed closely by volunteer parents with water bottles, as these poor kids were marching for over two hours this morning, in the beating sun, dressed in the polyester red-and-white uniforms; they were followed by a rifle brigade, baton-twirlers, a flag brigade and their show riders. We were in a great spot, as the band stopped and played in front of us for several minutes. It should be a good year this year. Some years, they walked right on by to just the beating of a drum, this year, it looked like the marshalling at the end of the parade was going to give us some good entertainment.

'So people stopped in my square,' Ken said. 'But they stopped in everyone's squares. So who wins?'

'Ken, it's the Stampede. It's not about people.'

'What do you mean?'

'Just like that,' Cam laughed, pointing across the street.

A forest ranger riding his horse was stopped and talking to some kids across the street. The horse's tail lifted up, always a sign, and the group of ushers started screaming, trying to see whose circle lay below the horse. And then it happened. The horse kindly deposited its load directly into the middle of one of our circles, lowered its tail delicately and wandered off down the street.

'That's what we're betting on?' Ken asked. 'Where the horse manure will fall?'

'That's right. That's what it is.'

'That's disgusting, is what that is.'

'Well, then I guess you won't be wanting your fifty-dollar prize, then?' Cam asked, handing him over the envelope of money.

'I won?' Ken asked.

His wife reached across him and took the envelope from Cam.

'On behalf of my husband I apologize if he has personally insulted any of your Calgary traditions and gratefully accept this prize in his name.'

'Hey,' Ken said, trying to grab the envelope, but she was quick.

'Remember those shoes I was looking at the other day?' she asked, a sly smile on her face.

'Yes.'

'Well, thanks, honey, I'll pick them up tonight.' She kissed him, put the money in her purse and turned back to the parade.

Six hundred and fifty horses, twelve chuck wagons, seventeen bulls, one herd of sheep, thirty-five clowns, forty-five floats, twenty-five marching bands, countless pipers and two hours later, the procession of police cars, fire trucks and ambulances with sirens blaring, followed by the very necessary street cleaners, signalled the end of the parade. We quickly pulled ourselves up off the curb, as traffic would follow minutes after the sweepers, and gathered up our garbage. We said our goodbyes to everyone, carried our stuff back across the street to Cam's car and dropped Sam and Ryan and Bonnie off at the fire hall to get their car.

We stopped off at home for a short nap. I grabbed some jeans and a jacket and we headed back to Sam and Ryan's place for their yearly parade-day barbecue. A few close friends, a barbecue in the backyard with everyone but Sam contributing – since she made breakfast we gave her the night off – followed by a little beer drinking, a little two-stepping on the patio and then blankets spread out in the backyard, where we all sat to watch the fireworks display. I sat on the dewy grass in front of Cam, leaning against him with his arms wrapped around me, watching the fireworks explode in the sky, listened to the crackle of the wood in the fire pit behind me and realized I really wanted a home like this. I wondered if Sam and Ryan would just give us this house and then they could spend tomorrow out with a realtor, the fate that awaited me. Maybe that was why I didn't want this day to end.

Saturday

The alarm rang early and I got up without complaint. This was going to be a whole new me with a whole new attitude. I showered, ate breakfast and packed up my backpack. I finished dressing and stood dutifully by the door, waiting for Cam to join me. I knew it was going to be a long day for everyone, but I had resolved to try really hard and find something I liked in one of the twenty houses we had lined up to see today. I was going to be adult about this. The noise of the jackhammer just down the hall reaffirmed the fact that I really had no choice in the matter.

We had spent most of June not really sleeping past seven in the morning, as construction raged on around us. I had even gotten on the Internet to check out the city's noise by-laws, but seven o'clock was what it said was legal, so unfortunately I couldn't have anyone arrested. Very disappointing news. There were about ten of us diehards left in the building, and we were all getting crankier by the day. What finally did it for me was the day they closed the laundry room, so we were now hauling everything to the Laundromat on a weekly basis. Plus we had a maximum of forty days left in our extension and then, whether we were gone or not, our place was getting turned into a condominium. In a way, I think it was a good thing we had stayed through the initial phase of construction, because at this point in time I really didn't want to be here any longer. A bit of aversion therapy might just motivate me to find the house of Cam's dreams.

We went down to the car and got in. Cam hadn't said much this morning and I assumed he was just so pleased that I wasn't whining and complaining already that he didn't want to tempt the fates by breaking the silence. I was happy not to have to fake any joyful small talk just yet, as well. I was sure I was going to be stretched to my limit later in the day. So I settled back into the comfortable passenger seat and let Cam drive me to my fate. Though I was getting a little confused as he turned off Memorial Drive and made his way to 16th Avenue, pointing us west. I waited a few minutes, thinking this might be a shortcut to some mysterious community that held our dream home, but he didn't turn either left or right and soon I saw the Calgary city limits sign.

'Where are we going?' I asked, as the Fish continued to speed down the number-one highway.

'We're going for a breath of fresh air and a bit of a break,' Cam said.

'Not house-hunting?' I asked.

'Not today. I thought we'd try something different today,' he said. 'I thought I'd give you a little piece of heaven instead of a day of hell.'

'And where is this mysterious piece of nirvana located?'

'Don't you trust me?'

'Well, in all honesty, if I were you I would be tempted to

take me out into the mountains and dump me where only the grizzly bears would find me.'

He laughed out loud. 'I swear I am not taking you out to the mountains to dispose of the body. I thought we might take a little walk—'

'Not a hike?' I interrupted, knowing that his idea of a hike and mine were two very different things.

'I swear, just a walk. You will not need to be a mountain goat to manage any of the pathways.'

'There are real pathways?' I asked. 'Why have you never taken me to a place like this before?'

'Because you've never been this close to a nervous breakdown before. Anyway, I've got some prosciutto, some goat cheese, a baguette and a lovely bottle of a great little red wine. My plan is to walk a little, lay down a blanket and have a lovely little picnic while we forget about people dying of cancer and real-estate agents and summer schedules at the theatre and the vacation we're probably never going to get this summer . . .'

'That sounds wonderful,' I admitted. 'A few minutes of peace would be worth my soul right now. Oh, but Cam, maybe we should have brought Graham out for a little break. I'm sure he'd like to get away for a while.'

'Nope, this is you and me. He's got his own friends and they'll look after him. As a matter of fact, he looked OK yesterday.'

'He looked hung over yesterday.'

'Maybe that's what he needed, a big drink with his friends.'

'I don't know if that's the answer.'

'Katie, he's nineteen, drinking, girls and staying up all night are the only answers.'

'I suppose you're right.'

'Well, today we're not going to worry about other people. Today, we're going to look after each other.'

'I really love you sometimes, you know?'

'Yeah, well I'm pretty lovable.'

Cam had left the highway at the Nakiska Mountain turn-off and headed into Kananaskis country. He seemed to be able to differentiate the various dirt roads from each other and snaked his way into the forest until he was satisfied we were far removed from civilization. He parked the car, turned it off and grabbed his loaded backpack from the trunk.

'Do you want me to carry anything?' I asked.

'I've got it all here,' he said. 'All you have to do is hold my hand and stroll through the trees with me.'

'You're sure I don't need to leave a trail of breadcrumbs? Or maybe some clues to my disappearance?'

He laughed at me but held out his hand and I took it. His idea of a pathway was radically different than mine as well, but at least it wasn't up a seventy-degree slope or hanging off the edge of a glacier. We slipped and slid our way up a hill until he found a nice little meadow, protected from the breeze by a nice grove of larch trees. Cam spread out the blanket, pulled out a little cutting board and set up our snack. He had two crystal wine glasses, wrapped up in dishtowels, which he unwrapped and handed to me to hold while he uncorked the bottle.

'Crystal?' I asked.

'Well, it's a special occasion and I did get it on sale.'

'Special occasion?'

'Yes, it is,' he said, pouring the glasses and re-corking the bottle. 'We're here to celebrate.'

'What are we celebrating?'

'Katie, I don't want you to be angry.'

'Oh, shit, Cam, do you think that's a really good way to start this conversation? Or this day?'

'No, but I just could not figure out another way to start it.'

I took a big sip of wine, and then another. 'OK, I'm ready.'

'Katie, you know I love you and I only have your best interests at heart, right?'

'Without a doubt.'

'And I know how incredibly stressful this whole house-hunting has been for you.'

'You know, I should be apologizing to you. Cam, I don't know what's wrong with me but this has freaked me out so badly. And I've just been so unreasonable about everything. You and Mr Jones really have been saints to put up with me.'

'I appreciate that, sweetie,' he said taking my hand and holding it tightly. 'So, because I know you wanted a house that was kind of different and because this was all stressing you out, I found something a couple of days ago and Mr Jones put an offer in on it for me. They accepted the offer this morning, I got the message on my cellphone. Katie, we are now officially property-owners.'

I felt my stomach churn and my peripheral vision suddenly tighten and I thought I might faint. Cam took my wine glass out of my hand and set it on a flat rock, safely away from where I might cause it harm.

'Katie?'

'I'm OK,' I rasped.

'Do you need water?' he asked, reaching for the backpack.

'No. No, I just need a minute to process this. You bought a house for us?'

'Yes.'

'OK, which one was it?'

'You haven't seen this one.'

'OK.' I tried to control my breathing so I wouldn't hyper-ventilate. 'You bought us a house that I haven't even seen yet?'

'Yes. But, Katie, it's cute, it's different, it's exactly what you wanted.'

'How would you know that?' I asked, trying really hard not to show too much attitude until I had the whole story.

'I know because I know you. It was a little expensive, it's at the top of our price range and it's a bit of a fixer-upper . . . but, Katie, it's almost five thousand square feet. It's got a huge ventilated and heated garage so I can work on the car. There's an exercise room. The kitchen is amazing with restaurant-quality cook tops and stainless-steel appliances. There's an entertainment room and three bedrooms . . .'

'I can't believe you did this.'

'Well, frankly neither can I. But we had a definite problem going on here. You couldn't make up your mind about a place and our current apartment is coming down around us. I'm getting tired of the dust and the noise and the jackhammers at seven in the morning, Katie, aren't you?'

'Well, yes, but we have to find the perfect place.'

'Well, I can assure you that this isn't it. But what it has is the perfect bones to become our perfect place. And I will renovate it myself, night and day, and make it into any style you want it to be. It will be your dream home in six months.'

'And this is supposed to calm me down.'

'Hope springs eternal,' he sighed.

'Oh, oh wait a minute. I get it now. This is a joke. This is your idea of how to pay me back for looking at all these damned houses, right?'

'No joke.'

'Come on, Cam, it's kind of funny. You really had me going, actually.'

'Katie . . .'

'But, Cam, the best part of a joke is knowing when to end it and I think you should end it now and then we can laugh and we can drink some wine.'

'Kate,' he yelled harshly, 'I am not joking!'

And those words echoed off the mountains as I just stood and stared at him.

'Cam, you've bought a house I have never seen. I don't know how you think this would relax me or calm me down.'

'Because, Katie, the decision is made. All you have to do now is get really pissed off at me, we'll make up and then we move into our new home.'

I just stared at him. I didn't know what to say or do. In a way he was right, I couldn't make a decision about buying a home because I didn't want to give up my old home. But a huge mortgage in my name on a property I had never seen before . . . and then I did start hyperventilating. A several-hundred-thousand-dollar mortgage, debt that I wouldn't be able to pay off for twenty-five years or more and a piece of land that I didn't even know where it was . . .

'Katie,' Cam said, putting the paper bag the baguette had been in over my nose and mouth. 'Breathe slowly, in and out, in and out.'

I did what he said and got a mouthful of breadcrumbs on the first try, but slowly felt the oxygen getting back into my system and my panic subsiding. When I eventually felt in control, I pushed the paper bag away and sat there quietly for a minute, blinking back the tears that were threatening to spill out of my eyes.

'Are you going to say anything?' he finally asked me.

'I'm going back to the car,' I said, standing up and storming off down what I thought was the pathway.

'Katie,' he called and I heard him getting up after me. 'You're going the wrong . . .'

'Cam?' I asked, turning around, when I heard a crash behind me.

'Fuck!'

'Cam?' I raced back and found Cam lying on the ground, face up, one of his knees twisted beneath him. 'Oh, God, Cam, what happened? Are you OK?'

'I slipped on some loose rocks,' he informed me, through gritted teeth.

'Are you OK? Let me help you up.'

'I felt a pop in my knee. I'm not really sure I want to try sitting up just yet.'

I looked at his knee. It didn't seem to be in an unnatural position, which would probably mean a fracture or dislocation, just hyper-extended.

'I'm just going to try to straighten out your leg,' I said. 'Take a deep breath and try and relax your muscles.'

'No, Katie, I don't think that's such a good idea.'

'Cam, right now I'm in charge. Deep breath and let me do all the work, don't try and lift your leg or anything.'

I slowly straightened out his leg, causing him more pain than I felt he deserved, even with buying a house without my seeing it. Once the leg was straightened, I felt up and down it. The kneecap was where it was supposed to be, and he wasn't wincing from my palpating pressure, so I don't think there was anything broken. Probably just a really bad sprain or strain.

'I think you're going to live. Do you think you can walk out of here?'

'Only one way to find out,' he said, holding his hands up in the air for me to help him up.

I grabbed his hands and braced myself. We got him into an upright position and then I draped his arm around my shoulder.

'OK, let's try to get back to the blanket,' I suggested.

Cam took two hopping steps, almost crushing me in the process, but he had already broken out in a cold sweat. I stopped him and sat him down on a boulder. I pulled my phone out of my pack and turned it on.

'No signal,' I said. 'Shit, what good are these things for anyway?'

'You know the coverage in the mountains isn't perfect yet.'

'All right, plan B then. Since I'm not going to be able to get the paramedics out here to rescue you, and since I have no intention of spending the night in the mountains, I'm going to try and find something for you to use as a crutch and we'll splint your knee and make our way back to the car.'

'That sounds like a good idea,' he admitted. 'Katie, you're really being amazing here.'

'Yeah, well enjoy it while you can. Once you're at the hospital and checked out, the truce is over and you're a dead man.'

I found some short and sturdy branches and we made a makeshift splint out of branches and belts, just like in Boy Scout training. I couldn't find anything for him to use as a crutch, so I guessed that was going to be my job. I packed up the backpack, leaving the food and pouring out the wine, to make the pack as light as possible, and then put it on. I fed Cam a couple of extra-strength Advil I had in my purse and then we started out. It was exhausting. Cam was trying not to weigh me down, but then his leg would give out and I'd be struggling to hold him upright. It took us about two hours to get back to the car, from the spot it had taken us thirty minutes to get to. I took the car keys from Cam's pocket and opened up the back door. I didn't think he'd fit anywhere else with his leg splinted.

'Whoa, just a minute, what are you doing?' he asked, pulling away.

'Putting you in the car. Unless you wanted to walk all the way back to Calgary?'

'I can drive,' he said. 'My leg is feeling much better.'

I sighed and cursed this whole car thing he had going on. But I knew I had to keep it calm and reasonable or we'd be out here all night arguing about it.

'Sweetie . . .' I started.

'No, Katie, I'll drive us back into town.'

'No, Cam, you won't. You can barely move that leg. How are you going to work the clutch?'

'I'll do it,' he said. 'Don't you worry about that.'

'Cam, I don't want to die,' I said. 'And if you're trying to drive us in with that knee that just gave out on you twenty-five times in that walk we just took, then we are going to die.

And we'll probably take some innocent people with us. So either you climb in that back seat immediately and let me drive us back into town or I'm throwing the car keys into the forest right now and neither one of us is getting out of here. Those are your two choices.'

He stared at me for a long time. I saw his jaw muscles working and his brow furrowing, but not a sound left his lips. Finally, when he knew he was beat and there would be no argument that would sway me, he sat in the back seat, his splinted leg stretched out across the other side. He did his seat belt up and sat in silence.

'Thank you,' I said.

I closed the back door and let myself in the driver's side, repositioning the seat and doing up my seat belt tightly too. I wasn't real sure about driving this thing now that I was sitting in this seat.

'So, Cam, can we just review exactly how to use the clutch?' I asked, dreading his response.

'Have you ever driven a car with manual transmission?' he asked quietly.

'No.'

There was a moment of silence and then I heard a sigh. I didn't turn around, not wanting to antagonize him any more than I already had.

'All right, you use the clutch to change gears. So, to start the car, you're going to put the clutch in and keep it in, then start it. When you are ready to drive, you are going to slowly let the clutch out while you are slowly pushing the accelerator down. OK?'

'OK.'

'And then when the rpms are reading just below the red zone, you're going to push the clutch in again and pull the gear shift down into second from first.'

'Where is the rpm thingy?' I asked, studying the dashboard.

'Never mind, I'll tell you when to change gears.'

'OK,' I said. 'Can I start it now?'

Again there was a big sigh from the back seat, but I saw his head nod in the affirmative and I turned the key. The car took a big jump forward and I let my hand fall off the key, shocked.

'Oops, the clutch,' I giggled nervously. 'Sorry.'

I carefully pushed the clutch in and turned the key again. The car started normally this time and I took a deep breath, wondering if I was going to be able to pull this off or not.

'I love you, Cam,' I said, letting my foot off the clutch in what I thought was a slow and steady manner. The car lurched forward, seeming to jump from under me, and then it stalled. 'What did I do?'

'You just didn't quite have the gas and the clutch synchronized correctly,' he said, and I noticed his teeth were gritted again.

'Shall we try again?' I asked, pushing the clutch back in and turning the key.

This time, though we lurched and jumped, we actually made some forward progress as the car resisted stalling. Once the clutch was out and we were driving, it was just like any other car I'd ever driven. Until Cam spoke from the back.

'Put the clutch in and pull it straight down into second gear now,' he said. 'And then slowly let the clutch out again.'

I did as he instructed, finding second gear much more forgiving than first had been. We continued on and he told me to gear up into third gear, which I did, with a horrible grinding noise coming from the car, but we kept our forward motion. I was feeling really proud of myself until I saw the stop sign up ahead and realized I was going to have to go through this all several more times.

'Well, there's the first mile down,' I laughed, slowing down for the stop sign.

Cam didn't respond, as he was busy rubbing down the migraine headache that was starting behind his eyes. I slid the car into first gear and managed to stall it two more times before we made it through the stop sign. By the tenth stop sign Cam was supine on the back seat, leg up in the air, not able to watch any longer. Mind you, I was getting much more proficient with the clutch. And the tenth stop sign took us to the highway, which meant it was going to be smooth sailing for thirty minutes until we hit the city and the traffic lights. Cam called out gear changes to me from the back seat, but even then I had discovered the tachometer and was anticipating when he would tell me to gear up. And then the Gods were with us because between the city limits and the emergency doors of the Foothills Hospital we didn't hit a single red light. I pulled to a stop in front of the door and went inside, looking for a wheelchair and some assistance. I was rewarded with a burley orderly who pretty much pulled Cam out of the car and settled him in the wheelchair, adjusting the leg into a comfortable position, before he kindly offered to park the car for me. I gave him a ten-dollar bill for the parking fees and pushed Cam into the emergency room, where he was assessed by a triage nurse.

Apparently, mid-afternoon on the second day of Stampede is an excellent time to get injured and visit your local hospital, as Cam was whisked back and changed and X-rayed all within a couple of hours, though the nurses told me that in another day or two this room would be bustling with drunken urban-cowboy injuries, like sprained ankles from walking in cowboy boots, sunstroke and pancreatitis from too much drinking in too short a period of time.

I was allowed back to sit with Cam until the doctor came by, which took a little longer, but it was an orthopaedic surgeon, so we didn't complain. The wait list to see him via normal means was probably six months, so this was a bonus.

'Hi there,' the surgeon said, shaking our hands. 'Stan Savage.'

We both shook his hands and I liked the fact that his hair was beginning to gray and he actually looked at least our age, if not a little older. Doctors were generally looking younger and younger with every year older I got.

'Well, I've looked over the X-rays and talked with the resident that did the examination, and I'm afraid it's probably an ACL tear. May I?' he asked, taking Cam's knee in his hands and manipulating it. 'Yes, there's definitely some instability in there. So, we're going to ice it and we're going to use some painkillers and an anti-inflammatory and you're going to be in an immobilizer for at least six weeks.'

'There's got to be some other way,' Cam protested. 'We just bought a house.'

'I can suggest a good moving company, but that's the best I can do. We need to get an MRI and that's going to take a month or so. I'm not in a hurry there since I know I'm not going to do surgery right away.'

'Surgery?' I asked.

'Probably. For the degree of instability I'm feeling here, I'm pretty sure we're going to have to do a reconstruction.'

'What is that?' I asked. 'I can't remember if it's a tendon, ligament, muscle or bone.'

'Anterior cruciate ligament,' both Cam and the doctor said simultaneously.

'And I'm guessing it's pretty important?'

'Without good stability, the knee is going to give way, and twist. And that just causes more injuries to other areas of the knee as well as opening him up to osteoarthritis. Now, you seem to have fairly good muscle tone. I take it you work out regularly?' the doctor asked.

'I used to,' Cam said. 'Until today.'

'Right. Well, I'm going to send you to the physiotherapist next week and they will give you a home-exercise program. It's very important you keep the rest of your leg nice and strong. Other than that, there's not much I can offer except a little Celebrex and Tylenol Number Three,' he joked.

He scribbled out a couple of prescriptions and pulled out a business card, handing them all to me.

'So, you can get those filled on the way home, keep the ice packs on him and then my secretary will set up an appointment for you in the next six weeks. Nice to meet you both. I'll send the nurse in to help you get the immobilizer fitted and then get you dressed.'

I left Cam with the nurse and sat in the lobby to wait for him. I called Sam and Ryan and begged them to come and rescue me and the car. Sam pulled up at the emergency entrance just as I was wheeling Cam out. Ryan jumped out of the passenger's seat and Sam leaned over so she could talk to us from the driver's seat.

'Well, I was going to suggest you guys come over for dinner, but maybe I'll just bring you over something later.' Sam said.

'Good idea. We have to get some prescriptions filled and then I imagine Cam will pretty much feel like hanging around home tonight, am I right?'

'Yeah, you're right. Well, Bonnie is sleeping over at her friend's house and then they're going to the zoo tomorrow, so why don't I meet you guys back at the loft and I'll take care of dinner for you tonight.'

'You don't have to do that, Sam,' I said. 'I can order in.'

'I know you can. But I can cook too. It's no trouble.'

I looked at Cam for affirmation and he nodded. 'That would be darned nice of you.'

'Well, we're darned nice people,' Sam said. 'I'll see you guys in a bit, then.'

'Do you need a key?' I asked.

'Nope, I brought mine just in case.'

We closed the door and Sam drove off down the street.

'Well,' Ryan said, taking the wheelchair from me and pushing Cam across to the parking lot. 'What a busy afternoon you've had.'

'I can't say it went exactly as planned,' Cam laughed.

'Where's the car?' Ryan asked.

'I'm not sure,' I said. 'I asked the orderly to park for me since I wasn't sure if I could manage parking it or not.'

'Oh, I see it,' Ryan finally said, leading the way.

'Thank God, I never saw the orderly come back in so I was afraid he might have gone joyriding.'

'So how's the clutch?' Ryan asked Cam.

'It's going to be in need of some work. And she was a little harsh on the brakes too.'

'Considering I have never driven a manual and considering I had just dragged you ten miles out of the woods and considering I was totally stressed out, I would say I didn't do too bad a job,' I protested. 'And if you'd ever let me drive that thing before today, maybe I would have been a little more prepared.'

'Well, I'll be happy to teach you how to drive a manual,' Cam said. 'But I'll rent a car to do it in.'

Ryan took the keys from me and helped Cam into the back seat. I took my preferred place in the passenger side and Ryan returned the wheelchair to the hospital entrance for us. Then he pulled the car smoothly out into traffic and shifted gears quietly and painlessly.

'So, do you have a preference for which pharmacy we stop at?' he asked.

'No,' we both agreed.

'Did you get a chance to tell her before you fell off the mountain?' Ryan asked.

'Tell me what?' I asked innocently. Then realization dawned. 'You knew about the house?'

'Katie,' Cam warned me from the back seat.

'Ryan, you bastard, you knew and you let him do it anyway? You're married. You of all people should know better.'

'Well, Sam thought it was a good idea,' he said, and then realized what he had let slip.

'Sam knew? My best friend in the world was in on this betrayal?'

'Kate, we were all just trying to help,' Ryan tried.

'Help who? Cam?'

'Katie,' Cam warned again, 'it was my idea. If you're going to be mad, be mad at me. They were just trying to help us out.'

'Take me there.'

'What?'

'Take me to this house. I'm not going back to my apartment to listen to you all talk about it when I've never seen it.'

'Now?' Ryan asked. 'Don't you think we should get Cam home first?'

'Why, because he's in pain?' I asked. 'This is nothing compared to the pain he's going to be in.'

'Cam?' Ryan asked, waiting for instructions.

'Take me now or I swear I'm getting out of this car and none of you will ever see me again.'

'It's OK, Ryan,' Cam said. 'Would you mind driving us there?'

'You sure you feel up to this?' Ryan asked.

'No, I don't feel up to it, but I feel less up to the alternative,' Cam said.

I ignored him, and sat staring straight ahead, very interested in seeing where this drive would take us and where I would be living in a couple of months. Ryan drove us down 29th Street and turned left on to Memorial Drive and zigzagged over to Bow Trail. The traffic got heavier as we neared downtown, but we followed it into the downtown core, where Ryan cut down to 1st Street and turned south. We followed 1st

Street until it ended, and then turned down 2nd Street. I was trying to figure out what neighbourhood I was going to be living in, when Ryan turned at 18th Avenue and parked the car. We were in Mission, a nice community filled with beautiful huge old elm trees that lined the streets. Refurbished old houses stood side by side with new apartment-style condos, most designed to fit in with the age of the area. Several of my favourite restaurants were within a few blocks and I knew of a couple of coffee shops in the area too. This might not be so bad after all.

'Which one?' I asked, getting out of the car and looking up and down the street. There was a beautiful little wooden house a couple of doors down, with gingerbread cut-outs along the eaves. There was an old wooden farmhouse a few more doors down and a beautiful brick manor-style that must have belonged to the local doctor or lawyer back in the days it was built. I was actually starting to get a little excited about the idea that we owned one of these gems. Even the little wartime clapboard houses on this side of the street had great potential. And Cam was very handy.

Cam had pulled himself out of the back seat and was standing up, holding on to the car door to steady himself.

'That one,' he said, pointing to the corner lot.

'The corner?' I asked him, trying to clarify.

'Yes.'

I walked over and inspected the lot. It was huge, probably a double lot by today's standards. There was an overgrown lawn on one side, and the back was fenced. The building sitting upon the lot was a huge older brick building, which would normally excite me because I liked old and I liked brick. But this wasn't old brick, worn and weathered, this was fairly new brick. And the building was pretty much a square block, institutional.

'There are great windows,' Cam said, limping up to where I stood. 'There's a nice yard in the back and I'm going to build us a deck on the roof as well.'

I took a few more steps toward the building. Cam had been right, the garage was huge. It would probably house a semi-trailer if I had one to park there. And I looked at the inscription that rested above the huge garage door.

City of Calgary
Fire Hall # 7
1967
A Centennial Project

'You bought a fire hall?' I asked.

'It's not a fire hall any more,' he said.

That hadn't exactly been my point.

'The city decommissioned it about five years ago,' Ryan said. 'They needed a bigger one and relocated it. A couple of firefighters bought this one and were going to turn it into a pub. But it just never worked out for them and they finally decided they wanted to get rid of it. So Mr Jones arranged for Cam to come and look at it. It was a really good deal, Kate.'

'It's a big square brick fire hall,' I said. 'You expect me to live in a fire hall?'

'I expect you to show a little imagination and realize what we could turn this into. It's palatial and it's half the price we would pay for something this size.'

'And there's a reason for that,' I said. I couldn't tear my eyes away from the building.

'Kate, Ryan has offered to help and I can hire guys I know who will work for half their regular fees.'

'Can we go inside?' I asked.

'I have a key,' Ryan admitted, looking to Cam with apologetic eyes.

I took the key from his hand and hurried to the front door. Ryan helped my limping boyfriend try to keep up with me. I put the key in the lock and turned it, pushing through the glass door and noticing the white cinder-block walls and industrial linoleum. The rooms were all large, but all the walls were cinder block and the linoleum ran throughout.

'Cam?' I asked, turning and looking into his eyes to try and see what he had seen.

He draped his arm around my shoulder and pulled me close to him. I knew he was using me in place of a crutch, but this time I felt his calm come over me by osmosis. I was trying to see this all through his eyes as I blinked back tears that seemed to be forming.

'All right. First of all the linoleum is coming up and we will

94

replace it with tile or carpet, depending on the room. We can also use hardwood, which might be really nice for the bedroom or living room. I'll take you to Home Depot and we can look at some of the different samples they have. Now, there's nothing we can do to change the cinder block, but we can drywall over top of it. The hallways are extra wide, so losing a little bit of depth with framing and drywall isn't going to make a difference.'

He started walking me down the hallway, poking his head into the various doorways.

'This used to be the captain's office,' he said. 'See, there's glass that looks out into the corridor and into the garage? I thought this would make a great office and computer room. We can put blinds on the glass for a little privacy or replace the windows with glass bricks. That way there would still be lots of light in the room.'

He pulled me across the hall.

'These two rooms would make great guest bedrooms. We'll drywall and put some flooring in and the main bathroom is just over here. We can just put a stall shower in and we'll be good to go.'

And a little further down the hall, 'This can be the exercise room.'

'That's what they used it for,' Ryan added, trailing along behind us.

'And the kitchen,' Cam said. 'The appliances are all top of the line. Look at this great gas range. And I bought it with all the appliances included.'

This kitchen did look like something you might see a famous chef using on his network TV food show. It was all gleaming stainless steel and Cam was positively beaming.

'There'd be room for a huge old wooden table over there,' I suggested, wanting to please him.

'And then there's a room off here that we could open up and turn into the family room and TV room,' he said, beaming at me now. 'Do you want to see upstairs?'

'Can you manage?'

'I can manage,' he said.

He hopped up the stairs and led me into a large room.

'This was the sleeping area,' Ryan said. 'The captain had a separate room just down the hall.'

'This will be the master suite,' Cam said.

I looked around and couldn't imagine it. It was a big barn of a room, covered in linoleum and still those blinding white cinder-block walls. There were tattered blinds on the windows and the bathroom was industrial urinals and a large communal shower.

'My bedroom?' I asked. 'Here?'

'Katie, I know your bedroom is important to you. It's going to be beautiful. I swear, if you give me two weeks, I'll have this turned into the most luxurious room you could ever even dream of. The rest of the place might take me a bit longer, but I'll bring in the troops and have this room ready for you.'

'Two weeks?' I asked. 'When is the possession date?'

'Monday if the lawyers can get all the paperwork cleared. I wanted to be able to do some renovations before we moved in.'

I looked into his eyes and saw the dream he had wanted to build for me. He had planned this all as a big surprise, I guessed. Planning to drive me over here in a few weeks and show me some of the finished rooms, to make me believe that it could be turned into a beautiful palace for me. And then I looked down at his knee and realized his dreams had all been shot down. And mostly because I had taken off down the mountain in the heat of the moment and he had come to rescue me.

'I can still get it done,' he said, reading my mind.

'I know you can,' I said, sucking it up and thinking of him. 'It's going to be beautiful.'

Right now I was lying, but I hoped that eventually I would believe it. But that was a lot of hope. Meanwhile, the look on his face was worth it all. He grabbed me and pulled me into a huge bear hug that would have knocked us both over if Ryan hadn't been there to pull him back upright.

'I love you, Katie,' he said.

'I love you too, Cam,' I told him. I just didn't know if I would ever love this as my house. My home.

'We better get going,' Ryan said. 'Sam's going to wonder what we've been up to.'

Ryan and I helped Cam back down the stairs and into the car. We stopped at a pharmacy and got him hooked up with some crutches and his prescriptions and then headed back to the apartment.

Sam had a big tabbouleh salad on the table, garlic pita was warming in the oven and she was just washing the last pot in the sink when I rounded the corner to the kitchen.

'What took you guys so long?' she asked.

'Well, Sam, we stopped and saw the new place that apparently I am a co-owner of. I guess you've already heard about it.'

She was about to deny all, when she saw Ryan shaking his head at her.

'Damn you, Ryan, can you not learn to keep a secret,' she cursed him, and then filled two wine glasses and handed one to me. We both took a big drink.

'Kate, I . . . '

'Sam, we'll discuss this later,' I said. 'And I mean that. But let's just get Cam settled, I think he's ready for one of these painkillers.'

'And a beer,' Cam said from the couch, where Ryan already had his leg propped up on a pillow on the coffee table.

'I guess I'm not much of a caregiver,' I said, joining him on the couch.

'Well, no you're not, especially since there's no beer in your hand.' He laughed.

I held the pill bottle in front of his face and pointed to the picture of the martini glass with a diagonal line drawn through it.

'No drinking while you're on these,' I said. 'It says so right here.'

'Ryan?' he tried.

'Sorry, my medical training doesn't allow me to dispense either medication or beer or advice.'

'Oh, for God's sake, a single beer isn't going to kill him,' Sam said, pulling one from the fridge and bringing it over to Cam.

'How many will it take?' I asked.

'Are you still mad?' Cam asked, washing his Tylenol down with his beer. I couldn't watch.

'I'm definitely feeling a little outnumbered.'

'Kate, I'm your best friend,' Sam said, carrying the salad out to the patio, which she already had set up for dinner. 'I love you and I want nothing but the best for you. But you have been acting absolutely ridiculous about buying a house. It's a house. You live there for a year and if you hate it, you move. And because it's Calgary, you probably make fifteen thousand on the sale too.'

'It's not a house, it's a home,' I protested.

'See, there's where you're wrong. They all start out as houses. It's what you do to them and how you live in them that makes them a home. And this place is going to be great.'

'You think so?' I asked.

'Yes,' all three of them said in unison and then broke down in laughter.

'Well, I'm not going to hold you to your promise about having the bedroom done in two weeks,' I told Cam. 'You're not going to be able to do that all trussed up in that brace.'

'I'll get some help,' he said. 'I promise you, in two weeks it will be the most beautiful room you've ever seen.'

'Oh, Cam, that's sweet. But honestly, when I'm in my non-manic phase, I don't care if we're sleeping in the garage, as long as I'm with you. It will get done when it gets done.'

He kissed me, looking quite content.

'However, the other thing is with that amazing kitchen you better be cooking some seriously good food for me every single night.'

'I'll have to,' he laughed. 'I don't think we can afford to go out ever again.'

'Have we got a big mortgage?' I asked.

'You'll find out tomorrow when you sign the papers that I have to have back to the bank by 10:00 a.m. on Monday. Although if I could figure out how to avoid you seeing it, I would.'

'Is it that bad?'

'It's scary when you look at all the zeros.'

'Ryan?'

'Nope, I'm not talking for the rest of the night,' Ryan said. 'Apparently I'm not good at keeping secrets.'

'Sam?'

'Norman Caminski, you can tell her now or tomorrow, but

she's going to find out. Half of that mountain of debt is going to be hers.'

'Way to reassure me, Sam,' I told her sarcastically.

'All right. With our big down-payment, the mortgage was $389,000.'

I felt my lungs gasping for oxygen. That was more money than I earned in ten years.

'But it's a really good deal. We've got a double lot, Katie. A double lot in the inner city. We will do OK. And that still gives us fifty thousand to start the renovations with. And with me doing the work and getting everything at wholesale prices, that money will go a long way.'

'Three hundred and . . . '

'Oh, you're still back there,' he laughed. 'It sounds like a lot. Especially when it's your first mortgage.'

'I need more wine,' I said, getting up and returning with the bottle.

'You'll be fine,' Sam said. 'We've all been there. But maybe you should have some food with that wine?'

'Yeah, let's eat,' Cam said. 'Katie and I kind of missed lunch today.'

But I found I couldn't force any food down my throat, though the wine went down quite easily. Which is probably why I don't really remember when everyone actually went home and left us alone for the night.

Sunday

I drank a lot of wine. I remember that we discovered Cam was going to have real problems with his brace and crutches and the spiral staircase up to the loft. So, the night before, we decided the better part of valour, considering the amount of wine I'd had and the additional painkillers he had ingested, was to sleep on the sofa bed in the living room. That's why I had such a problem waking up when the doorbell rang. I heard it, my eyes opened, but where the bedroom wall should be was a huge window and balcony. I turned over and looked at the ceiling, wondering why it was so low. The bedroom ceiling was supposed to be ten feet high. And then I recognized my living room and slowly my brain filled in the blanks. Then the doorbell rang again. And my head started pounding. The doorbell seemed unnecessarily harsh this morning, even considering the amount of wine festering inside me. I grabbed Cam's wrist and looked at his watch. It was only six thirty. No wonder. We hadn't got to sleep until very late if the number of empty wine bottles lined up on the table on the patio was any indication.

I fought my way out of bed, finding my feet twisted in the comforter and my coordination very much lacking. I finally broke free, looked down and inspected myself for suitability of answering the door. I had on Cam's T-shirt, which came down to my knees, and I smoothed out my hair and rubbed the mascara from below my eyes. Whoever was at the door had given up on the doorbell and was now pounding on it. Cam snorted in bed and rolled over, the noise slowly working its way into his subconscious.

'All right,' I called. 'I'm coming.'

Cam rolled over and pulled the pillow over his head to stifle the noise. I turned on a light and made my way around the bed and coffee table, to the hallway. I looked through the peephole and couldn't believe what I was seeing. I unlocked the three locks my security-conscious boyfriend had installed on our door and opened it wide, blinking to try and clear my vision from the blinding hallway light.

'Katie girl, how are you doing?'

'What the hell are you doing here?' I asked, shock outweighing good manners.

'Katie, we haven't seen each other for almost a year and that's the best greeting you can muster up for me?'

I heard a noise behind me and turned to see a naked Cam, on his crutches, making his way to the bathroom. He stopped when he saw me standing at the open door.

'What's going on?' Cam asked. 'Who's at the door at this time of the morning?'

I stepped aside looking them both in the eye, one and then the other and then back again. I wished and prayed I was invisible but when that didn't work I decided I better speak.

'Cam, I'd like you to meet my father.'

After our inauspicious beginning, Cam had gone into the bathroom to wash up and put on his robe. I led Dad into the kitchen and busied him with the job of making coffee. While he did that, I hurriedly made the sofa bed and tidied up the living room. When we were all sitting at the table like civilized folks, with a cup of coffee and a bagel, I decided that we should probably try speaking. Not a word had been uttered since Cam disappeared in the bathroom and I let my dad in.

'So,' I began. 'Did Mom tell you that Cam and I were living together?'

'No,' Dad answered.

'Oh, how nice of her. She's never kept a secret in her life until now. I had hoped she would spill this one and save me the anxiety of having to tell you myself.'

Dad gave Cam one of those looks, the father sizing up the boyfriend looks.

'Well, Dad, Cam and I have been living together for about a year now. I'm sorry I didn't tell you sooner, but I was trying to work it all out in my own head first.'

'You think too much Katie,' he said.

Cam let out a muffled chuckle, which he silenced when my dad shot him a dirty look.

'You're not laughing at my daughter, are you?' Dad asked.

'No, sir,' Cam answered dutifully.

'Oh, this is ridiculous,' I said. 'Daddy, how long are you here for?'

'Just a couple of days.'

'And where are you staying?'

'With you, of course.'

'OK, well, I can't do this.'

'You won't let me stay with you?'

'Only if you and Cam shake hands and make up right now. I'm not going to be caught in the middle of the two of you for the next couple of days.'

'Sir,' Cam said, 'I am very sorry that you didn't know I

was living with your daughter, that really wasn't my choice but I had to respect her decision.'

'Well, I know Katie can be a little bit stubborn.'

'And I am very honoured to finally meet you. I am going to be eternally sorry that it happened the way it did, however.'

'Oh, don't worry about it, son. I met my future father-in-law when Katie's mother and I were in the back seat of my 1964 Super Bee and I was just removing her panties. Oh, I remember the smell of those leather bucket seats like it was yesterday!'

'Dad!' I squealed.

'And you're lucky, son,' Dad laughed. 'Because her father had a shotgun with him at the time.'

'Well, then I do consider myself lucky, Mr Carpenter.'

'Call me Sherm,' he said, holding out his hand for Cam to take. They shook hands and Cam tried to stand up.

'What do you need?' I asked, pushing him easily back into his chair.

'More coffee.'

I got up and brought the pot over, filling everyone's cups for them.

'Cam fell off a mountain yesterday afternoon,' I told my dad.

'You sure you didn't push him?' Dad asked.

'Oh, don't be such a smart-ass. Although it was close. He told me we'd just bought a house. Only he forgot to show it to me first.'

'You two bought a house together?' he asked, his eyes lighting up. 'So this is serious then, not just for sex?'

'Dad!'

'Oh, Katie, get over it. You're in your forties . . .'

'Thirties . . .'

'Whatever. And I realize you're a grown-up. And I know you don't really have long-term relationships . . .'

'Dad, maybe we could discuss some of this when Cam isn't sitting here?'

'No, I'm fine.' Cam laughed. 'Don't let me stop you.'

'Well, I'm just happy you bought a house,' Dad said. 'Maybe there'll be a wedding and all that someday? The pitter-patter of little grandchildren-type feet?'

I sat down and took a sip of my coffee.

'Actually, Daddy, we did have a surprise pregnancy last fall,' I said softly. 'But we lost the baby.'

Cam smiled at me and put his hand overtop of mine, a gesture that was not lost on my father.

'Well, there's plenty of time for that. After all, you're only in your thirties, right?'

I laughed out loud. 'So, I have to go to work today. Are you going to be OK here with my wounded warrior?'

'I'll be fine,' he said.

'Do you know how to drive a manual shift?' Cam asked.

'Does a bear shit in the woods?'

'Oh, Daddy,' I sighed.

'Well, if you'd be willing to drive my car, I'd be happy to show you what we bought,' Cam said. 'It's a bit of a fixer-upper and maybe you could give me some ideas.'

Cam was such a charmer.

'That'd be great,' Dad said. 'I've done a bit of renovating in my time.'

'Dad was a building inspector for the city,' I said. 'Among other things.'

'All right,' Cam said. 'We are going to have ourselves a good day. Let me just have a quick shower and then we can be on our way.'

'What kind of car have you got?' Dad asked.

'A '71 Hemi Barracuda,' Cam said. 'I've done a little bit of work on her.'

'Really,' Dad said, letting out a little whistle between his teeth. 'I am looking forward to seeing that. You're right, we are going to have a great day.'

And I was going to worry all day about what Dad might tell Cam about my life that I had omitted to tell him so far. Yeah, we were going to have a fun day, I thought sarcastically!

Dad did more than whistle when he saw Cam's car, and I fastened my seat belt extra tight as he sat behind the wheel, revving the engine and admiring the sound. He and Cam were discussing litres and horses and all sorts of things I didn't understand, so I undid my window and enjoyed the sunshine, as they drove me to work. They dropped me at the stage door to the Plex and I reluctantly got out and let them head off together. I made my

103

usual left turn instead of right, and found my way into Gus's coffee shop, trying to decide what I needed to start my day.

'Morning, Kate,' Gus said, polishing his machines up for the day. I swear he must talk to them, like you would with plants, because his machines made better coffee than anywhere else I had ever tried.

'Morning, Gus.'

'How's Cam's leg doing?'

I had ceased being surprised that Gus seemed to know things that happened at the Plex. I was never sure how he did it, but sometimes he seemed to know them before they even happened. It could be very helpful when I needed information but very annoying when I was trying to hide something.

'Cam's leg is paining me greatly,' I joked. 'But he seems to be OK with it!'

'Well, how about a nice little hazelnut latte to try and help with that pain?'

'Only if you have an almond biscotti to go with it.'

'I saved one for you. Hey, was that guy that was driving Cam's car . . . ?'

'My dad?' I asked, happy that maybe I finally had one up on Gus.

'That's your dad? Sherman Carpenter? I never put that name together with yours.'

'You know my dad?'

'We worked together when he was with the city. I was doing some private contracts and our paths crossed a couple of times. He and I have definitely shared a laugh or two over a beer.'

'Small world.'

'Yeah, I should have known he was your dad, though.'

'Why?'

'Because he always talked about his daughter who was stretching his nerves to breaking point getting involved in everything she shouldn't be involved in,' Gus explained, laughing at me.

'Hey, they encouraged me to be curious,' I protested.

'I'm just teasing you, Kate. Your dad was so proud of you. He always talked about your piano lessons and that kind of stuff. But I don't know if I remember him calling you Kate?'

'He used to call me MK,' I explained.

104

'MK?'

'Mary Katherine.'

'I didn't know your first name was Mary,' Gus said.

'It isn't. He always used to say, "Mother Mary, please protect my daughter Katherine from all the trouble she gets herself into." It eventually got shortened to MK.'

Gus laughed and handed me my coffee. 'So then you really haven't changed much since then?'

'Apparently not.'

I turned to leave the shop but Gus stopped me.

'Hey, you tell Sherm to come in and I'll buy him a coffee.'

'He only drinks decaf these days,' I warned him.

'I know, old age, heartburn, I'm there too, you know?'

'See you later, Gus,' I laughed. Once on the sunny street, I decided to walk down the sidewalk and sneak in the front doors of the theatre. Not the way the staff were supposed to go. We were supposed to sign in and sign out, so security always knew who was in the building. But it was sunny and I didn't want to walk down some dark and dank hallway. And it wasn't like I hadn't done it before!

The Stampede decorations were up and we were ready to go for the week. There were hay bales at the main entrance, with planked corral fencing all around our lower lobby and wagon wheels scattered here and there. The coat check and box office were done up like the town jail cells and there were more hay bales upstairs, some with saddles on them. Moving to the upper lobby, there was a stuffed bull with a rodeo backdrop behind him. We were hosting a couple of corporate functions this week and this was for all the out-of-town vice-presidents to pose on and have their picture taken, riding the stuffed rodeo bull. On the other side of the lobby there was a mechanical bull that I was assured had been rigged to stay on the slow speed only.

But tonight wasn't corporate night. Tonight was Jann Arden, local girl done well, launching her new book and CD. It was a private party tonight, for friends, press and her record company and book publishers. We had a sold-out house and lobby sales of books and CDs. It was going to be a busy day, especially since I planned to waste a lot of my energy worrying about my dad and my boyfriend.

*　　*　　*

105

I snuck in and got up to my office to discover I was bliss-fully alone. Normally, Graham would be in trying to keep up on paperwork or something, but he seemed to be spending less time at work and more time somewhere else. I wasn't flat out worried about him, as I figured he had some emotional stuff to deal with, but I was keeping an eye on him. I didn't bother to turn on the lights in the office, as the sun was streaming in. I checked the soil in the plants I had here and watered them and then I put a pot of coffee on. I sat at my desk and opened the drawer. There were a package of ciga-rettes in there. Still. I guess I hadn't been up here since I quit smoking. I picked up the package and looked at it longingly. I thought about cigarettes every day. Still. I pulled one out and smelled it and my mouth literally watered. I lit a match and held it up to the cigarette until the cigarette started burning. I breathed in the aroma, staring at the burning cigarette and wondering if I should put it to my mouth and take a drag. I don't know what came over me but I stamped it out in the ashtray and tossed the package in the garbage.

I had to distract myself and the thought of Cam being out with my dad flitting through my mind was good enough to do it for me. I wondered if Cam had his cellphone turned on and I picked up my phone and dialled him.

'Hello?'

'Hi, it's me.'

'Everything OK?' Why was that always his first question?

'Fine. Just wondering what you guys are getting up to.'

'Katie, we dropped you off thirty minutes ago.'

'OK, I'm practising work avoidance right now. Graham's not here to do the stuff I hate so I thought I'd call you rather than count the liquor inventory.'

'We're at the house.'

'You mean the fire hall?'

'I mean our house. Has the banker called you yet?'

'On a Sunday?' I asked. 'You were serious about signing the papers today?'

'He's a friend of mine and doing me a favour.'

'You have too many friends.'

'Has he called?'

'I haven't checked my messages.'

'He wants to bring the papers by for you to sign this afternoon.'

'I thought we would go in tomorrow?' I said, feeling that panic again.

'He's going to be downtown this afternoon.'

I didn't respond, something very unusual for me.

'Katie?'

'Cam?'

'Katie, whether you sign those papers or not, the place is mine. I made an offer and it was legally accepted. So either I own it or we own it. Your choice.'

'I promise I'll sign them,' I admitted, defeated. 'But, Cam, can't we do it together?'

'I'm sure your dad will bring me up there. If not, I'll grab a cab. I'll be there.'

'What does Dad think of the place?'

'I'll let you talk to him and ask him yourself.'

I heard Cam call my dad's name and then the phone was handed over.

'Hey, Katie girl, you miss us already?'

'Actually, Dad, I was wondering what you thought of the place.'

'Well, I haven't had a real good look around yet.'

'Are we making a mistake, Daddy?' I asked, desperately.

'MK . . .'

'Wow, you haven't called me that for ages.'

'That's because you're giving me more gray hair as we speak. Cam told me how much trouble you caused your realtor with house-hunting.'

'Yes, I admit I was having trouble picturing myself in most of the places we were looking at.'

'So, don't you think that Cam did well by finding a place that was different?'

'I guess.'

'Isn't that what you said you wanted, something different?'

'Yes,' I gave in, reluctantly.

'Well then, what exactly is your problem?'

'I just can't picture it as a home. It's so institutional.'

'Well, you're going to have a bedroom to sleep in by the end of the week, and once you see the bedroom, you'll trust that Cam can fix up the rest of it for you.'

'I know he promised me a bedroom, Dad, but he's hurt. His leg is in a brace. There's no way he can manage the construction now.'

'I know that. But we've been making some phone calls and I think we've got some help rounded up. We're going to do it like those home-improvement shows and we'll have it finished for you.'

'But you can't get the permits and everything in time.'

'Katie, I worked in this city for thirtysome years. I already have two old friends coming over that are going to work with us on the permits and things. As soon as they've been here, we're going to Home Depot. Cam's just finalizing the supply list.'

'Dad . . .'

'Oh and by the way, MK, I'm staying a few extra days.'

'Daddy?'

'Well, I kind of like this guy you've got, and he's in a bit of a fix. So I'm going to stay and help with the bedroom, kitchen and living room, so you guys have some liveable space here. I promise I'll get out of your hair after that.'

'Daddy, you're sixty years old. You can't do all this.'

'I most certainly can. But if we get enough young guys out here, then I'll just supervise and make sure they're doing things the right way.'

'I think we should talk about this at dinner,' I tried.

'Look, MK, do you have anything important to discuss? If not, I'm signing off because we have work to do here. Men's work,' he laughed and I could hear Cam snickering in the background. I was outnumbered.

'I have nothing else to say.'

'All right. Cam says we'll see you at dinner when you have to sign those papers.'

And then the phone went dead.

Surrounded by men and feeling overwhelmed, I decided it was time to even up the odds. I called my friend Sam. There was no answer at her house, so I tried her cellphone.

'Hi, Kate,' she answered, obviously seeing my number on her call display.

'Hi, Sam, am I interrupting something important?' I asked, worried she might be on her way to a job.

'No. No work for me today. I'm just taking some supplies over to the house for the guys.'

'Sorry?'

'Your dad called and said he and Cam were going to start some work there.'

'Dad called you?' I asked.

'Yes he did and I can't believe you didn't tell me he was in town.'

'Well, it was all a bit of a surprise. And I always suspected he liked you better than me, even when we were little kids. I guess this proves it.'

'I can cook, you can't. He knows that.'

'What's that got to do with anything?'

'He told me they were going to be working on the new place and wanted to know if I could do some lunches for them. I said I would and offered to bring some frozen things over and some canned stuff, so they could snack, too. Don't worry, I'll clean out the fridge for you before I put anything in it.'

'Well, do you want to meet for a coffee after you drop that off?'

'I sort of already promised Cam that Ryan and I would go to Home Depot with them. They wanted a woman's opinion on the colours.'

'I'm a woman,' I said.

'Yeah, but you know that Cam wants to surprise you.'

'So you're on their side too?'

'It's not really that I'm picking sides, Kate. I mean if Cam hadn't hurt his leg, I probably wouldn't even be here today. We're just trying to help out.'

'I know. I'm sorry,' I said. 'I'm just stressed out.'

'Yeah, well just wait until you actually sign the mortgage papers. Then you'll really be stressed out. There's something about owing all that money that just sends a person around the bend.'

'And this is helping me how?'

'Sorry. So are you OK with me helping out or not?'

'Of course I am. I'm just being stupid. You do whatever you want to do and I'll go and count liquor bottles.'

'Kate, you know this is all going to be all right, don't you?'

'I'm hoping.'

109

'It will be. You're going to have an amazing place to live and you and Cam are going to make it a wonderful home.'

'Thanks, Sam,' I said, and hung up. I thought about calling my mom for a minute or two, but I knew if she found out Dad was here and helping out she'd want to be here too. And I just couldn't handle both my parents here right now. I picked up my inventory sheet and headed for the storage room.

Graham finally turned up about forty-five minutes before show time. I had to have Cam cancel his banker friend and rebook for tomorrow, because I was left alone with lobby set-up and program stuffing and bar set-up and I didn't have time left to pay attention to anything else. I'm sure Cam thought I was trying to avoid dealing with this whole mortgage issue, and maybe I was, but why waste such a good excuse.

I was just folding the last T-shirt when he sauntered up the stairs, dressed in jeans and a rumpled shirt and looking a little worn around the edges.

'Nice of you to drop in,' I said, sarcastically.

'Yeah, I guess I'm a little late.'

'Yeah. And I guess there were no phones around to call me and let me know?'

'I guess not,' he said, continuing his saunter across the lobby to go upstairs and change.

'Are you sorry?' I asked.

'Oh sure.'

I dropped the T-shirts and followed him across the lobby, grabbing his arm and halting his progress.

'Graham?' I asked, trying to look deep into eyes that were avoiding contact with mine. 'What's up, kiddo?'

'Um, I don't know, I just buried my mom; I guess I'm not over it yet. Sorry, Kate.'

'Graham, don't do this to me.'

'Oh, it's about you? Sorry, I didn't realize that either.'

'Look, let's just go up to the office and talk.'

'You go ahead, if I'm not there in a half an hour just start without me.'

'Graham, no matter how hard you try, you're not going to make me hate you.'

'Spare me the first-year psychology.'

'But I will send you home tonight if I have to.'

'I don't want to go home.'

'Good. We're agreed.'

'I'm sorry,' he said, his eyes on the carpet now.

'Go get changed, Graham.' I felt he might actually feel a little penitent for his behaviour now. 'We'll deal with this later.'

I dropped his arm and he slowly made his way up the stairs. I finished the T-shirt display and then went up to my office. As I pushed through the fire door at the top of the stairs I thought I smelled smoke. I raced down the hall, pulling my keys out and opening the office door. Smoke poured out of the trash can, fingers of flame beginning to blacken the side of my desk.

'Oh my God!' I screamed, momentarily stunned by the sight of the fire.

'Watch out, Kate,' Graham called from behind me. He raced into the office with a fire extinguisher in hand and aimed it expertly at the base of the flame, just like they always taught us. A couple of sprays brought things under control.

'Good job, Graham,' I said, feeling my heart still racing.

'That was scary,' he said, a smile on his face as his chest too was heaving from the excitement.

'Were you smoking up here?' I asked, smelling the aroma of a freshly lit cigarette.

'Kate, I don't smoke. You do.'

'I haven't smoked for a month, Graham.'

'I smell cigarette smoke too,' he said.

'I lit one up, but I didn't smoke it.'

'And then you dumped it into the trash can, right?' he asked.

'No, I didn't.'

'Well, how else do you think that happened, Kate? Do you think I started it?'

'Graham, I never said that.'

'You probably dumped the ashtray without even thinking about it. Years of habit.'

'Years of habit taught me never to dump an ashtray into the trash can. You know that.'

'So we have a ghost?'

'I don't know, but let's get this cleaned up before the rest of the staff get here. I would rather not have to mention this to anyone in security.'

'Don't worry, Kate, your secret is safe with me.'

I looked at Graham but kept my mouth shut, deciding this really wasn't the time to get into an argument with him. And I bit my tongue several more times that evening, as he was uncharacteristically harsh with a couple of volunteers and even crossed the line with me a few more times. Everyone seemed to understand, since everyone knew what he had just been through, so I didn't have complaints to deal with. I did want to talk to him before he left for the night, but after we cleared the last of the audience from the lobby, and I hurried up the stairs to my office, he was changed, signed out, back-pack over his shoulder and heading for the stairs with Lawrence and a couple of the other young ushers.

'Are you leaving already?' Usually Graham was the last one out with me.

'We wanted to catch last call at the beer gardens,' he said, motioning to the group around him.

'I had hoped we could have a little talk before you left,' I tried.

'Tomorrow?' he asked. 'Would that be OK with you?'

'Tomorrow will be fine,' I sighed but smiled at him. 'You guys have a good time.'

'Night,' they all said, hurrying out and onto the streets.

I watched them from my office window, heading for the Stampede grounds, hoping they would watch out for Graham since I wasn't going to be there to do it. Then I locked up the theatre and headed for home.

Monday

'Cam, do you think Graham's doing OK?' I asked.

Cam was in his new position in the back seat of his car, while Dad drove and I rode shotgun. We were off to the bank,

112

an errand I was working really hard to not think about.

'What do you mean?'

'Who's Graham?' Dad asked.

'Graham's my assistant at the theatre,' I explained. 'He's nineteen years old and he just lost his mother to cancer.'

'Oh, that's rough,' Dad said. 'Nineteen is young to lose your mother.'

'Something weird happened yesterday.'

'What?' Cam asked me.

'Well, there was a fire in my office . . .'

'What?' both men asked at the same instant.

'Just a little one, in the trash can. We got it put out right away. But Graham seemed really insistent on blaming it on me.'

'How could it be your fault?' Cam asked.

'Well, we think there was a cigarette dumped into the trash can that still had a burning ember . . .'

'You had a cigarette?' Cam asked.

'You smoke?' Dad asked.

'Oh, crap,' I said and turned to Dad. 'I used to Daddy, sorry. But I quit for a month now. And, Cam, I lit one and smelled it. But it never touched my lips, I swear.'

'Well, it probably was your fault,' Cam said. 'You probably dumped the ashtray without thinking.'

'Cam, have I ever done that before?'

'Katie, do you know how bad smoking is for you?' Dad asked.

'Yes I do,' I screamed. 'And yet right this very minute I would trade either one of you for a cigarette.'

I heard some rustling in the back seat and Cam's hand appeared over the edge with a piece of nicotine gum in it.

'Thanks,' I said grudgingly, chewing it harshly. 'Never mind about the fire. You're probably right. But Graham was acting a little strangely yesterday.'

'Well, Katie girl, think about it,' Dad tried to explain, as if to a five-year-old. 'He just lost his mom. He's searching for a new identity, a new place in the world for himself. He's going to try on some different personalities until he finds out who he is and where he belongs.'

'You're very wise, Dad,' I admitted.

'You just want me to be quiet, don't you?' he laughed at me.

'That doesn't mean I don't think you're wise,' I said, turning and staring out the window. And then Cam handed me another piece of gum.

Following Cam's instructions Dad pulled over to the curb in front of the bank. None of Cam's friends ever worked in the suburbs in a lowly little branch. No, they all worked downtown, in these skyscrapers, on the twentieth or thirtieth floor with some ostentatious corner office meant to humble me. Just like now. I stood on the street, looking up at the huge building they called Banker's Hall, all the way up to its 645-feet-high art deco rooftops. This was a building that I had always liked, especially at night with the opposing silver and gold roofs lit up. Now, it loomed over me like a haunted mansion, gargoyles springing from the roof, black clouds swirling around the top, lightning bolts crashing through the skies.

'Katie!' Cam's voice finally rang through my nightmare vision. 'Will you please open the door for me?'

'Sorry,' I said, opening the back door and giving him my hand.

Once Cam was upright on the street, crutches balancing him, I leaned into the car window.

'Dad, there's a parking lot at the end of the next block, just park in there and we'll meet you down there when we're done, OK?'

'Katie girl, how many years did I live in Calgary?'

'Yes, Daddy. Sorry, Daddy.'

'Just bring me back a coffee,' he instructed.

'I'll do better than that, I promise.'

I watched Dad pull out into traffic in Cam's car and I felt like crossing myself, something I hadn't done since junior-high school. I turned to Cam, and really wanted him to hold my hand as we made our way upstairs, but he was a little preoccupied with the crutches and brace, so I took a deep breath, and decided to act like an adult and followed him up in the elevator. We emerged on one of the executive floors and I was pretty sure this guy was not your run-of-the-mill mortgage specialist but probably someone doing a big favour for Cam. I hoped this favour was going to be reflected in the mortgage rates we were about to sign up for.

Cam smiled at the receptionist and gave her his nice little charming routine, which got us both a cappuccino and him an extra-special smile. The steam was still rising on the cappuccino when we were shown into the office. Wayne was a lovely man in a suit that probably cost more than our mortgage. His door said vice-president, but he smiled and shook our hands like he was one of the people. He settled us on the sofa and opened a file up in front of us, filled with documents printed on very official-looking legal-sized paper. He handed us each a lovely gold pen, pulled out the first page and smiled.

'You look nervous, Kate,' he said, before he turned to the paper.

'This is my first mortgage,' I admitted.

'Oh, well I promise I'll make it as painless as I can.'

'So you'll be making our payments for us?' I made a weak excuse for a joke.

'All right, this first page just outlines . . .'

His lips were moving, I knew there was sound coming out because Cam was nodding his head as he followed along, but all I heard was a buzzing. I smiled and nodded when Cam nodded, pretending everything was OK. My hand was sweaty and I was embarrassed when the pen slipped from my grip. Cam leaned over and picked it up, handing it back to me, while Wayne just smiled and carried on with his droning. I continued to smile and was pleased when a few words actually broke through the buzzing, until I realized those words were $389,000.00 and forty-eight months and balloon payment. Luckily, by the time he got to monthly payment I was just hearing the buzzing again. The office was uncomfortably hot and I actually found I was having trouble catching my breath. Suddenly, I noticed that both men were staring at me, and Wayne had his hand pointing to an X, waiting for me to sign my name. I looked up at him and smiled, trying to move my arm from where it rested on my knee to where the mortgage papers lay. And then the funniest thing happened, and I felt my eyes flutter and then I actually slipped off the couch.

The next thing I remember was looking up and seeing a worried Cam waving a magazine over my face, with my legs unceremoniously raised up on to one of the office chairs. Thank God it was Stampede Week and I was wearing jeans and not a skirt. I tried to push myself up into a sitting position, but found the room swirling around me.

'Just lie still for another minute, Katie,' Cam said. 'Wayne's just gone to get some orange juice. I explained that you didn't eat breakfast this morning.'

'Cam, I'm so sorry to embarrass you like this,' I said closing my eyes but enjoying the breeze from the magazine. I still felt hot.

'It's OK,' he said. 'Just another good story to tell later.'

'A lot later, right?' I asked. 'Like when I find this funny in twenty or thirty years?'

'Well, later,' he said. 'You're not quite as pale as you were a minute ago, why don't we try sitting you up again?'

I removed my legs from the chair they rested on and pushed myself slowly into an upright position, staying on the floor and leaning against the sofa.

'You OK?' Cam asked.

'I think so.'

'Katie, maybe I should just do this mortgage myself.'

'Cam, you don't qualify for the mortgage yourself,' I pointed out.

'I'm sure Wayne can figure something out.'

'Cam, I don't know what came over me, but I am going to sign these papers and get over this once and for all.'

'I just hate to see you going through all this anxiety.'

'It's more like pain. But I think I'm having some sort of growth experience here. I think I have to do all this. I mean, I'm thirty-four years old, you think I could manage to buy a house and sign some mortgage papers. God, Cam, sometimes even I can't believe I do these things.'

He tousled my hair and laughed.

'It's what makes you an original.'

'Yeah, well where's that stupid pen?'

He handed it to me and I signed at the X, and everywhere else that had a little Post-it note attached, awaiting our signature. And then Wayne came in, handed me my orange juice, which I drank greedily wishing it was laced with vodka, and checked over the papers. It was done, we were done and I now had twenty-five years to pay off my debt. I felt my breath catch in my throat so I rapidly pushed that thought out of my mind, shaking hands, smiling and following Cam back down to the street level.

'I'm proud of you,' Cam said, kissing me.

'I'm so glad it's over,' I said. 'Do you think you can walk to the parking lot or should I go down and get Dad to bring the car back for you?'

'I can make it,' Cam insisted. 'It's only a block.'

We walked slowly to the parking lot and we found the car right away, the good thing about having a classic car. But the car was locked up and empty.

'Where is he?' I asked.

'He might have just gone for a walk, stretch his legs. Maybe he had to use the washroom.'

'Well, he should have left us a note or something.'

'Katie girl, you just worry too darned much about everything.'

I turned around and saw Dad ambling across the parking lot toward us. He had a plate of food in his hand and was busy shovelling bacon into his mouth.

'Dad, where have you been?'

'You know, I forgot all about these free breakfasts that happen during Stampede Week.'

'Dad, we could have all gone together when we got back.'

'Look at that, flapjacks, bacon, sausage and baked beans. For free.'

Cam laughed but I still wasn't impressed at the fact of my father wandering the streets of Calgary all alone.

'If we time it right, we can eat for free all week long,' he said rolling one of his pancakes around a sausage and stuffing it in his mouth.

'I think I can find us some free dinners too,' Cam continued to giggle. 'For sure I know I can get us into the Beef n' Beans party for sure.'

'Well there now, that's showing some good motivation.' Dad laughed too. 'Now that you have a mortgage, you are going to want to save money wherever you can.'

'Oh, you two are going to make me crazy,' I said, taking Dad's empty plate from him and running it over to the garbage bin. 'Can we just go now?'

Dad opened up the car for us. 'Where can I take you now, m'lady?'

'We're going to go and have a coffee at the Plex, then I have some work to do and I guess you guys are going to continue your mysterious work at the fire hall.'

'Our house,' Cam called from the back seat.

'Your home,' Dad corrected.

I rolled down the window and pretended to study the traffic, which Dad finally pulled out into. Cam handed me more nicotine gum from the back seat. After parking at the Plex, we walked Dad across the street and into Grounds Zero. We took seats at the counter and I waited for him and Gus to notice each other.

'Afternoon, Kate,' Gus called from behind the machine, where he was wrestling with bags of beans to put into the roaster. 'I hear you own yourself a house now.'

'I do,' I said. 'I've brought you a little surprise, though.'

Gus poked his head up over the back counter and noticed my dad sitting between me and Cam.

'Why, Sherm, you old son of a bitch,' he laughed, tossing the coffee beans to the side and wiping his hands on his apron.

'Gus?' Dad said, not believing his eyes. 'Gus, what are you doing working as a waiter in a coffee joint?'

'I own the joint,' Gus said. 'Much better end than retiring and living in a tepee. Isn't that what someone told me you did?'

'I only lived in the tepee for one year, while they were building my five-star fishing lodge,' Dad protested.

'Yeah, well at least I didn't have to leave town.'

'Well, I didn't exactly have to leave town. It's just that casino owner was getting a little hard to avoid.'

'So I couldn't believe it when Kate here told me you were her father.'

'Yeah, I didn't believe it when her mother told me that either.'

'Daddy!' I swatted his arm, hard.

'Katie girl, it was a joke, just relax,' Dad said, rubbing his arm.

'Well, if you guys are just going to sit here and besmirch

my reputation, then I might as well just go up to my office and get ready for the concert tonight.'

'Have a good afternoon then,' Dad said, leaning over and kissing me on the forehead.

'And just call when you're ready to come home,' Cam said, from my other side, leaning over and kissing my cheek.

I was very disappointed that neither of them had argued for me to stay, but thanked them for the coffee and headed back out onto the street. The sound of their laughter boomed out, following me and mocking me and making me wish I had a cigarette. Separately I loved them all, but together, they scared me.

My office was cool and dark. It was empty but Graham's bag was sitting in the middle of the floor, so I knew he must be around here somewhere. I turned on the lights and made a pot of coffee, then I picked up Graham's bag to move it out of the way. He didn't have it done up properly, a fact which I didn't realize until after I had already picked it up and felt half the contents slip out and drop to the floor.

I dropped to my knees and began picking up his things, putting them back inside his pack. I picked up a T-shirt that felt damp and cursed myself for breaking something. I unwrapped the T-shirt, hoping I didn't cause too much damage. A package of matches and a can of butane lighter fluid fell out of the rolled-up T-shirt and suddenly I realized why the T-shirt was damp: it was soaked with the lighter fluid.

'Holy cow,' I said out loud, shocked at my find. What possible reason would Graham have to be carrying around stuff like this? There were only two reasons I could think of, either you were a very heavy smoker or you were starting fires. I wrapped everything up quickly, afraid Graham would appear back in the office at any moment, and stuffed it all back in his pack, which I hurriedly secured and tossed in the corner of the room. I would ask him about that later. For now, feeling very uncomfortable about what I'd found, I pulled out some time sheets and some inventory sheets and started to get everything ready for the show tonight. But if I didn't get a good answer out of him, Cam and I were going to have a serious talk about Graham tonight and maybe even an intervention.

The afternoon became a whirlwind of people everywhere, setting up the stage and the merchandise, sound checks and even security. I don't think we'd ever had anyone here who required their own security. I met the tour manager and got an idea of what that night's show was going to be like and then found Graham and got the lobby set up. When it was done, I got him back to my office, intent on having our little talk.

'Graham, when I first came up to my office today your backpack was lying in the middle of the floor.'

'Oh sorry, Kate, I was meeting someone for coffee and I was late, so I just tossed it and ran.'

'No, that's OK. It's just that when I moved it, you forgot to close it and . . .'

And the door to my office opened. It was Krista, one of the new ushers I had hired. I noticed Graham's face break out in a big smile as he greeted her in sign language. I smiled and waved too, as she waved back.

'When did you learn sign language?' I asked Graham.

'Learning,' he corrected me. 'I'm really bad and she has to talk really slowly to me.'

'OK, when did you start learning sign language?' I tried again.

'I signed up for a course just after you hired her, I thought it might help out a bit.'

'I'm sure it will. You know, I'll let them know upstairs. We might be able to get some sort of grant or something and pay for your classes.'

'That would be cool.' He took a minute and explained our conversation to Krista. 'So, you were complaining to me about my bag pissing you off?'

'No, never mind,' I said, smiling at Krista and wishing she had been just a few minutes late. 'I'll tell you about it later.'

'Well, I promise not to be so sloppy.'

'You want to take Krista down to coat check tonight?'

'Coat check?' Graham groaned.

'Graham, that's where everyone gets to start.' I watched him carefully, realizing he might actually be feeling a little more for this lovely young woman than just being her concerned supervisor. 'You wouldn't want me to play favourites, would you?'

'No, Kate, that's fine,' he gave in. 'I'll take her down and show her how it works.'

'Thank you.' I smiled sweetly at the two of them as they made their way out of my office. I checked the time on my watch. If he wasn't back up here in ten minutes I was going down after him.

When I checked my watch, I realized it was only an hour before we opened the house for the audience and that I better get ready. I straightened my jeans, unrolled the cuffs of my shirt, tied a bandana around my neck and put my cowboy hat on my head. I loved Stampede Week, dressing was so much easier. I left the sign-in sheets on my desk and headed down for the main lobby. I knew we were going to be in for a busy night but was surprised to see people lined up outside the door already.

At eleven thirty I was slumped in my office chair, tired of chasing people with cameras and video phones and confiscating lighters and joints. We were not the Saddledome, not the place where rock concerts of any sort were normally held and not used to the kind of night we had just been through. Finally, the last of the ushers, led by Graham, made their way boisterously down the hall. I tried to sit up a little straighter and not appear quite so tired . . . or old.

'Hey, Kate, we got the last person out and the doors locked,' Graham said. 'I think our work here is finally done.'

'Great. Well you kids can go on home and get yourselves a good night's sleep.'

'Sleep?' Leonard asked. 'During Stampede Week?'

'You're not going out?' I asked, disbelief in my voice.

'If we hurry we can get an hour on the midway before the rides close down for the night and then we still have another hour or so before last call at Nashville North.'

'You're insane,' I said, slumping over in my seat again.

'No, we're young,' Graham said as the last of them signed out. 'Are you OK to get home?'

'Yeah, Cam and my dad are coming to pick me up. You guys go and have fun.'

'OK, see you tomorrow,' he called, as they all raced down the hallway.

I turned off the coffee and rinsed out the pot, turned off the lights and locked my office up. I double-checked the theatre as I cut through and made sure everything was locked up tight. Backstage there was still tons of activity, as they were striking the set, but there wasn't anyone around that I knew real well, so I kept going and didn't stop for a visit. It was a beautiful night, so I said good night to the security guard on duty and sat on the step in the loading dock, waiting for my ride. I was finding myself looking forward to sitting on my deck with my men, for one of the last times, and listening to what those men had been up to today. I thought I smelled something funny, thinking maybe the hot July days and the garbage dumpster in the loading dock were starting to disagree with each other. Then I realized though the smell was acrid, it wasn't garbage, it was something burning. I looked around, trying to figure out where it was coming from, and then noticed a thin finger of flame reach up over the top of the dumpster.

'Fire,' I stood up, screaming. And then realized I was alone on the street, so I turned and ran inside the building. 'Fire, there's a fire in the dumpster.'

'What?' the security supervisor asked, turning his attention away from the TV monitor he had been watching.

'There's a fire in the dumpster,' I shouted at him, trying to break through his ennui.

'Where?'

'The dumpster, in the loading dock,' I tried again, making sure I was talking very slowly.

'Hi, Katie girl.'

I turned and saw my dad rushing up the steps. He put his hands on my shoulders and pushed me gently out of the way.

'Dad?'

'Did you have a good day at work, sweetie?' he asked, pulling the fire alarm and then unhooking the industrial-sized fire extinguisher from the wall.

'Uh, yes.'

'OK, well I'll be back in just a minute.'

I followed him out the doors and down the stairs, where Cam was still struggling to get out of the car. He grabbed my arm and held me back from following Dad into the loading dock.

'What is he doing?' I asked.

'Putting out the fire,' Cam said, and sure enough, he had climbed up on a couple of empty crates and was pointing the fire extinguisher down into the dumpster, at the flames that now climbed up the wall of the building.

I heard sirens and two fire trucks pulled up onto the street, spilling out firefighters, just as people began to spill out of the Plex in response to the alarms, followed closely by the E-News news van. Two firefighters joined Dad at the dumpster and soon the fire was out. Dad set down his extinguisher, shook some of the firemen's hands and then wandered back over to the car, where we waited for him. The firemen started to pull everything out of the dumpster, making sure there were no hot spots left that might flare up later.

'What happened?' I asked.

'There was a fire and we got it put out,' Dad laughed.

'That's not what I mean and you know that.'

'Now, don't you worry. Stuff like that happens all the time. A stray cigarette somewhere and look what can happen.'

'Hi,' a sweet voice said, interrupting us. 'Geneva Arnold, E-News. That was very brave of you, jumping in to deal with the fire like that.'

Both the microphone and her huge smile were pointed in Dad's direction.

'Well, it was nothing,' he shrugged, smiling back at her.

'How did you happen to know what to do?' she asked.

'Well, dear, usually when there's a fire, and it's not in your barbecue or fireplace, it's a good idea to try and put it out.'

And I thought he had been succumbing to her charms.

'I was just trying to get some information . . .' she sputtered.

'Get in the car,' Dad told us. We did and he locked the doors.

'Dad, that was a dangerous thing for you to do,' I insisted.

'Katie, it's over. And no damage done other than a couple of scorch marks,' Cam pointed out.

But I froze as I watched the firefighters through the car window. They were poking through the dumpster, making sure it was safe, and I saw them pull out a half-burned T-shirt from the dumpster. A T-shirt with the same logo as the one I had found in Graham's backpack.

123

'What's the matter, Katie?' Cam asked.

'Nothing,' I said, trying to shake off the icy feeling I had in the pit of my stomach.

Cam wrapped his arm around my shoulder and pulled me close to him in the back seat. 'You sure?'

'Yeah,' I smiled. 'It's nothing.'

'Well, it's been a long day and I've just about used up my whole supply of adrenaline, so what say we all go home and get us some shut-eye?'

'Sounds good to me,' I agreed, leaning my head against Cam's shoulder and realizing suddenly how tired I really was.

Tuesday

We arrived home and Dad and Cam both went to bed right away, tired from their long day of home improvement. By the time I'd washed my face and changed into shorts and a T-shirt, Cam was snoring softly in the sofa bed. I tucked myself against him and decided I could talk to him about Graham in the morning. But by the time we got up in the morning, got dressed and had breakfast, they had to get to the fire hall, or I mean our house, to meet an electrician and they dropped me off at work on the way.

I made my way up to my office and found it empty. So then I tried to call my friend Sam, but all I got was her voicemail. I was still feeling really suspicious about Graham. I grabbed my coat and my wallet and wandered down the street to the Alexander Calhoun Library. If no one was going to talk to me today, then I was going back to the basics. I remembered reading something in first-year psychology in university about how people used behaviours like this to deal with overwhelming emotions, so I bought myself a coffee from Good Earth on the main floor and headed upstairs to do some

124

reading. A couple of hours later I was overwhelmed with enough information that I was now really worried about Graham's state of mind and very determined to talk with him as soon as he got to work.

During Stampede Week, the Plaza outside the Plex was used as Rope Square. The reflecting pool was drained and every lunchtime there was square-dancing or fiddle-playing or line-dancers entertaining the crowds. My theatre was used as a backup in case of rain, but we also had some minor entertainment ourselves, for those folks that didn't want to sit outside in the heat. Today we had a local country-western band coming in, and they were already doing sound checks on the stage.

I sat in my office, nervously playing with paperwork, and waiting for Graham to arrive. Unless there was rain, we didn't have a huge turnout indoors, so Graham and I usually ran these events ourselves. And since it had been sunny and bright this morning, I hadn't bothered to call anyone else in.

I finally heard someone coming down the hallway, and I took a deep breath, preparing my non-threatening opening statement, when the door pushed open and Leonard walked in.

'Where's Graham?'

'Good morning, Kate. Yes, I'm well, thank you and it is a lovely day out there,' he said sarcastically, sitting in the chair across from me.

'Leonard, I'm sorry, there was just something personal I really had to talk to Graham about. I was kind of shocked to see you come through the door.'

'Oh, he didn't tell you he wasn't coming in?'

'No, he seems to have forgotten to do that.'

'All right then, you're forgiven. Graham had to drive his dad to the funeral home. They had to do something about a headstone. I didn't get the details.'

'Oh, then I should be thanking you for filling in.'

'You're welcome.'

'Leonard, do you think everything's OK with Graham? You seem to be spending a fair bit of time with him.'

'Well, not really. I mean he ditched us last night.'

'He did?'

'Yeah, he said he left something here and had to get it. That's the last we saw of him.'

'Oh.'

'But I don't think it's anything to worry about,' Leonard reassured me with all the self-confidence of a twenty-two-year-old. 'You know, he's just got some stuff to go through. His mom died pretty suddenly and I imagine it's still all a little unreal to him.'

'I suppose.'

'And he is only nineteen and he just broke up with his girl-friend. I mean, give the poor guy a break.'

'You really think he's OK?'

'I really think so. I mean, it's not like I'm his greatest confidant or anything like that.'

'Who is, then? Who does he talk to?'

'You,' Leonard said, shocked that he had to point that out to me.

'But he isn't talking to me.'

'But he will.'

'OK,' I said, locking up my desk and putting my keys in my pocket. 'OK, I'm going to officially quit worrying and just give him some time and space. Now, shall we go listen to some country music?'

'I never get tired of country music,' Leonard laughed. 'Yee haw and all that.'

'Oh yeah, you're believable as a cowboy.'

'Well, let's face it, I am just not the poster boy for gay cowboys.'

'And why's that?'

'Because it took me three hours to get this bandana just right. If I had to go through that every day I would never leave the house. I mean can you imagine any other gay guy in the world that can't arrange a scarf properly?'

'It's a bandana.'

'Same difference. And I can't handle it.'

The phone rang, saving me from further comment on that front.

'Kate Carpenter.'

'Kate, it's Nick,' the security supervisor greeted me. 'Look, I've got someone here who wants to see you.'

'Nick, I've got a show about to go in.'

'All twenty people?' he laughed.

'Well, it may be small but it's still a show.'

'Look, please just come down and give me five minutes. She's really being insistent and she's got a camera crew with her.'

'What?'

'Please, Kate. She's asking for you specifically.'

I hung up the phone and tossed Leonard my keys. 'I'll be back in a few minutes.'

I cut through the backstage area and down Tin Pan Alley to the security desk. There she stood, tailored suit, perfect teeth, microphone in her hand and cameraman right behind her.

'Ms Arnold.' I smiled at her, but it was my fake smile.

'Ms Carpenter.' She smiled back, but hers looked real. Man, she was good. 'I wonder if I could just have a couple of words with you?'

'Not if that camera is on you can't.'

She turned to the cameraman and winked at him, and he took the microphone from her and then headed out to the van parked in the loading dock.

'Better?' she asked.

'Two minutes,' I said.

She led me out the stage door and perched on the step, pulling a cigarette out of her purse and lighting it. I sat down beside her, since standing there and towering over her seemed silly. And the smell of the cigarette was almost overpowering. I watched, trying not to drool, as she held it up to those perfectly shaped lips and took a deep drag. I could almost feel the nicotine racing through my bloodstream as she slowly exhaled the smoke.

'You don't like me,' she finally said.

'I think we're even on that score.'

'Fair enough.' She took another deep drag from her cigarette.

'Is that all you wanted to say?' I asked.

'No, I was just trying to figure out how to work up to the rest of it.'

'Oh, I'm a big girl, just say it.'

'All right, then.' She smiled, turning to face me. 'I have spent years working to get where I am today. I spent four years at the National Broadcasting School, working nights to pay my tuition. I graduated at the top of my class and got a dream job with E-News, and do you know where they sent me? The Yukon. Do you know how much airtime I got up there? But I worked and worked and got reassigned back down here. Out of Moose Jaw, Saskatchewan. And then they spent the next year sending me to cover stories about farmers who grew a potato shaped like Abraham Lincoln or a pumpkin with the Virgin Mary on it. But I didn't give up and I moved from those crappy human-interest stories to hard news and up to Calgary, which is the number-three market right now. So, when I come to cover a story here, I will not let someone like you give me a smart-ass answer and dismiss me, do you understand me? I intend to be hosting the *National News* in the next year and you need to start being more cooperative with me.'

'Are you threatening me?'

'Well, I guess if you want to think of it that way, that's what I'm doing.'

'And where is the other part of that threat? The part where I'm scared you're going to do something to me if I don't comply?'

'Well, that's the funny part. When I was covering the Bishop murders a couple of months ago, I found a nice picture of you on file kissing someone who doesn't look anything like your boyfriend.'

My stomach did a somersault but I tried to maintain my poker face.

'Yes, we had a bit of a falling out then. But I'm sorry to disappoint you, Geneva, Cam knows all about it.'

'How twenty-first-century of you,' she laughed, stomping her cigarette out with her Italian leather pump. 'But I'm guessing that a photo of it might bring up some hard feelings again. Maybe plant a little doubt in his mind?'

'Geneva, you are a bitch.'

'Well, I told you that at the beginning. But I'm going to be the bitch hosting the *National News*. Sorry, Kate, have I been talking too fast for you to understand all this? Should I go back and explain it again?'

128

I stood up and she stood up too, her face way too far in my space for my comfort.

'So, should I send him the picture and see what happens?' she asked.

And I did it. I lost control again. All that forward progress I had been making in improving my self-control gone in one split second as I pulled my hand back and slapped her face. I saw an angry red welt appear, in the shape of my hand, as a couple of flashes of light temporarily blinded me. I looked around and saw her cameraman had come around on the street, with a still camera in his hand, flashing pictures of my attack on the reporter.

Geneva's hand was up on her cheek, rubbing the spot where I had struck her. 'Now those should make some good pictures.'

'You set me up!'

'Dear, I am always going to be at least one step ahead of you. I suggest you don't even try to fight that. Now, can we expect a little more cooperation around here or should I call the police, charge you with assault and broadcast it on the evening news?'

I stood there for a minute, breathing heavily, trying to resist the urge to jump her and beat that pretty little skull of hers into the concrete sidewalk.

'Watch out!'

We both turned to see where the sound was coming from when Scott appeared with a giant dog on a leash. The dog was racing out of control down the street and pulling the hapless man behind him.

'I can't stop him,' Scott screamed, as he and the dog crashed into the cameraman.

The cameraman fought mightily to maintain his balance, but I noticed Scott give just a little shove and it was all over, the cameraman was down, his camera hitting the pavement hard, exploding open and rolling out into 9th Avenue, where a city bus promptly ran over it. Scott managed to stop the dog and wrapped the leash around a lamp post, racing back to the scene.

'Hey, are you OK, man?' he asked, pulling the cameraman up off the ground. 'I'm sorry, I'm dog-sitting for my friend and this dog is out of control.'

129

'I'm OK,' the man said, brushing off his pants and looking down at the pieces of his camera that were now scattered up and down the block.

'You asshole,' Geneva screeched from beside me, as she strode over to the two men.

I thought Scott's life might be in danger but Geneva went straight to the cameraman and slapped him in the face twice as hard as I had attacked her.

'We had her, you asshole, and you lost it.'

'I fell!'

'And don't you know you're supposed to protect your film at all costs?'

'And get a broken skull instead? I don't think so, lady.'

'Get back in the fucking truck,' she screamed. 'We're going to go and have a talk with your supervisor.'

'You are one crazy fucked-up lady,' he said, but headed back for the news van.

'This is not over,' she said to me, before she stormed after him.

The van pulled out into traffic, almost causing an accident as he tore onto 9th Avenue without checking for oncoming traffic, and Scott came back to the stage door with the dog he had been walking.

'Well, thank God you're dog-sitting.' I smiled at him, looking down at the cigarette Geneva had stomped out and wishing I had one of my own right now.

'Here you go, ma'am,' Scott said, handing the dog back to an elderly lady and her grandson. 'Thanks for loaning him to me.'

'Scott?'

'Nick gave me a call and said you might need some help. I saw the camera dude sneaking around to get his shot. I knew she was setting you up.'

'Yeah, I guess everyone knows about my temper, huh?'

'Well, it's not like you try and hide it,' he laughed. 'You OK?'

'I'm OK. Especially now that there is no record of my lapse of judgement.'

'What did she want?'

'She seemed to think I was covering up some story. I guess

it's because she's run into me at a couple of fires recently, and I've been less than cooperative.'

'Wow! Well, I'm thinking that the best thing for all of us to do is to stay far away from her.'

'I'm with you on that one,' I agreed. 'We better get back to our show. It's not safe out here in the cold cruel world.'

Leonard and I finished up at the theatre by one thirty, and after I got everything locked up for the day I decided to take a walk down to the fire hall, which I still couldn't think of as my house, and surprise the boys. I didn't call them to warn them, because I was pretty sure Cam didn't want me there yet. I loaded up my backpack and decided to stop at Cedar's Deli for some baklava to take them. I knew they had a coffee pot and a fridge full of beer and pop, so they were OK for the drinks. I was hot in my jeans and wished I had changed into some shorts or something before I had headed out, but stayed on the shady side of the street. When the fire hall first came into sight I stopped and just looked it over again. It was huge but it was kind of pretty, I decided. I liked the brick-work and if we put some grass out front and maybe a nice flowerbed, I was sure it would look more homey. Cam's car sat proudly in the huge garage, surrounded by sawhorses and equipment tables that were set up everywhere. As I started walking and drew nearer, I noticed there were probably ten cars parked out front. I cut in through the open garage doors and pushed through the unlocked door into the main hallway. I heard voices and followed the sound down to the kitchen area.

'Wow!' The word came out of my mouth before I realized it.

Ten heads turned in my direction and Cam took a couple of steps forward.

'Katie, what are you doing here?' he asked.

'Surprise!' I tried weakly.

'I am surprised,' he said, limping over and kissing me in greeting. 'Because I thought we were going to surprise you at the end of the week?'

I looked around the kitchen and found myself speechless. The appliances had been scrubbed to within an inch of their lives and were gleaming, as were the stainless-steel counter-tops. Drywall had been put up and painted a sunny yellow and stylish wooden blinds hung over the window. The linoleum was gone, replaced with maple hardwood. An amazing table, at least eight feet long, sat on a multicoloured woven rug. A breakfast bar had been built onto the end of the counter and four bar stools were tucked underneath it.

'Oh my God!' I grabbed Cam around the waist and hugged him. He had to hop a couple of times to keep his balance, but the grin on his face told me he didn't mind so much.

'You like it?'

'Oh my God,' I said again.

'I don't think I've ever seen Kate lost for words,' Scott said.

I turned back to the table, surprised to see our stage carpenter here, next to our technical director, the stage carpenter from the concert hall, an electrician from the Heritage Theatre and another electrician from the Ballet. There were several other people sitting around the table that I didn't recognize.

'Scott?'

'Just been helping out around here a little,' Scott said.

'Since your boyfriend is such a gimp right now,' Trevor added.

'Thank you all,' I said, looking around at the kitchen again.

'We don't have any artwork up yet, or anything like that,' Cam apologized. 'That will make it seem a lot more homey.'

'It's beautiful, Cam. It doesn't look like it ever used to be that nasty room I saw the first time I was here.'

'I told you I could make it the house for you,' he smiled at me.

'Your home,' my dad piped up from the end of the big table.

'Hey, the wall is missing,' I said, suddenly noticing the big archway that had been cut into the next room.

'Yeah, it's going to be a kitchen family room combo. We'll have the TV and computer and piano in there. What do you think?' he asked.

'I think I want to see the bedroom now.'

'No way.'

'Please?'

132

'No. I don't want you to see it until it's all done.'

'And who's going to stop me, you?' I smiled, planning a mad dash up the stairs.

'Oh, I'm pretty sure one of these guys can stop you,' Dad said from the end of the table again. 'Right, boys?'

'Absolutely, Mr Carpenter,' Scott answered my dad, but smiled at me, almost daring me to try. Funny how quickly he could change sides.

'Daddy, you're pissing me off.'

'Katie girl, talk nice to your daddy, you're not too big for me to turn over my knee.'

'You're not going to win this one,' Cam whispered into my ear, enjoying this more than he should have.

'That's OK, if I stay here another minute I might burst into tears and ruin my reputation.'

'Come on,' Cam smiled. 'I'll walk you out.'

'You mean limp me out?'

He laughed and we walked slowly down the corridor and into the front entry.

'It's so weird,' I said, running my hands over the cinder blocks that still lined the hallway. 'Out here, it's fire hall, but in that one room, I can see home emerging.'

He smiled but resisted saying anything.

'You can say, "I told you so." '

'Sometimes it's better left unsaid, don't you think?'

'Have your moment, then, you don't get them very often,' I teased. 'So where did that amazing table come from?'

'I made it.'

'What?'

'I made it. I can't do a lot with my leg bound up like this, but I can stand in front of a table saw and use a sander.'

'It's beautiful.'

'I'm glad you like it. I found the chairs at a flea market a couple of weeks ago and I decided to build the table to go with them.'

'Well, I'm still totally freaked about the mortgage I'm holding but I'm definitely feeling a little better about this place.'

'Good. Katie, I thought we could start moving some stuff over, if you don't mind.'

'Already?'

'Well, mostly because of the leg. If I could move a couple of boxes every time I have a ride, it would probably make it a lot easier. But I don't know what you need at home.'

'Why don't I just take my clothes in to work tomorrow and then other than my make-up bag and my takeout menus, I should be fine.'

'OK. That sounds like a good plan.'

'Cam, I really need to talk to you about Graham too.'

'Cam!' someone yelled from the back.

'What is it?' he asked, looking over his shoulder to see who was looking for him.

'Never mind,' I sighed. 'It's nothing. We can talk tonight.'

'You sure?'

'I'm sure,' I said, kissing him goodbye. 'I'll see you later.'

Cam hurried off into the bowels of the building, while I pushed through the door and out into the sunshine. On the street, there was a man standing in front of the open garage door. He had a notepad in hand and looked like he was writing down Cam's licence-plate number.

'Can I help you?' I asked, approaching him.

'I'm sorry, this is official business.'

'What kind of official business?' I asked, having used the excuse myself a few times.

'Who are you, ma'am?'

I cringed at the ma'am but ignored it. 'I am the owner of this place. Who are you?'

'Detective Sims,' he said, flashing a badge quickly and putting it back in his pocket.

'And what can I help you with, Detective?'

'Nothing, I'm finished up here anyway,' he said, turning and starting to leave.

'Detective, sorry, can I just see your badge again?' I asked, emboldened by his attempted flight.

'I'm finished here, ma'am, don't make me cite you for interfering in an ongoing investigation.'

With that, he climbed into his car and pulled away. I was in such shock that I only managed to get the last three numbers of the licence plate. I was feeling very uncomfortable with what had just happened and headed out to the main street to find a payphone. I wanted to call the police and report that this detective wouldn't properly identify himself. As I turned the corner, I stepped aside to make way for a bike rider, coming off the street and up on to the sidewalk.

'Kate?'

I turned to see who was calling me and there was Detective Ken Lincoln, climbing off his fancy bike, pulling off his chic helmet and straightening his hair. If he hadn't had those lovely tanned and muscular legs, he would have looked silly standing there in his bike shorts and T-shirt.

'Ken, what are you doing here? Like this?'

'Well, contrary to popular belief, I do get an occasional day off and actually have a personal life on those days,' he laughed. 'When you're not putting your nose into my investigations that is.'

'OK, OK. Since I'm not actually involved in anything right now, you have to be nice to me.'

'There'll be a next time.'

'No, there won't be. I've reformed. So what are you doing in this neck of the woods?'

'Well, I actually ran into your dad at City Hall the other day and he told me all about this place you guys bought. So I thought I'd come and have a look at it for myself.'

'You know my dad?'

'Well, I think everyone who works for the city knows your dad, Kate. He was in the Fire Department forever and then he worked for the city for another fifteen years or so, didn't he?'

'Yeah, I guess he did.'

'So, how's the place shaping up?'

'Well, I had to sneak in, because Cam didn't want me to see it until he had some more finished, but I have to say the kitchen looks pretty amazing.'

'Wonderful. Well, maybe I can help out this afternoon. I hear Cam is all trussed up.'

'Yeah, he's in the brace for at least six weeks. I thought the renovation was going to be doomed but I can't believe the amount of people that have come out to volunteer.'

'People like to help out.'

'You can't tell me that as a cop you still believe in the milk of human kindness?'

135

'I work really hard at not being cynical, Kate.'

'Ken, speaking of cynical, something strange just happened when I came out of the fire hall.'

'What's that?'

'Well, there was this guy in a bad suit standing in front of the garage writing down Cam's licence-plate number. And when I approached him and asked him what was going on, he said he was a detective and I was interfering in a police investigation.'

'Maybe there was a car that looked like Cam's that they were looking for?'

'That's possible. But I thought it was weird that he wouldn't show me his badge again when I asked to see it. And he pulled out of here in a Honda Civic.'

'Well, yeah, if you ask to see a badge, they should probably show you the badge. Did you get his name or anything?'

'He said he was Detective Sims and the last three numbers on his plate were 604.'

'OK, well I don't think it's urgent or anything, but I can give him a call tomorrow when I'm on duty and see what's up.'

'Would you mind?'

'No. Now, just remember that I might not be able to tell you what the investigation is about.'

'I know, I know,' I laughed. 'Remember, I've reformed.'

'You say that now. You'll have to prove it the next time I say no to you.'

'You're funny. Well, thanks, I'll let you go check out my new place. I've got to get back to work.'

Ken hopped on his bike and rode it right into the open garage. And I turned and looked back up and down Second Street. I really didn't have to get back to work. I really had nothing to do and apparently no one to do it with. Normally, this would give me a great excuse to go shopping, but in four weeks I had the first mortgage payment coming out of my bank account and I was still a little freaked out about that. I went back to the payphone and tried Sam again, but I just got her voicemail. Some day I was going to have to remember to charge the battery in my cellphone.

'Hi, Sam, it's Kate. I was just bored and looking for

company. I thought you were working, but just wanted to double check. Maybe we'll catch up later.'

I hung up the phone and sighed. I walked a couple of blocks, stopped in at a second-hand book store, bought myself a murder mystery and wandered down to the first coffee shop I could find with an outdoor table. And that's where I spent the afternoon.

At about five o'clock, I thought the boys might be coming home for supper, so I finished my third café crème and headed for home. At the front door I bumped into an electrician who was taking apart the panel that displayed the fire alarms. I wondered if they shouldn't leave stuff like that until the building was empty of the last of us hold-out tenants, but they obviously knew what they were doing. The electrician stepped aside to let me pass, and I thought he looked vaguely familiar. I crossed the lobby and pushed the button for the elevator and waited for the doors to open. The nice thing about only having ten people left in this building was that the wait for the elevator was never very long any more. I turned around, pushed the button for my floor, and as the doors closed I realized who the electrician reminded me of. He reminded me of the detective that had been outside the fire hall this afternoon. And as the doors slipped closed and he turned and smiled at me, I was sure that he recognized me too.

Wednesday

I lay in bed and stared up at the ceiling. We had been sleeping on the sofa bed and put my dad upstairs in the bedroom, since the spiral stairs really did prove a lot of work for Cam to navigate. But the fact that I was used to sleeping under a ten-foot ceiling had me feeling claustrophobic every time I slept in the living room. That, and the fact that I hadn't told Cam anything about the mysterious electrician/police detective from yesterday. When I first got back to the apartment and double-locked the doors, I was going to call him right away. But then I decided I was going to handle this on my own, since Cam was totally preoccupied with our big renovation job and I was probably just imagining this whole conspiracy anyway. So my goal was that when I got to work today I was going to call Ken and see what he had found out about this mystery man who liked to play police detective and then I was going to call Ryan and have him arrange to have our fire panel investigated and make sure it was all still working as it was supposed to. When they told me that everything was fine and no one was actually following me, then I would be very proud of myself that I hadn't troubled Cam with all my crazy ideas.

But lying here in bed with a secret hanging between us again was making me uncomfortable. I had sworn a few months ago that there would be no more secrets. Ever. That seemed to be proving harder to live up to than I had imagined. Plus, there was the whole issue about him keeping secrets, like buying the fire hall. Even though that was working out really well for us.

'Katie, if you think any more loudly you're going to wake your dad up,' Cam mumbled.

'Sorry,' I said, realizing I had been doing the tossing and turning thing while I was arguing with myself.

'Everything OK?'

'Everything's fine.'

'Really?'

Damn him, I thought, was he going to make me lie directly to him now?

'It's about time you two woke up,' Dad said running down the stairs, fully dressed and ready to face the day.

Saved by the bell, I thought. 'Morning, Daddy.'

'Morning, Katie girl. Do you two always sleep this late?'

'Well, half of us does,' I said, pushing myself up into a sitting position. Dad was in the kitchen and already had the coffee perking and butter melting in a frying pan on the stove. 'But some of us work nights, you know?'

'No, firefighters work nights, you work late. And use it for a grand excuse to waste away half of your days in bed,' he teased, cracking some eggs into the butter and scrambling them up. 'And if I recall, you were finished work early in the afternoon yesterday. I think I recall you showing up at the fire hall and bugging us for a while, don't I?'

'Yes, Daddy.' I reached over to the end table and looked at my watch. Six thirty. Yikes. I slid back into a supine position and pulled the comforter over my head.

'No you don't,' he said. 'The eggs will be done in another minute and then Cam and I have to get to work.'

I felt Cam getting out of bed and limping to the bathroom. He came back, tossed my bathrobe to me and sat himself down at the table. I dragged myself out of bed and put on my robe. Dad immediately put a cup of coffee on the table in front of me and I reached for my bag, grabbing for a cigarette automatically.

'We quit, remember?' Cam asked.

'How to ruin a perfectly good morning,' I grumbled, sipping my coffee.

'We do have to get an early start,' Cam said. 'I want to have you in that bedroom by Saturday night.'

'Cam, you know, I do understand that you are injured,' I tried. 'You can slow down a bit.'

'I will, as soon as the bedroom, kitchen and family room are finished. But I told you I want you to have some nice rooms to live in.'

'Well, I appreciate it. But I miss you,' I said, leaning over and kissing him, morning breath and all.

'What about me, do you miss me?' Dad asked.

'Hardly at all,' I laughed. 'First time you've been out to visit me that you have not spent the entire time nagging me about everything.'

'Not everything,' he protested.

'Where I live, how I live, my job, who I'm dating . . .'

'Who was she dating?' Cam asked.

'OK, let's not go there. The fact that I'm wasting my education, that I don't have a car, the clothes that I wear . . .'

'Kate, I'm your father. If I can't spend my days nagging you, I don't feel I'm fulfilling the job requirements.'

'And this visit?'

'Well, this visit you got me a nice guy to play with,' Dad laughed. 'You've never had a boyfriend before that had a cool car and asked me to help him build things.'

'I would have done that a lot sooner if I knew it was going to get you out of my hair,' I laughed back. 'Now if I could just figure out how to handle Mother as easily.'

'Your mother isn't coming, is she?'

'No, Daddy, you're safe.'

'You two don't get along?' Cam asked.

'The last time they were together, they both got a little tipsy and took a charter to Mexico for the weekend,' I explained. 'They took separate planes home and haven't been able to look each other in the eye since then.'

Cam laughed but stifled it quickly when he got an icy look from Dad.

'That's not exactly the way it happened,' Dad tried.

'That is exactly the way it happened,' I insisted. 'And my brother was there and will verify the story.'

'Your mother and I just had some things to talk over and wanted to do it alone, away from you kids.'

'Dad, you stole a box of condoms from my bedside table. What exactly were you talking over? My choice of birth control?'

'Cam, you ready to go?' Dad said, getting up and rinsing off his plate before he put it in the dishwasher.

'Yes, sir,' Cam said, standing up quickly and helping Dad make his escape.

'You can run but you can't hide,' I called after him.

'And like I said, you're still not too big for me to turn over my knee. Now show a little respect for your poor old dad.'

And then the door shut, before I had a chance to show him anything.

At the office I decided to call Sam's place first. For once, no voicemail, a real person actually answered her phone.

'Hey, Kate. Sorry I didn't get back to you yesterday.'

'Don't worry. I was just feeling needy and you were at the bottom of my list to call.'

'The bottom, well thanks.'

'No, the bottom because I know you hate to give me sympathy and prefer to give me hell.'

'Oh, OK, well that's better. So did you just call to insult me or was there actually some point here that would make me want to continue this conversation?'

'Actually, I wanted to talk to Ryan. Is he around?'

'He's at work today, or with his girlfriend, I can never keep those straight,' she laughed.

'All right, all right. Can I call him at the fire hall?'

'Of course you can. Everything OK?'

'Yeah, I just want to know if he can stop by my building, I'm just worried about a safety violation and I wondered if they could check it out.'

'I'm sure he can help. Or he can direct you to somebody that can help. Just give him a call.'

'OK. Well, I'll talk to you later. I'd like to get on this now.'

'OK, don't let your imagination run away from you.'

'I won't. Later.'

I disconnected and dialled the phone.

'Station One, Ryan speaking.'

'Hey, Ryan, it's Kate. You busy right now?'

'Nope. I don't hear any bells ringing so you're good to go,' he laughed.

'Ryan, I have a favour to ask.'

'Sure. Anything. I mean almost anything.'

'When I came home yesterday, there was an electrician doing something to the fire panel in the lobby.'

'It probably needed some servicing, what with all the construction going on around there.'

'Yeah, well, the thing is, I also saw him in front of the new place yesterday. Only then he said he was a police detective.'

'That's interesting. Have you shared this with anyone else? Like the police?'

'Yeah, I'm just waiting for a call from Ken Lincoln.'

'OK, I'll talk to the captain about it. We should be able to make a stop there while we're out on rounds today.'

'Thanks, Ryan, it would make me feel a whole lot better.'

'No worries. Look, I'll give you a call when I get home tonight and let you know if we found anything or not, OK?'

'That's great. Thanks again.'

I hung up and realized I didn't have the coffee started yet and suddenly realized how much I depended on it without my cigarettes to tide me over. Some days, I really felt like a junkie between the nicotine and caffeine. I found a half a chocolate bar in my desk and ate that while I made some coffee. I finished the last bite of chocolate and inhaled deeply as the aroma of fresh brew wafted over from the coffee pot. I heard a noise at the end of the hall and turned to see Graham wandering down. Well, at least if he was early today, we should have a chance to have that talk I wanted to have with him yesterday.

'Morning,' I said.

'Good morning to you.' He smiled, tossing his backpack into the corner and his jacket on top of it.

'You're here early.'

'Well, I get up early these days. Dad doesn't sleep very well and when I hear him in the kitchen, I like to get up to keep him company.'

'Things still rough there?' I asked.

'He's having a really hard time being alone. The girls have been talking and I think Amelia and her family are going to move back into the house for a while. I think being around the grandkids might be good for him. Her husband got laid off last month and money's tight, so it might be good for all of them. Dad will have the three grandkids to play with and they can save some money until they get back on their feet.'

'That sounds like a good plan.'

'For everyone but me,' he said. 'God, I can't believe I just said that out loud. I hate even thinking that.'

'What do you mean?'

'Well, how selfish is that?' he asked. 'I'm worried because I won't have any privacy when Dad has just lost his wife of forty years. Poor Graham has to share his bathroom.'

'Graham, it's OK,' I said. 'It's just how you feel. It's not wrong.'

'It's terrible. That's not the way my mother raised me, Kate. Not to be selfish and think only about myself.'

'Graham, your mom would understand better than anyone how mixed-up you are about all this.'

'Never mind, I don't want to talk about this any more.'

'I think we should,' I insisted. 'I think it's good to get this stuff out.'

142

'Why, because then everything will be better?' His voice was spiteful.

'No, it won't be better. But it won't be a secret.'

'Spare me your first-year psychology, if you please.'

'OK, I know you're really stressed about this, but let's try not to get rude.'

'You know, I just came in early to help you out. I know I haven't been around much and I thought maybe some things were getting a little behind.'

'Graham, I actually can run this theatre, you know?'

'Yeah? Well, since you haven't done it for a couple of years, I wondered if you remembered how.'

I sat there speechless. Shocked by what he had said and shocked by the rage in his voice. I didn't want to get angry with him, I didn't want to turn this into a pissing contest and I didn't want to drive him away. I took a deep breath.

'Graham, I love you like you're my own brother and I'm going to give you all the time and support and whatever else it is you need to get through this. And if you need to lash out at me, then I'll sit here and take it.'

'Kate, I'm sorry.'

'I know you are, Graham. Look, do you need some time off?'

'No,' he said, his eyes filling with tears. 'No, I couldn't stand if I had to be there all the time and didn't have a reason to leave.'

'OK. Did you want to keep yelling at me, then?'

'No. No, Kate, I just have all this stuff swirling around inside of me and I don't know what to do with it.'

I stood up and took a step toward him.

'No hugging,' he said.

'No, no I was just going to get a coffee.'

'I mean it, I am just barely holding it together right now. Please.'

I poured a coffee and sat back down at my desk.

'Graham, there is something I need to talk to you about.'

'What?'

'Well, yesterday when I moved your backpack . . .'

And then the phone rang. I looked at Graham and then looked at the phone.

'Answer it,' he said. 'I'll be here all afternoon and we'll have plenty of time to talk.'

He got up and waited outside the office. I picked up the phone.

'Kate Carpenter.'

'Kate, it's Ken. We need to talk. Can you meet me at Grounds Zero in ten minutes?'

I checked my watch and realized I still had two hours before show time. 'Sure, Ken, I'll be right there.' I told Graham, 'I have to go out for a few minutes, and I'm not even going to ask if you can handle it or not after our last conversation.'

He laughed. Thank goodness. 'What's up?'

'I'm not sure,' I admitted. 'I promise I'll fill you in when I get back.'

I grabbed my wallet and headed down the fire escape, my short cut to the street, and hurried to Grounds Zero. Ken was at a booth talking to Gus. When Gus saw me arrive, he got up and headed for his usual spot behind the counter. I slid into the booth, happy to see there was a cappuccino waiting for me already.

'Thanks for the coffee.'

'Thank Gus,' Ken said. 'I wouldn't have a clue what to order for you and I think you drink too much of that stuff anyway.'

'Yeah, well, you're not the only one.'

'So tell me about the detective that you met yesterday.'

'Well, I told you yesterday . . .'

'Humour me,' he said, without a trace of humour in his voice.

'OK, well, I went to the fire hall to see what was going on because they haven't let me check it out since they started working on it. When Cam walked me out I stopped on the street while I was trying to decide what to do for the rest of the afternoon. The doors were open in the – what do they call it, the equipment bay?'

'Garage?'

'I was trying to sound official. So there was this guy standing in the driveway staring at Cam's car and writing down the licence-plate number. I walked up to him and asked him what he was doing and he said that he was Detective Sims and I was interfering with a police investigation.'

'That's nothing new.'

'Yeah, which is why he didn't really scare me off. He flashed a badge and when I asked to see it again he refused and got into his Honda Civic and drove off. And by the way, don't they pay you guys well enough to drive something other than a Civic? I mean, as a citizen, how would you be able to save me in a car that wouldn't go above eighty on a down-hill slope?'

'What a man drives is a very personal choice, and you should realize that from your experience with Cam and his car.'

'You mean his first love?'

'But regardless of that, when we're out, we're in unmarked police cars. If he were on duty he wouldn't be driving around in his personal car. Can you describe him?'

'Well, he was about Cam's height . . .'

'Five foot . . . ?'

'Five foot ten. Even though he says it's five eleven. He was kind of tanned, medium-blond hair with a little bit of gray in it. He was kind of stocky, heavier than Cam but not quite as heavy as Gus. He had deep furrows between his eyebrows, like he squinted a lot.'

'Anything else?'

'I wasn't really paying that much attention. He had eyes, nose, ears, the usual, you know?'

'That's very helpful,' Ken said sarcastically.

'So, is this guy in trouble, then?'

'Kate, this guy doesn't exist.'

'What?'

'There is no Detective Sims on the Calgary Police Force and there is no Honda Civic that has those last three numbers on its licence plate.'

'So I was right to be suspicious?'

'Yes, you were right to be suspicious.'

'Then there's something else you need to know.'

'Oh, God.'

'When I got home last night, there was an electrician working on the fire-alarm box in our main lobby. And it took me a few minutes, but I really think he was the same guy as this Detective Sims.'

'Oh? Did he recognize you?'

'I don't know, maybe. I didn't really clue in until I was in the elevator. He looked at me but I'm not sure if he recognized me or not.'

'OK.'

'Well, why is this guy following me?'

'He's not. At least I'm pretty sure he's not.'

'Well, that's not very reassuring.'

'Kate, there's a lot of things going on here that you don't know about. And I'm just not sure if I really should tell you or not.'

'Oh right, and after saying it that way I'm just going to head back up to my office and let you handle everything?'

'No, I realize that is not an option. It is you we're talking about, after all.'

'So?'

'Have you been following the arsons that have been happening? First across the country and now they apparently settled in Calgary?'

'Yeah, especially with Ryan being a firefighter.'

'Well, Kate, your dad has been following those fires too.'

'Well, I'm sure he's interested. He's a retired firefighter.'

'Kate, your dad has been to all the fire sites. And he's been at City Hall pulling plans and building permits.'

'Ken, I'm sure there is a perfectly good explanation,' I said, not really believing that he could think this.

'And do you know your dad was in town for three days when that first fire happened in June?'

'Sorry?'

'He stayed at the Sheraton in the north-east.'

'Dad was here in June?'

'And he registered under the name Robert Semaka. Does that mean anything to you?'

'That was the name of my paediatrician,' I said, thinking this must all be a joke somehow.

'Kate, I really need your help with this.'

'No.'

'Kate . . .'

'You want me to spy on my dad for you?'

'It's really important.'

'You think he's the arsonist?'

'Kate, we're investigating lots of different possibilities. Like I said, I didn't even realize he was your dad at first.'

'Ken, if you think my dad is the arsonist, you think he is a murderer too.'

'Kate, those deaths might be accidents.'

'Ken, I have to go.'

'Kate.' He reached over and grabbed my hand. 'Kate, please just sit down for a minute. Have a sip of your coffee and take a deep breath.'

I didn't want to, I wanted to run away, and not talk about this any more. But Ken had always been straight with me and I knew deep down he wouldn't be saying this if there weren't a good reason for it.

'Kate, I've been doing a bit of checking into your dad's background for the last couple of years.'

'What?'

'Kate, your dad has been in four different cities for four major arson events.'

'Well, he likes to travel a lot, you know.'

'And now Calgary makes five.'

I felt tears sting my eyes but I blinked them back. There was no way this was true. Any of it. It was just all one gigantic coincidence.

'We just need to ask him. We need to ask him why he was in all these different places.'

'Not we,' Ken said.

'What?'

'Kate, I don't want him to know we're suspicious of him.'

'So you want me to just sit down at the dinner table tonight and say, "Gee, Dad, been to any good fires recently?" '

'No, you know that's not what I want.'

'I can't spy on my own dad.'

'And what if he's got a problem? What if he needs some psychological help because he can't stop setting fires?'

'But that's not what you think, is it? Not if he's been in lots of different cities. You think he's some sort of contract fire-starter. Or a contract killer. Oh my God, why did you decide of all the investigations you've been on to tell me about this one?'

147

'Because I need your help.'

'Ken, I don't think I can give it to you.'

'You have to, Kate. You have to let me know what your dad is up to and see if you can find out anything about his travels.'

'Fine. I'll do it. But I'll do it to prove you wrong.'

'That would be very nice.'

'Ken, forget my dad for a minute. Who is this guy pretending to be a police detective and what does he want?'

'I don't know, Kate, and that worries me.'

'So what's he looking for?'

'I think he's looking for your dad. Or he's found your dad and he's trying to find out who you guys are.'

'So are we in danger here?'

'I think you should be very careful. Until we know more . . .'

'And you won't know more until I tell you, right.'

'Right,' he said. His eyes were full of regret but his voice didn't waver.

I walked much more slowly away from Grounds Zero than I had going there. I knew when I climbed those stairs up to my office Graham would be sitting there waiting to hear about my meeting with Detective Lincoln. And I didn't know what to say to him. I didn't even know what was really going through my mind. I was shocked. I didn't know how I was going to face Dad tonight when he and Cam came to pick me up. Or Cam. Wow, now this was going to be a gigantic secret between us. Guess my whole resolution about truth-telling was about to go out the window. And what would I say to him tomorrow as he and Dad were heading off for another day of renovations? Don't let Dad near the propane tanks? Hide the matches? This was surreal and my stomach was doing some major flip-flopping right now trying to decide if I was going to lose my breakfast or not. Halfway up the stairs I pulled my cellphone out of my pocket and checked the battery. Cam must have charged it for me the night before because it was reading fully charged right now. I pushed the speed dial and called my office.

'Front of house,' Graham answered on the second ring.

'Graham, it's me,' I said. 'Look, I have to go do something. Can you call someone in to work with you today?'

'Sure. I think Leonard is around today. No worries. Everything OK?'

No, I thought, nothing is OK. But I started with my first lie of the day.

'Everything's OK. There's just something personal I have to deal with. I'll see you later.'

And then I sat in the stairwell for a half an hour, way down at the bottom where no one ever came, and I cried.

The movie had been great. That was usually my answer to life's big problems, avoidance. So I had walked down to Eau Claire and saw one of those wonderful Pixar animated things and laughed and cried and laughed some more. And as I walked back to the theatre to pick up my backpack and sweater, I was pretty sure I could face my dad. I didn't know if I could ask him questions but I thought at least I could look at him. Cam I wasn't so sure about and I might have to confess all in bed later tonight, but I could cross that bridge when I came to it. So I grabbed my stuff, and wandered home, window-shopping and enjoying the sun. When I got home, I made myself a stiff drink, ordered a couple of pizzas for dinner and made myself comfortable on the deck, where I sat getting blissfully oblivious while I waited for my men to come home. And they did come home, eventually, two Scotch and sodas later, with Dad carrying two pizza boxes in his hand.

'We ran into the pizza guy at the front door,' Dad said.

'It was nice of you to cook for us,' Cam laughed.

'Honey, you know nothing is too good for you,' I said, afraid I had slurred a word or two but not really sure.

'Katie, are you drunk?' Cam asked.

'No, I've just been sitting on the deck having a couple of drinks, waiting for you guys to get home.'

'What have you been drinking?' Dad asked. 'And did you pour one for your old hard-working dad?'

'I just had a Scotch and soda.'

'Scotch?' Cam asked. 'You only drink Scotch when something serious is going on. What's up?'

'Nothing,' I insisted, wondering how convincing I would be right now.

149

'You sure?'

'Oh, quit being so serious,' Dad said, bringing a couple of beers out of the fridge and opening one for himself and one for Cam. 'It's not like she has a drinking problem. Or does she?'

'No, not at all.'

'Uh, she's in the room,' I said.

'So shall we take our pizza onto the deck and have dinner in the sunshine?' Cam asked, still looking funny at me.

'I've got the pizza,' Dad said.

'I'll get plates and napkins,' I offered.

'I've got the beer,' Cam said, leaving the crutches and hobbling out to the deck, his beer in hand.

We all sat around the table and Dad set up the pizza boxes and opened them up.

'What's this?' he asked, turning up his nose at the first pizza.

'It's spinach and feta cheese,' I said.

'Spinach, on a pizza? You must have a drinking problem.'

'It's good,' I insisted. 'But I promise you'll like the other one.'

I opened the lid and revealed a pizza covered with everything that was guaranteed to give you a heart attack, pepperoni, salami, sausage, bacon, beef, double cheese, anchovies, peppers, mushrooms, onions and just for a little heart health, olives. Dad and Cam both smiled and grabbed a piece.

'Cam, I thought you liked the spinach one?' I said.

'I do, sweetie, but nothing can compare to the Boston Pizza Royale.'

'Oh, is that how you feel about the avocado pizza too?' I asked, worried that we weren't going to be able to order my favourites any more.

'Give the guy a break, Katie. Those are girl pizzas. If he's eating those it's only because he loves you,' Dad laughed.

I looked over at Cam, who was suddenly very intent on counting the olives on his pizza.

'Dad, can I ask you a question and you won't get mad or ask me how I know?'

'Sure, MK, although when you preface a question like that, it's bound to get a father worried.'

'Daddy, were you in Calgary in June?'

'Oh, Katie girl, now who went and told you that?'

'You said you wouldn't ask.'

He heaved a deep sigh and took a big chug of his beer. 'Yes, I was in Calgary in June.'

'And you didn't see me, or even call me?'

'Katie girl, it was one of those crazy business trips. I'm doing some contract work, privately you know? And I had two days of work to do here and then I was due somewhere else. I honestly had no time at all. And I knew I was coming back here now, in July, so I didn't think it was such a big deal.'

'Then why did you keep it a secret?'

'Because I know that you take these things very personally and I didn't want you to get all hurt about it.'

'Really?'

'Really.'

'So what's this contracting stuff about?' I asked. Funny how these questions all just started rolling off my lips and I didn't seem to feel badly about it at all.

'I have a confidentiality agreement, so I can't really talk about it right now.'

'Have you been doing a lot of travelling?'

'A bit.'

'So where have you been?'

'Katie, please, we've been hammering nails all day long and I'm exhausted. The last thing I want to do is sit around here and talk about work. Can't we just talk about movies or books or your old boyfriends or something?'

'Sure. Sorry, Daddy, I didn't mean anything by it.'

'I know, I'm just old and cranky. But another beer would probably help my constitution.'

I got him another beer. And we talked about movies and books, my brother, my cousins and anything else that was considered a safe topic. We skipped my old boyfriends but then I was pretty sure that he just brought that up when he wanted to change the subject. Dad started yawning and made his excuses and went upstairs to bed. I didn't feel any better for the fact that he had sidestepped all my questions either. A fact that Cam didn't miss, as we sat out on the deck and listened to the fireworks. You couldn't see them from my deck, but you could hear them reverberating off the buildings and up and down the long streets and avenues.

'So, you OK?' Cam whispered into my ear. We were in the big lounge chair, me in front of him, his arms wrapped around me.

'Yeah, of course I am.'

'What were all those questions about at dinner?'

'Oh, nothing much.'

'Katie, you're not getting mixed up with something you shouldn't be, are you?'

'No, no I'm reformed, remember?'

'You know, your dad really seemed to be avoiding your questions.'

'I think he was just tired.'

'I want you to tell me if you want me to keep a closer eye on him. And I want you to swear you'll tell me if you're in any danger. And if you swear to that, you can have your secret for now.'

'I swear. And it wouldn't hurt to stick close to him.'

'OK.'

'And I love you.'

Thursday

I hadn't slept really well the night before. Better than I expected, since Cam was actually almost on my side, but still not great. My dad had lied to me. Dad had probably lied to me sometime in our lives, but I'd never actually caught him at it. And I'd caught him at it on the same day that the police had told me they were interested in his travels. And I still hadn't been able to deal with Graham and I was really worried about him. I had to be able to settle at least one thing in my life. So I had gotten up early and dressed and had breakfast with the boys before they went off to the fire hall and worked on what was apparently becoming my dream bedroom. I made my way to the Plex, got everything ready for the show, called Graham to confirm he was coming in and decided today was the day I was going to find out what was going on in his head. I had coffee made, I had time sheets done, I had a banjo player warming up on stage and apparently I had everything under control. For a change.

Until Nick and Lazlo hurried down the hall into my office. Lazlo Hilleo was Head of Building Services, which put him in my path frequently. We didn't like each other. So usually when our paths crossed there was lots of yelling and grandstanding and one of us trying to be better than the other. It was usually a draw and just ended up giving me a headache. Today, I had other more important things on my mind and I promised myself I was going to keep my cool and give him whatever it was he wanted and then get him out of my office.

'Good morning, Kate.' He smiled. See, that was always how it started. His lips smiled but his eyes said I hate wasting my time talking to the little people.

'Good morning, Lazlo.' I smiled back, showing him a real smile. 'Nick.'

Nick was Senior Security Supervisor. He stood a couple of feet behind Lazlo, which was all the distance he could get from him in my office, looking incredibly uncomfortable. The security staff generally had a good working relationship with everyone in the building, and Lazlo didn't. So they hated going around on his little missions with him and always tried to distance themselves. Nick just kind of nodded to me.

'Kate, I'm not sure if you've been aware of this, but we seem to be having some problems with fires in this building.'

'Oh?'

'Yes. It appears people are getting sloppy with some safety procedures.'

'How can I help?'

'Well, you did have a fire in your garbage can, didn't you?'

'Just a little smoke, which I don't recall reporting.'

'And that would be a violation in and of itself now, wouldn't it?'

153

I took another deep breath, exhaling slowly, craving a cigarette not only for the nicotine but because I knew Lazlo didn't like the smoke.

'It was just a little smoke. I didn't think it was something I had to report. How did you find out about it?'

'The cleaners discovered it that evening and reported it. Following correct procedure, I might add.'

'Uh-huh.'

'Well, regardless of all those inconvenient rules and regulations, I am sure that under normal circumstances I wouldn't be so worried about such a little incident. But since it would be the third fire we've had at the Plex now, I just wanted to get full details.'

'I emptied an ashtray in the can and obviously there was still a hot ember. Graham put it out in like a second, Lazlo, we caught it right away.'

'Yes, that was very fortunate. Now, Kate, you are aware that the new smoking by-laws have come into effect and that as of Monday this is a non-smoking building.'

'Well, that is fine, because I'm a non-smoking house manager, Lazlo.'

'Good, good for you. What is it they say? It takes eight tries to successfully quit smoking?'

'Sorry, Lazlo,' I said, feeling my smile becoming more forced and less real, 'is there a point here?'

'I just wanted to remind you about the rules and that we need to be diligent during this dangerous time.'

'No, you just wanted to remind me that you were in charge. Something you seem to take the greatest pleasure in doing.' Damn it, I lost my temper!

'Kate, I know you have had a lot of stress in your life recently. I know that your friend has passed away and that must be very hard,' Lazlo offered. 'But we have to try and maintain our professionalism during these times.'

'You're right,' I said, swallowing my pride. I wish I had a glass of water to wash it down with. 'You're right and I apologize.'

The smile that had been growing on Nick's face now faded as his eyes resumed their study of my office floor tiles.

'Thank you. Now, I need you to promise me that you will report anything you see that may be out of the norm, so to speak. It would a great relief if we could put an end to this dangerous behaviour.'

'Lazlo, that's exactly what I was planning on doing this morning,' I said, telling the truth for the first time since he had walked through my door.

'Good, then we are in agreement. Should I stop by later and check out how things are going down here?'

'Maybe I'll just give you a call,' I suggested. 'We don't want to rush into this cooperation thing too quickly.'

Nick actually snickered and quickly disguised it as a cough.

'Nick, where are we off to next?' Lazlo asked, turning quickly from me now that we were done. He was halfway down the hall by the time Nick had his clipboard out.

I poured myself some fresh coffee and paced the office. I didn't want Lazlo snooping around here too closely if Graham really was going off the deep end, but I couldn't stop him. So I had to stop Graham from going off the deep end. And get all that done before my father lit another condo complex on fire, if Detective Lincoln was on the right track.

'OK, I am not enjoying this!' I screamed out loud, working under the disillusionment that I might actually be alone in this building for once.

'Kate?'

I jumped and turned to see who was listening to me rant.

'Graham?'

'Sorry, didn't mean to sneak up on you.'

'It's OK.'

'What's wrong?'

'Nothing.'

'Well, you don't usually scream at any empty room unless there's something big going on.'

'OK, OK, there is. Graham, I've been trying to talk to you about this for days and we keep getting interrupted. And I didn't want to do it like this. I mean I even went over to the Calhoun Library and did some research in the psychology section to see how I should approach this. And by the way, this is not the way to do it.'

'What?' he asked.

'When I moved your bag the other day, it was open and some stuff dumped out of it.'

'So?'

'So some of the things that dropped out were a package of matches, a can of butane lighter fluid and a T-shirt soaked in it. Things that someone might start a fire with.'

'What?'

'You heard me, things that someone might start a fire with. And there have been some strange fires started in this building. And now Lazlo is snooping around and if you have a problem we have to deal with it before he finds out.'

'You think I've been starting the fires here?' he gasped, sitting hard in my chair.

'Well, Graham, it's a little suspicious, and with you being upset about your mom . . .'

'Kate, I am shocked that you could even think that about me. Yes, I'm upset about my mother. But I'm working through that. I'm not lighting fires for some sort of sick emotional release.'

'Graham, why else would you have that stuff in your pack?'

'I never had anything like that in my pack. Maybe someone put something in there. It's not like we have any privacy here.'

'Who could have put anything in your pack?' I asked.

'Leonard has been around and so has Krista.'

'Give me a break.'

'Kate, I swear . . .'

'I might have believed you until I saw them pull that T-shirt out of the dumpster later that night. The T-shirt that was in your backpack.'

'Kate, you're wrong about this.'

'Prove it.'

'How can I prove something like that?'

'Empty out your bag.'

'I will not.'

'Graham, if you're not carrying anything around like that, empty your bag and show me.'

'Kate?'

'I mean it, Graham. We are addressing this right here and now. Before you leave this office we are going to be straight with each other about what is going on in that mind of yours, OK?'

'I thought you were my friend!' he screamed, and raced

156

out of the office, with his backpack over his shoulder.

I watched him disappear down the hallway, not expecting this outcome in any of my backup plans.

'Well, that went well,' I sighed, refilling my cup and sitting back down at my desk. I picked up the phone and dialled. 'Hi, Leonard, it's Kate. Can you work this afternoon?'

After Leonard and I managed our rousing crowd at the lunchtime concert, and Leonard stuck around for a banjo lesson while trying to pick up the cute cowboy in the tight jeans, I wandered down to Grounds Zero and got an iced latte and made myself comfortable at one of the sidewalk tables. I was happily sipping my drink and finishing the book I had picked up the other day, feeling the afternoon sun burning my legs through the dark denim of my blue jeans. I moved my legs under the table and into the shade, readjusted my cowboy hat and turned the page. I hadn't even noticed someone approaching until I heard the chair behind me scrape the concrete as someone pulled it out and sat down. I looked up, startled, but that changed to shock when I recognized the man sitting beside me.

'Don't scream,' he instructed me, quietly and calmly. 'Don't run away and don't even look like anything strange is happening.'

'What do you want?'

'I want you not to be afraid of me.'

'Why should I be afraid of you? You're a police detective and the police are our friends, right?'

'Look, I used the police-detective thing because it usually makes people happy and they leave me alone.'

'So you find telling people you're a criminal and a liar scares them away?'

'Yeah, ha, ha, you're quite the wit.'

'I find that when I'm in danger I can get quite entertaining.'

'You're not in danger.'

'Oh, now you're the funny one.'

'I need to ask you some questions,' he said.

'Gee, I'd like to do the same. Like what were you doing in my building the other day?'

'Oh, you recognized me,' he sighed. 'I thought I'd snuck by you on that one.'

157

'No such luck.'

'Well, a friend of mine has been staying in that building and my friend has a reputation of having bad things happen when he's around. I just wanted to check to see if he'd been playing with anything that he shouldn't be playing with.'

'Like the fire-alarm system?'

'Yeah.'

'And?'

'And it's fine now. I put it back into working order.'

'And who is this friend of yours?'

'Interesting question,' he laughed, taking my coffee and taking a sip out of it before sliding it back in front of me.

'Keep it.'

'Well, this fellow is apparently staying with you. And I'm guessing from the age difference and the way you behave around each other that you're either having an affair with someone who's really out of your age range or he's your father.'

'Maybe I like older men?'

'Maybe your boyfriend likes threesomes too?' he laughed. 'And maybe pigs fly.'

'So what is your point here? Want a dinner invitation or something?'

'What I want is for you to pass a message on to good old Dad that you and I had this conversation today.'

'That's it?' I asked, expecting that this would be the part where he pulled out a gun and shot me.

'Yeah, you know, I'm pretty sure that will do it. I'm one of those people that's really hard to forget.'

'And with whom shall I say I had this conversation?'

'Again, just tell him about this, I'm pretty hard to forget. Good afternoon, ma'am.'

And he was gone. And Gus was running up the stairs, bringing me a fresh coffee, worry on his face.

'Kate, you OK?'

'I'm fine, Gus, what's wrong with you?' I said, pushing a chair out for him, as his face was beet red.

'That man,' Gus said. He was breathing heavily but at least his face was turning back into a slightly more normal shade.

'Yes?' I said, not wanting to give anything away.

'Detective Lincoln was asking me about him. Told me he

158

might be hanging around down here and I should let him know if I saw him.'

'Did you call Detective Lincoln?' I asked.

'Yeah, he's waiting in your office. He didn't want to scare him off or to let him know that we were on to him.'

I closed up my book and stood up. 'Guess I'd better go and have a talk with him.'

'Kate, you were never alone out here,' Gus said, handing me my fresh coffee. 'I was watching you.'

'Thanks, Gus,' I said.

I sat in my chair and stared across the desk at Ken. I was on the wrong side of my desk to begin with and I suspected he had done that on purpose, to make me feel out of control.

'Kate, I asked you to tell me what happened down there.'

'And I'm thinking,' I said.

'Thinking about what? About what not to tell me or just gathering your thoughts?'

'Ken, two days ago the biggest problem on my mind was that fire hall and the $389,000 mortgage I hold on it. Yesterday you were trying to convince me that my father is a crazed arsonist and maybe a killer, that some deranged criminal is stalking him or me and that it's my civic duty to spy on him and turn him in. And then there's that stupid woman from E-News TV and this crap with Graham . . .'

'What about Graham?'

'Never mind, just stuff with his mom dying. It's unrelated.'

'You sure?'

'As sure as you're going to know right now,' I said. 'With a promise that my worries about him are totally unrelated to anything you're worried about.'

'You know we tend to not call it worrying. We prefer investigation.'

'Fine.'

'And I'm still trying to investigate what just happened to you out there.'

'And I'm still trying to decide where my loyalties lie here, Ken.'

'Do we have to have that whole talk about going to jail again?'

159

'Maybe for my dad going to jail is the right thing to do.'

'Kate, if I told you I would really rather find your dad innocent, would you believe me?'

'Yes.'

'But if I do find him guilty I need to do my duty and get him off the streets.'

'Yes.'

'So, can you tell me what this guy said?'

'He admitted to me that he wasn't a police detective and told me that he wanted me to tell Dad that he had talked to me.'

'Who is he?'

'He didn't say. He made some vague comment about how Dad would know who he was.'

'That's it?'

'That's not quite all.'

'Well, I'm not getting any younger.'

'Ken, you used to be way more patient with me.'

'Yeah, that was several months ago, before I learned that you can be this hugely sneaky and underhanded person, someone who can lie way too easily when she's trying to protect her friends and who always thinks she knows best and that I don't know what I'm doing.'

'That last part isn't true. I think you're very competent.'

'Thank you. So what aren't you telling me?'

'I got his fingerprints on that cup.' And a very self-satisfied smile spread across my face.

The self-satisfaction had left when Ken explained that fingerprints weren't a sure thing. But the smile had crept back a little when he found a plastic bag and set the cup gently inside it, before leaving my office.

The big white car, with a fine layer of sawdust covering it from its stay at the construction zone today, pulled up at the stage door promptly at five thirty to pick me up. My heart was beating a mile a minute as I climbed in and fastened my seat belt. I was surprised to find Ryan driving the car and not Dad. Surprised and relieved.

'Hi?'

'Your dad wanted to go visit some old friends tonight,' Cam explained. 'Ryan kindly offered to drive the crippled one

160

home so that we wouldn't have to risk you driving again.'

'Where did Dad go?' I asked, a little too quickly.

'Well, there's an interesting question,' Cam said. 'Especially considering that Ryan asked me to pass on a message to you.'

'Oh?' I asked innocently.

'Something about the fire panel in our building?'

'Oh, I guess I forgot to tell you about that, huh?'

'Didn't you say you would tell me if you're in any danger?'

'Ryan, I thought you were going to call me?' I demanded.

'Look, between you and my wife, I am never going to win any of these arguments. But basically, you never said it was a big secret, so I just asked Cam to tell you what we found.'

'And what did you find?' I asked, ignoring Cam's glares from the back seat.

'The panel had been opened and there were several wires that looked like they had been undone. But when we inspected it, everything was hooked up correctly. The captain did report it to the police, though.'

'So, Katie, do you mind telling me who is trying to kill you and why?' Cam asked.

'I can't say. Ken Lincoln has threatened me with jail if I say anything.'

'And would you like to know what I can do to you if you don't tell me something?'

'It's not me, Cam, it's my dad.'

Friday

Cam slept through the night. I could tell because of that nasty self-satisfied snoring I heard as I tossed and turned. Lucky for him that he got to work all day and didn't know half of what I knew: all sorts of things kept bouncing against each other in my mind all night long. I was still awake when

Dad came home and I whispered a hello to him, which he answered, but then went straight upstairs. As I heard him climb into bed, I heard a fire truck racing down the street, sirens blaring. So the first thing I did when I woke up from my fitful sleep was turn on the TV to the E-News breakfast news show. Geneva might be a bitch but she had a nose for fire. I muted the sound while I scoured the stories for pictures of fire, but nothing. When I heard the newspaper get tossed against the apartment door, I climbed quietly out of bed and grabbed it, checking the headlines for any mention of fire or arson. I sat at the kitchen table, quietly turning from the first section to the city section, scanning even the smallest article, but there didn't seem to be anything.

I heard a whisper coming from the couch. 'What are you doing up so early?'

'I wanted to read the paper,' I said. 'I couldn't sleep and I didn't want my tossing and turning to wake you up.'

'Well, that didn't, but the light and the rustling of the pages did.'

'I'm sorry, Cam.'

'Couldn't you at least put the coffee on?'

'I didn't want to wake Dad up.'

'Too late,' I heard from upstairs.

'Sorry,' I called up. But I did get up from the table to get the coffee brewing.

Dad came stumbling down the stairs in his robe, rubbing very tired-looking eyes.

'Dad, why don't you go back to sleep,' I said. 'It's really early.'

'And I'd like to know what you're doing up this early,' he said. 'Aren't you the one that sleeps until noon?'

'Normally.'

'And you were awake when I got home,' he pointed out.

'Yeah, I didn't sleep very well last night.'

'How come, Katie girl? You got troubles?'

'Oh, sort of,' I said and then changed my mind. 'No, not really.'

'Well, which is it?' Cam asked, pushing himself up into a sitting position and turning the TV off.

'No, it's nothing,' I said, and brought three coffee cups down from the cupboard and filled them, hoping that would shut the guys up for a while.

Cam said, 'We have some good news for you.'

'What?' I asked, but he just smiled. 'Dad?'

'Can I?' Dad asked Cam.

'Go ahead.'

'Today at about two o'clock we are going to drive over to the theatre and we are going to pick you up and bring you back to your new home and show you the amazing bedroom that this loving boyfriend of yours has built for you.'

'Hey, I had lots and lots of help,' Cam said.

'It's done?'

'Almost.'

'If we're lucky it will be by two,' Dad explained. 'If not, I'm driving real slow and we're going to have to stop at Peter's Drive Inn for a banana-fudge milkshake.'

'Stalling?'

'You got it.'

'Just like when you and Mom were having a fight and you were avoiding going home?' I teased.

'I was never scared of your mother, Katie girl, I just had lots and lots of respect for that Irish temper of hers. And I loved those banana-fudge milkshakes.'

'What's it look like?' I asked.

'Well, it's a small white building with blue trim . . .'

'Not the drive-in, you goof, the bedroom.'

'That is a state secret,' Cam said. 'Are you going to bring me that coffee before it gets cold?'

'Oh, sorry,' I said and took it over to him, perching on the side of the bed. 'What colour are the walls?'

'A very pretty colour.'

'Who picked it?'

'I did,' Cam said. 'Now you just stop asking because we are not going to tell you anything until this afternoon.'

'And just so you know,' Dad added, 'we've armed everyone working at the site today and if you come snooping around I've given them orders to shoot to kill.'

'Oh, nice way to treat your own daughter.'

'I know you too well, Katie girl. So don't even think about sneaking over.'

'You think you know me so well.'

163

'I do,' Dad said, sipping his coffee and opening the news-paper. 'Did you find what you were looking for in the paper?'

'No.'

'That's too bad.'

'No, it's a good thing.' I said, sitting beside him and pulling the crossword out.

'If we're up for good, does anyone mind if I take a shower first?' Cam asked.

'Go for it,' I told him.

Cam hobbled into the bathroom and shut the door. I started the puzzle. One down, five letters, intentional fire. A-R-S-O-N. I shivered, scrunched the crossword into a ball and tossed it into the garbage. I was beginning to feel like someone was sending me secret messages through crossword puzzles. What was next? Was I going to start wearing tin foil hats to block satellite signals?

'Giving up already?' Dad asked.

'I guess I'm just not in the mood.'

'Are you going to tell me what's going on?' he asked.

'I can't, Daddy. I'm so sorry but I just can't.'

He reached over and pulled me closer to him, wrapping his arm around my neck and pulling me into a bear hug.

'It's not Cam, is it? Is he giving you a rough time about something? Is it buying the fire hall that's got you all worked up?'

'Oh, no, Dad. I'm fine with Cam.'

'Promise me you'll talk to me if you need me,' he said. 'I don't like to see you so troubled.'

I let them drop me off at the theatre early. I sat in the window ledge, coffee in hand and lights off, just staring out into the sky. We had a big sky here and the clouds were one of my favourite things to watch when I was feeling down. It was like meditation. I stared and watched the wind blow them across the skies, watching for shapes and patterns to emerge, thinking they might be signs from the heavens. They never were, or if they were, I wasn't very good at interpreting them. An hour before show time, I forced myself up, went and checked the theatre and the lobbies and then got the time sheets ready. I wondered if I would see Graham here or if he had called someone in to work for him. Actually, I was wondering if I would ever see Graham again or if I had crossed a line last time we talked. Or fought. Or whatever it was we did.

I heard the door push open at the end of the hallway and turned. I smiled when I saw it was Graham, but then my smile dropped when I saw he was followed by Krista. They both bounced into the office and plopped themselves on the bench along the wall, sitting quite close together I noticed.

'Hi, Kate,' Graham talked slowly, signing while he spoke so Krista wouldn't miss the conversation.

'Hi, Graham, Krista,' I said waving, my weak attempt at signing.

'I hope you don't mind me bringing her,' Graham continued, talking to me and signing for her. 'She wanted to see the country band today. She says she went to school with the drummer. And then we're going down to the Stampede grounds after the show.'

'No, that's fine,' I said, knowing that it was a brilliant way for him to avoid finishing the conversation we had started yesterday. Knowing I would never bring the fire issue up with her sitting right there. Instead, we made small talk, me asking about the band and what she knew about them, while Graham translated back and forth for us.

A half-hour before show time, we opened the doors and waited for people to slowly wander in. This band must have had some fans, because we actually got about fifty people in for the show, and the E-News van arrived for live coverage on their noon-time news. As Geneva got out with a new cameraman, I left Graham in charge and hid in my office. I wasn't going to let her ruin my day today. The band played a bouncy mix of bluegrass, pop and country and everyone was smiling and tapping their toes as they left the theatre. We got things cleaned up and closed up in record time with Krista's help, and then Graham disappeared with her as fast as he had appeared. I sat in my window, watching them walk down the street toward the Stampede grounds. I noticed they were holding hands and couldn't decide how I felt about that.

As it got closer to two o'clock, I packed up my backpack, locked up my office and made my way to the stage door. I grabbed a bottle of water out of my pack and sat on the stairs, in the shade, and waited for my chariot to arrive to take me to my new palace. I couldn't decide if I was nervous or not. What if I didn't like it? I mean they had done a good job on the kitchen, but how hard was a kitchen? A bedroom was a whole different story. It had to be romantic yet functional. Peaceful, calming, and surrounding me with all the things I loved, my books, my music, my movies, yet without seeming crowded and messy. I had no idea how Cam was going to please me, since even just thinking about it sent my mind reeling.

I finished my water and tossed the bottle into the recycling bin. Then I checked my watch and was surprised to see that it was almost two thirty. I couldn't believe that my guys were late without calling me. I pulled my cellphone out and dialled Cam, but it went straight to voicemail. I tried Dad but got the same thing. Then I noticed I had a message flashing. I had to try and remember to check for messages more often. Sometimes I wouldn't find them for days. I opened the message and it said unknown caller. But I played the message anyway.

'You forgot to pass my message on to your dad last night,' the voice said, sending a chill up my spine. 'So I talked to him myself. Ladybug, ladybug, fly away home . . .' and then he hung up.

What was he talking about? Ladybug, ladybug, fly away home? And then it dawned on me, creeping back from my distant childhood – because your house is on fire and your children alone.

A taxi pulled up in front and dropped one of the security guards off. I rudely pushed him out of the way and gave the driver my address. He slowly pulled out into the street, and started talking about the weather.

'This is an emergency,' I screamed at him. 'Move this car!'

We drove to the fire hall, but it was locked up and peaceful. So then I gave the driver the address for the loft. He turned around and headed back downtown while I pulled out my cellphone and dialled Sam's number.

'Hi, Kate,' she said.

'Is Ryan home or at work?'

'Home. What do you need?'

'I need him at the loft faster than the speed of light,' I said.

'And I need half of the City of Calgary Fire Department right behind him.'

'What's up? What are you talking about?'

'Sam, if he's not in the car already it's too late,' I said and hung up on her. I figured she would take me more seriously if I did that, plus I could hardly concentrate and form sentences, let alone argue or explain my suspicions to her. I just sat in the back of the taxi, willing the lights to stay green and the traffic in front of us to part.

After what seemed like a hundred years dragged out in slow motion, the taxi pulled up in front of my building. I didn't stop to hear what he had charged me, but just threw a handful of bills out onto the front seat while I struggled to get out. I had my keys out and ready and finally let myself into the building. I punched the elevator button and suddenly felt dizzy and then realized that I been holding my breath. I took a deep breath, getting some oxygen to my starving brain just as the doors opened. I pushed the button and agonized as the ancient elevator made its slow ascent. As the floors unfolded slowly on the light panel above my head, I began to feel calmer. There were no fire alarms ringing, there were no smoke alarms buzzing and I was pretty sure I didn't smell any smoke. I hadn't seen flames leaping out the windows, licking the side of the building, or people screaming for help. Someone was just trying to play with my mind, trying to see if they could make me run. And what was making me really cranky was that they had succeeded. With one floor to go I was actually feel angrier than scared. All that changed when the elevator doors opened on the nineteenth floor. Smoke billowed up and down the hallway and smoke alarms were ringing out from behind every apartment door. I stood there, feeling the blood drain from the upper half of my body. And then the elevator doors closed. I reached out and grabbed the door just before it sealed and raced out. My backpack was left behind but I didn't even notice. I raced to my apartment and fumbled with the key in the three locks, cursing Cam for making us so safe inside and not thinking that we might need to get out in a hurry. I got the last lock opened and pushed the door open, racing inside, horrified at what I might find.

'Cam!' I screamed, seeing him lying half on the bed and half off, unconscious.

167

I raced over, my life without him flashing before my eyes. I touched him, scared he would feel cold and stiff, but he was warm. And his chest moved as he breathed.

'Cam!' I screamed again, shaking him. He was out cold. My eyes were streaming, partly from the fear and partly from the smoke. I turned around and saw our kitchen was on fire. There was a pot of oil on the stove, smoke shooting out of it. Flames had set the cupboards on fire and the paint was bubbling and sending horrible chemical smells into the air. Something was bubbling behind the microwave door too. I stood up and wondered if I should grab the fire extinguisher, if I would be able to get this out. But then the wood crackled and a cupboard door fell to the ground and I knew that wasn't going to happen. I heard coughing coming from upstairs and I raced up the stairs, and saw Dad lying on the bed, blinking his watery eyes, trying to get his bearings. He had one of Cam's crutches in his hands and a nasty gash on his forehead, seeping blood.

'Daddy,' I screamed at him, but this time it worked.

'MK, what is going on here?' he asked, sitting up on the bed and rubbing at his eyes.

'The loft is on fire,' I said, choking through the thick smoke that hung in the air. 'Come on, we have to get out of here.'

I grabbed his arm and pulled him down the stairs, with him practically falling over on me halfway down.

'This isn't the way this was supposed to happen,' he said.

'What are you talking about?' I asked, pulling him over to where Cam was lying.

'Oh my God, is he all right?' Dad asked.

'I think so but we have to get him out of here,' I said. I could feel the heat from the kitchen beating through my clothes and I turned to Dad and took him by the shoulders. 'I can't carry him by myself, can you help me?'

He coughed again, a horrible deep, lung-wrenching cough, but managed to nod. We each pulled at Cam's arms and managed to get him into a sitting position and then pulled him up. He was heavy. I now understood that whole dead-weight thing and I started bargaining with God about going to the gym or going to church or whatever it took to give me the strength to get him out of here. Dad had one arm around his shoulder and I had the other, but Dad was still pretty unsteady on his feet. We half dragged him out into the hallway, the flames engulfing the loft and the living room now, but I didn't care. I stood in the hallway and saw smoke seeping out from under all the apartment doors, up and down the hallways.

'There's fires in all the apartments,' Dad said.

'How do you know that?' I screamed at him and then started coughing. I had to save my strength for getting Cam out.

'Katie, I can explain.'

'When we're out of here,' I said, and then turned to the elevator and started dragging Cam down the hallway.

'We can't take the elevators,' Dad called to me.

'I don't have the strength to get him down the stairs,' I said. 'We have to risk the elevators.'

But halfway there, I didn't know if I had the strength to get either man to the elevator.

'Kate!' I heard a voice from down the hallway. I turned, thinking someone else might have been trapped in one of the apartments. Or maybe it was the angel of death, come to take us all with him. Or maybe I just needed some oxygen. And then I saw Ryan race from the stairwell toward us.

'You OK?'

'Not really.'

'Get your dad to the stairs. I've got Cam.'

He flung Cam over his shoulders, just like in the movies, and I put Dad's arm over my shoulders and tried to steady him as we raced to the stairwell. We got inside and closed the door. There was much less smoke in here and I stopped for a minute to blink my burning eyes and try and clear my lungs.

'Don't stop, Kate,' Ryan instructed me. 'We're not safe yet.'

'Did you call 911?'

'Yeah, they weren't far behind me, I'm sure. Now come on.'

We stumbled down the stairs. Dad's breathing was getting more laboured and he was becoming heavier on my shoulder. Five storeys down I stumbled and fell to the floor, with him landing on top of me.

'Kate, we can't stop,' Ryan insisted, turning to me.

169

'I know, I know,' I said. Dad had pulled himself up using the railings and sat on the edge of a stair, his head in his hands, trying to catch his breath.

'Come on, Sherm, you know we can't stop.'

'It's been a long time since I've been in a burning building.' He laughed.

I wanted to slap his face for laughing while we were choking on smoke and a couple of steps ahead of the fire. I wanted to scream at him for putting us in this danger, except I didn't have enough air or energy left to scream. And then I heard footsteps on the stairs below us. Four firefighters rounded the corner. The first one tried to take Cam from Ryan.

'I've got him,' Ryan insisted, refusing to relinquish his friend, but he followed the firefighter down the stairs.

Two firefighters got Dad between them and started down the stairs with him and the third grabbed me, half carrying and half dragging me down. I counted the floors, ecstatic to see two and then one and knowing I was going to live. We pushed through the emergency door and raced outside into the sunlight.

The street was blocked to traffic and covered with fire trucks, police cars and ambulances. Cam lay on a stretcher with an oxygen mask over his face and a paramedic wrapping a blood-pressure cuff around his arm. The oxygen was doing its trick because Cam was starting to struggle against the mask as he fought his way back up toward consciousness. Dad sat on a stretcher outside another ambulance, oxygen mask on his face, as Ken Lincoln leaned close to him and talked to him. When Ken straightened up, I saw that one of Dad's hands was hand-cuffed to the stretcher.

My rescuer still had me by the arm and he pulled me over to the ambulance where Cam lay, a firefighter standing over top of him, trying to hold the oxygen mask in place while the paramedic tried to calm him down. I sat down on the step on the back of the ambulance and reached out and took Cam's hand. As soon as he felt my hand grip his he stopped struggling. Someone slipped an oxygen mask around my face and slid a blanket over my shoulders. I pulled it tightly around me, because despite the hot July sun I was shivering.

'Katie?' Cam rasped, his voice harsh.

'I'm here,' I reassured him.

'What happened?' he asked.

'There was a fire in your apartment,' the paramedic told him.

'Are you OK?' he asked me, his eyes blinking open and trying to focus.

'I'm fine. What happened up there?'

'I don't know. Your dad and I came back to the apartment to bring a few last things over to the new place. He was packing some stuff up in the loft and I was downstairs. I heard something and I turned around and I just saw one of my crutches coming at my head. I don't remember a thing after that.'

'Good thing you have a hard head,' I laughed, hiding my nervousness as the paramedic wrapped a pressure bandage around his head.

'Is your dad OK?'

'I think so.'

'You think so? Where is he?'

'Detective Lincoln is talking to him across the street,' I said, not wanting to get into this with him right now.

'OK, we're going to get you two to the hospital and let the doctors have a look at you,' the paramedic told me, leading me into the ambulance and sitting me in a seat on the side of the vehicle.

'I'm OK,' Cam said.

'You need stitches at least,' the paramedic said, strapping him into the stretcher and ignoring his protests as he loaded him into the ambulance.

I took one last look up at my building before they closed the ambulance doors, and now I did see flames shooting out of the windows, as more fire trucks poured into the street. I felt my heart break as my home was destroyed. And as I turned for one last look down the street, I saw Geneva Anderson pointing to me and talking to her cameraman, as he turned the camera on to us. I raised my third finger to her, not caring that it might be all over the evening news. I could just say I was in shock and not responsible for my actions. And then the ambulance doors closed and we started the drive to the hospital.

*　　*　　*

Cam lay on the bed in the emergency room, complaining bitterly about having to stay there. I waited on one of those stools with the rolling wheels that the doctors always sat on, rolling back and forth.

'Katie, just sit still, you're making me crazy,' Cam said, an ice pack on his head.

'Sorry, I'm kind of stressed.'

'Be stressed quietly, I have a killer headache.'

'Yeah, well, it's you that wanted me to quit smoking.'

'Oh, Katie. Why don't you see if you can get some coffee? Or some nicotine gum?'

'Don't be pissed with me,' I said, lashing out. 'Do you know what it was like to see you lying on that bed and wonder if you were dead or alive?'

'Yes, Katie, I know exactly what it feels like. I know what it feels like to see you being thrown off a forty-foot tower. I know what it feels like to see you get shot. Shall I go on?'

I just sighed. Loudly and dramatically.

'Why don't you go and check on your dad?'

'I don't want to.'

'Come on, Katie, be a grown-up about this. He's your dad.'

'He did this,' I whispered.

'What?'

'Detective Lincoln has been investigating him. He's the arsonist.'

'What are you talking about?'

'I'm serious. And there is this other guy following him, pretending to be a police detective but I think he's like a Mob guy or something.'

'What have you got yourself mixed up in?'

'Nothing. Oh God, Cam, I haven't done anything, I swear. I just checked with Ken why this detective guy was writing down your licence-plate number and then we found out he wasn't a cop and then Ken told me to be careful because they were investigating my dad and that if I overheard anything suspicious I should call him and—'

'OK, OK, take a breath.'

'Sorry.'

'How long have you known about this?'

'Not long. It started the day I snuck down to the fire hall.'

172

'Well, how do you know your dad did this?'

'Because he was handcuffed to the stretcher in the ambulance.'

'I can't believe it. So you want me to believe that he's the one that clocked me with my crutch?'

'No, I don't want to believe that. But it appears to be what happened.'

Cam lay there, staring at the ceiling. 'It can't be your dad. Katie, he's a retired firefighter. What's he doing setting fires?'

'Cam, Dad has a fishing lodge on the coast that is probably worth over a million dollars. Have you ever stopped to think how he could afford that after retiring from the city?'

'I never thought to ask. He might have come into an inheritance or something.'

'He didn't. Neither did he win the lottery. So what else does that leave us with?'

'I don't know, but it can't be right.'

'Well, what do you want me to say?' I asked, exasperated.

'Why don't you go find Detective Lincoln?' Cam suggested. 'Maybe he can clarify what's going on.'

'OK,' I said, getting up and leaving the curtained area.

'And get yourself a coffee.'

I was going to find a nurse but I saw Ryan and Sam sitting at the end of the hall on one of the battered sofas, so I wandered down and sat down beside Sam.

'How's Cam?' Ryan asked.

'Fine. Minor smoke inhalation, minor concussion, waiting on stitches and then I guess we're done here.'

'Good,' Sam said.

'Ryan, I can never repay you for saving him,' I started, but he cut me off.

'Don't even think about it, Kate, it's what I do.'

'I don't care. You came there on your day off and went into that building without any safety gear or any backup and you saved our lives.'

'Kate, really. I'll accept your thanks but then we just need to move on.'

'OK. But anything you ever need, you just come to me.'

'Kate!' Sam said.

'All right, all right. So have either of you seen Detective Lincoln?'

173

'He left about five minutes ago,' Ryan said.

'Oh.'

'And, Kate, they moved your dad upstairs. But he's not allowed any visitors. Did you know he was under arrest?' Sam asked gently.

'Yeah.'

'But he's going to be OK physically from the fire. They just wanted to check his breathing overnight I guess and then he'll be released.'

'From the hospital to the jail.'

'Kate, we'll get him a lawyer, it'll all work out.'

'I don't know if I want to,' I said quietly.

'You can't believe he's guilty.'

'I don't know what to think. Except that I almost lost Cam tonight.'

'I know, look, we'll get Cam stitched up and get you guys home.'

'My home burned down tonight, Sam, remember?'

'Oh my God, you are the most melodramatic person I have ever met.' She laughed at me. 'Your apartment burned tonight and it didn't burn down. You'll be able to salvage some stuff when they let you back inside, in a couple of days. Meanwhile, you have this beautiful new home that Cam and your dad have been working like madmen on just awaiting your arrival. And as soon as Cam gets himself stitched back up, we're going to drive you there.'

'Oh my God, I forgot all about the fire hall,' I admitted. 'And now we have a really good excuse to buy all new furniture.'

'See, there's always an upside,' Sam said.

'I think I was being sarcastic.'

'Well, get over it,' she said, slapping the side of my head. I was saved from further assault when a nurse called out my name.

'I'm Kate Carpenter,' I said.

'Your boyfriend is ready to go home now,' she told me, and I went back to get Cam.

Ryan stopped the car in front of the fire hall and got out to help Cam out of the back seat. I grabbed my backpack, which

Ryan had valiantly saved for me, and went around to steady Cam, who didn't have new crutches yet.

'You guys want to come in?' I asked.

'No,' Sam said. 'It's your first night in your new place. You two do not need company.'

'You sure?'

'She's sure,' Cam said, putting his arm around me, half in embrace and half for balance.

'Goodnight, then,' I said, waving at them as they drove away. We turned and slowly walked down the sidewalk. Cam pulled out his key and unlocked the door.

'I'm really nervous for you to see this,' he admitted.

'I'm even more nervous,' I told him. 'So let's just do it.'

He held the door open for me and then locked it tightly behind us. Then he turned on the lighting and the ugly fluorescents snapped to attention up and down the hallway.

'Uh, I haven't got those replaced yet.'

'It's OK, sweetie,' I tried to reassure him.

We walked down the hallway, passing the kitchen that I had already seen, but which now had art on the walls and glass-front cabinets, and the family room, which was almost done, and I followed Cam up the stairs. At least he was better at negotiating them than he was with our old spiral staircase. He led me to the door and then opened it, turning a light on and stepping back so I could look.

I took a deep breath and stepped inside. There was a king-size bed on the far wall, covered in beautiful chocolate-brown and cream-coloured linens. The walls were a pale lilac and looked like linen. There was a beautiful rattan entertainment centre stained a dark brown, and matching end tables and dressers. There was soft lighting, creamy linen curtains and a stunning hardwood floor. In one corner there were two armchairs and a little table, surrounded by built-in bookcases. Cam led me through a door and into the walk-in closet and dressing area. There were his and her closets, with benches in the middle to sit on while dressing.

'My clothes are here,' I whispered.

'We didn't lose everything in the fire, Katie. The guys got a lot of stuff moved over today.'

'Oh my God, I can't believe it.'

'Come this way.'

He led me through the other door in the room into our bathroom. There was a gigantic soaker Jacuzzi tub, surrounded by amazing stone tiles. There were shelves with candles and bath oils and scented soaps jutting out from the wall. The shower was made out of the same granite tiles, and had glass walls. There were four shower heads, a bench for shaving and a steam setting. There were his and hers vanities, maple cabinets and a countertop glistening with opaque glass tiles.

'I don't know what to say,' I said.

'Do you like it?' he asked.

'It's so amazingly beautiful. I would have never thought you could make this out of an old fire hall.'

'Come look at this,' he said, pulling me back out into the main room and over to the bookcase, then stood beside it. 'Open that door.'

I undid the latch and opened the shelf and there sat a cappuccino machine.

'Now you don't have to go downstairs for coffee on Sunday mornings,' he said proudly.

I just hugged him. I didn't know what else to say or do. And I held on to him for a very long time.

'Are you as tired as I am?' he asked, gently unwinding my arms from around him.

'Exhausted.'

'I've got a bottle of wine in the fridge, why don't we just put on some music and go to bed with a glass of wine?'

'I'll go get the wine,' I said. 'Do we have glasses?'

'I think so. Most of the kitchen stuff came over too, but I don't know if it's all unpacked.'

'I'll find something,' I promised. 'If you can manage to find me something to sleep in.'

I raced downstairs and found the wine and two hand-blown glasses that Mom had brought me from Mexico. I turned off the lights in the kitchen and just as I was leaving, I noticed something in the family room. I set the wine on the kitchen table and went to have a closer look. It was my piano. I lay a hand on it, to prove to myself that it was real, and it was. Tears filled my eyes. I was overwhelmed by the emotions of the day and the lengths Cam had gone to with our home to make me happy.

I wiped at my eyes, not wanting him to know I was upset. I did smile at the incredibly amazing timing Cam had today, grabbed the wine and brought it upstairs. I turned off all the other lights on my way and found Cam already in bed. I handed him the wine to open and I went into my changing room to change. I folded my clothes nicely to put them away and then smelled them. I tossed them into the laundry bin and closed the lid tightly. I didn't want to make any sort of a mess in this beautiful new room. I pulled on my T-shirt and wished I had something a little nicer to wear, but was glad that at least it was clean.

I turned off the light in the closet and climbed into bed beside Cam.

'Oh, nice sheets,' I said.

'Spared no expense,' he said. 'It's all in the thread count, you know?'

'I guess I knew but I never really paid attention to it.'

'You realize we both stink of smoke and these nice new bed linens are going to have to be washed in the morning.'

'I'll do it, I promise. I'm just too tired to have a shower right now,' I said, taking the glass of wine he offered. 'Hey, we have a washer and dryer already?'

'Hmm.'

'Wow, we're pretty well set up.'

'Well, there are still a few more rooms we're going to have to save up to do.'

'Maybe I can find some extra shifts at one of the other theatres.' I laughed.

'Katie, we need to talk about your dad,' Cam said gently.

'I know.'

'You can't really believe he's guilty?'

'I don't know what to think. When Ken told me my head just went spinning. But then since I couldn't talk to anyone about it, I didn't know what to do. It appears that's how I work things out, by talking about them endlessly.'

He pulled me close to him, wrapping his arm around me. 'He didn't do it.'

'I know he didn't,' I said, tears starting again. 'But I don't know what to do about it.'

Saturday

It was seven o'clock in the morning. I hated this time of day and I especially hated it today, considering where I was going. But I had to be here. I had to see it. I rounded the corner and stopped. It didn't really look any different. I expected to see rubble covering the ground, piles of ashes, smoking embers. But it looked the same, just with big black scars where the flames had marked the concrete, windows that had broken out and the fact that it was wrapped in yellow police tape. My building. The place that had been my home for six years. And here it sat, empty except for the investigators coming in and out of the building. This side of the block was closed, so I crossed the street and sat on the bench at the bus stop. I watched for about an hour, people going in, people coming out, people going back in and people coming back out again. It was almost like a normal day, except the people going in and out were wearing hard hats and uniforms, not three-piece suits and brief-cases. I sighed and sipped my coffee.

Then I saw him coming toward me out of the corner of my eye, but I don't think he knew that. I didn't turn to make eye contact or even acknowledge him until he sat on the bench beside me.

'Wow,' he said, looking up at the building. 'Fire's a bitch, huh?'

'What do you want?'

'I'm glad to see you're safe and sound.'

'What's your name?'

'Why is that important to you? So you can tell the police?'

'No, so we can talk like normal people.'

'Call me Sims,' he said. 'It'll do.'

'So, how'd you know how to find me here?'

'They always come back to the scene of the crime. But what made you think I'd be here?'

'They always come back to the scene of the crime.' I smiled.

'Point taken,' he laughed at me.

'Well then, Sims, since we've established I'm not going to the police, why don't we establish what your motives are in all of this?'

'I think I have the same goal as you do.'

'My goal is that I want to get my dad off the streets,' I said, staring at my building.

'That's a good goal.'

'And what about you? What was that phone call you made to me about yesterday? Because you saved my boyfriend's life, you know.'

'I'm glad I could help.'

'But I don't know if that was really your intention. And if I'm going to help you out, I need to know your real intentions.'

'I don't know if I can tell you what my real intentions are. Can we leave it at the fact that I want to stop your dad too?'

'I think we can for now. So how are we going to do that?'

'Well, I hear rumours that your dad is going to be released this afternoon. Something about lack of evidence. So I want you to greet him with open arms and then once he thinks everything's OK with you, he'll let his guard down. And when you can find a time and a place where we can get him alone, you can call me on this number.'

He handed me a paper with a phone number written on it.

'It's just a disposable cellphone, so don't get any bright ideas about tracing it.'

'The thought never entered my mind,' I lied.

'Yeah. So we're good, then? You can get your dad alone somewhere and you call me and I'll take care of the rest.'

'Yeah.'

'And don't bother calling the police.'

'I won't.'

'They can't get him. I mean they're already releasing him for lack of evidence.'

'I said I won't call the police,' I said harshly.

'If you don't do this, you're leaving your boyfriend and all your other friends in extreme danger.'

'I know,' I whispered. 'I know what I have to do.'

I shoved the paper in my pocket and he stood up and walked down the street.

'Don't keep me waiting too long,' he called over his shoulder.

'I won't,' I promised, watching him walk away.

'Well, you and I have to stop meeting like this.'

I jumped as someone sat down on the other side of me. I turned and saw Geneva Anderson sitting down beside me, after carefully brushing off the bench. At least she didn't have a cameraman with her this time.

'Leave me alone,' I said.

'You know I'm an award-winning investigative reporter,' she told me.

'Congratulations.'

'And I'm beginning to wonder why almost every time I've turned up at a fire scene in the last couple of months, you've been there?'

'Just lucky?'

'Seriously, Kate, I don't think you're the arsonist. You've been in the news too much in the past and not staying in the background like a successful fire-starter would. But I'm beginning to think I should maybe start looking at the people who are close to you.'

My heart almost stopped beating at the thought of Geneva finding out about what Graham was carrying around in his backpack.

'Leave my friends alone.'

'Oh, I've struck a nerve, have I? Who could it be?'

'Geneva, I can't do this today. I lived in this building. I lost almost everything I own yesterday.'

'I didn't know that,' she admitted.

'So much for the award-winning investigative skills,' I spat out.

'I'm sorry,' she said. 'There hasn't been much time for me to look into this yet. I really didn't know.'

'Well, now you do know. And I almost lost my dad and my boyfriend too.'

For a moment she sat silently, pondering her next move. And then she stood up.

'I really didn't know and I am sorry. I'll leave you alone

today, let you have some peace. But I think you know more than you're letting on and you and I are going to cross paths again before this is over.'

'I'm sure we will,' I said wearily, as she walked back to her van.

I sat there for a long time, watching the building and waiting for Sims and Geneva to be far, far away. As the clock moved close to 9 a.m., I got up and took the C-train to the Plex. I stopped for a mocha at Gus's place and was really happy he wasn't in yet. If so, he would have taken one look at me and asked me a million questions. There was a new girl behind the counter and she smiled as I approached.

'Good morning, what can I get for you?'

'Double mocha, please. And one of those juices.'

'Great, it'll just be a minute,' she said, grinding some beans and foaming the milk.

'Thanks,' I said, as she slid my steaming coffee across the counter to me.

'That will be $5.85,' she said.

'Gus usually lets me put it on my account,' I explained.

'Your name?'

'Kate Carpenter.'

'Oh, you're Kate. Gus has told me about you.'

'All good, I hope.'

'Of course it's good.'

'And who are you?' I asked.

'I'm Ann Abdai,' she said, extending her hand across the counter. 'I'm going to be the assistant manager here.'

'Well, really nice to meet you, Ann,' I said, snapping a lid onto my coffee.

'You too. And according to what Gus says, I should be seeing a lot of you!'

I left Grounds Zero and entered the Plex through the stage door and signed in. Frank was there, chatting to the security guard, and I smiled weakly at him in greeting.

'Morning,' he said. 'How's the new place coming?'

'Good. I'm surprised Cam hasn't got you over there working, Frank.'

'I'm getting some good overtime here. He can't afford me right now.'

181

'Are you going to be working in my theatre today?' I asked.

'Probably. You've got a lot of doors,' he laughed.

'Too many places for people to hide,' I said.

'I've heard some of the stories. But I think this new security system will make you feel a little safer.'

'I don't know if anything can do that,' I sighed, images of my former home still burned into my memory. I turned down the hall and the security guard buzzed me through the door. I wandered down Tin Pan Alley and let myself in through the back of the theatre. I cut across the dark stage and climbed the stairs up to my office. I saw the light shining out from the crack under the door and my heart started to beat faster. I put my key into the lock and turned it, opening the door quickly to get the suspense over with.

'What are you doing here?' I asked.

'I couldn't wait for you to call.'

'Dammit, Cam, you just about scared the pants off me. You were supposed to wait at home.'

'Katie, you called it home!' he said, a big smile breaking out on his face.

'Focus, Cam, this is serious.'

'OK, sorry. It's just you were gone such a long time.'

'I know, it took longer than I thought it would.'

'Well, did it work?'

'It worked,' I said. 'He took the bait.'

'I can't believe I'm letting you do this.'

'Well, letting me do this would be stretching it a bit, don't you think?'

'You know what I mean. This guy is probably really dangerous and I can barely get around right now.'

'It'll be OK. We're just going to get him someplace where Detective Lincoln can drop in and have a chat with him.'

'Katie, I want you to get Graham in on this. I want him close by in case you need help.'

'Not Graham.'

'Why not Graham? He's been involved in every other crazy thing you've ever done.'

'It's just not a good time for him right now, Cam.'

'It's probably the best time. It'll get his mind off his problems.'

'Cam, I can't explain but please don't ask me to do that.'

'Katie, you need someone to have at your back.'

'What, now we talk like secret agents?' I asked and then realized he had his serious face on. 'OK, OK, I'll deal with Graham and I'll get him to stick close to me.'

'You're not just saying that?' he asked, and secretly I was. But now I had to mean it.

'I really mean it,' I promised, and realized no matter what, today I had to deal with Graham.

'Good. OK, I'm going to take a cab back to the fire hall. I have to do something today, I have to keep busy. And I think pounding nails would be a good way to do that.'

'I understand. I'll be home as soon as I get the show out.'

He kissed me. 'I love you, Katie, keep safe today.'

'I love you, Cam. And keep yourself safe today too.'

'I will,' he promised, and then limped down to the street.

When Graham came in, five minutes before his shift started, which was late for him, I was busy doing paperwork. It wasn't really anything that needed to be done, but I wanted him to think everything was back to normal between us and there was going to be no more mention of what was in his backpack.

'Hi,' I said, barely looking up at him. 'I was down at Grounds Zero and grabbed a mocha, I bought you a fresh-squeezed juice while I was there.'

'Thanks,' he said, sitting down and shaking it up before opening the top. He tossed it overhand into the garbage can and watched it drop in. 'Two points!'

I smiled sadly, remembering the fun we used to have just a few months ago, when he was still young and naive and not troubled by all this adult-type stuff.

'What do you need me to do?' he asked.

'Nothing. I got dropped off early because Cam's back at the new place, hammering or sawing or whatever it is you men do at construction sites. Everything's done and ready to go.'

'Wow, I'm impressed.'

'Well, I wanted to prove that I actually did remember how to run this theatre,' I joked.

'You know I was only teasing . . .'

'Graham, it's OK. I know you were teasing,' I said, checking my watch. 'Why don't you go and open the house and I'll just finish this up? If you think you can handle the twenty people or so all by yourself.'

'I think I can manage,' he laughed, relaxing a little, as he started to believe I wasn't going to attack him. 'Is it bad that I pray for rain during Stampede Week?'

'No, it would definitely make things more exciting. The concerts are good but pretty poorly attended, huh?'

'Yeah. I hear Leonard is really glad that he got to hear the banjo player this week.'

'Aw, is Leonard in love?' I asked.

'Leonard is in lust. Love might come later.'

'Just don't take me into the land of too much information, please,' I laughed. 'Now go and open up the house.'

Graham grabbed his backpack and stepped into the ushers' changing room to lock it up. He never did that and always left his pack in my office. I was beginning to think he didn't totally trust me yet. Which was fine, because I didn't totally believe he was innocent yet. He came back out of the changing room and headed down to the theatre. I gave him a few minutes and then wandered down into the changing room. Our lockers didn't actually have locks on them, but Graham had precariously piled a bunch of stuff on his pack, so he would know in an instant if someone had messed with it. I didn't care if he knew if I messed with it or not and pulled it out roughly from under his stuff. I carted it back to my office and closed and locked the door behind me.

I cleared the top of my desk and dumped his pack upside down, tipping everything out. I sorted through address books and scripts and loose coins and even a joint, which I had to give him hell about carrying into the theatre, regardless of what else I found. He had a toothbrush, tanning cream, sunscreen, moisturizer, a comb and a brush, a sign-language dictionary and two lighters, five packages of matches and newspaper clippings about all three fires that had happened at the Plex. Good enough for me.

I cleared my desk and dropped almost everything back into his pack, which I threw into the corner. The rest I left on my desk, and then I left my office and went to work the show with him.

*   *   *

'Come and listen to a story 'bout a man named Jed,' Graham sang, as he walked up and down the rows in the theatre, checking for lost and found, anything to clean up.

'That's more Beverly Hills than Foothills, I think,' I called out to him. 'You just about done?'

'I'm done,' he said, bounding up the stairs to where I stood.

'So, you got anything going on this afternoon?' I asked, as we walked down the hall and back to the office.

'Well, I was thinking about heading down to the Stampede grounds with some of the gang.'

'How can you keep going and going and going down to the grounds?' I asked. 'It's hot, it's expensive, it's loud and you drink too much beer.'

'Yeah, what's wrong with that?' he laughed. 'I seem to recall a couple of years ago you were at every corporate party there was until all hours of the night, here for the lunchtime crowd and then down to the rodeo before you hit the next party.'

'I was young and the tickets were all free.'

'Oh, before you were dating Cam?'

'Yep, I would promise a man anything for a ticket to one of the parties, and then dump him by midnight.'

'You callous cowgirl.'

'I would always fix them up with another girl before I left. I didn't just leave them on their own.'

'That's very kind of you.'

'Yeah, well, I'm kind of tenacious, you know. Like a dog with a bone. I hate to give up on things.'

He gave me a funny look. 'What do you mean?'

I swung open the office door to let him in and he just stood there for a moment, looking at his stuff spread on my desk.

'You went through my stuff,' he said. 'You bitch.'

I pushed him into the office, and closed the door behind us. I shoved the doorstop firmly underneath it, so that nobody could break in on us, nor could Graham leave in a hurry.

'OK, you get thirty minutes of free time, where I'm not your boss and you can call me any disgusting name you want. After that, if you say one more thing like that to me I'll fire you and turn you over to the police. Do we understand each other?'

'Whatever.'

'Sit down.'

185

'I'd rather stand.'

'Sit down!' I enunciated each syllable with a cold iciness I usually reserved for a boyfriend taking unwanted liberties.

Graham sat. I poured myself a coffee and slowly wandered around to my side of the desk.

'So when did you start smoking?' I asked, picking up the lighters and the packages of matches I had found.

'I don't smoke,' he said, not making eye contact with me.

'And I'm not sure why you feel the need to carry around the butane-lighter fluid when you are buying disposable lighters, or even buying disposable lighters when you don't smoke? Do you light a lot of barbecues, Graham?'

'Don't be so patronizing.'

'I am just trying to give you the benefit of the doubt, you know. I wouldn't want you to accuse me of jumping to conclusions here.'

'Fuck!'

'Fuck what? Fuck that you are doing something so incredibly stupid or fuck that you got caught?'

'Fuck to all of it.'

'So, you know, I wouldn't be doing this if I didn't really care about you,' I started. 'I know, I know, patronizing and clichéd. But it's true. I could really easily call Lazlo or Detective Lincoln and just turn you over to them and be done with you. But, Graham, I really love you. You're like my little brother. Well, actually you're better than him because you actually listen to me.'

'You have a point here?' There was still anger in his eyes but I thought I saw them softening around the edges.

'When people love each other they need each other too. Now sometimes it seems like I need you more than you need me. But right now, you need me really badly. You may not realize it, but you do. You have had a horrible, horrible thing happen in your life and you are not dealing with it properly. And you need me to help you figure it out.'

'This is stupid,' he said, standing up.

I picked up my phone and dialled for an outside line. 'If you leave I'm calling the police.'

He looked at me for a moment, trying to decide if I was bluffing, and then sat back down again. I set the phone back in its cradle and took a sip of coffee.

186

'Now I want you to tell me about the fires you've set.'

'You've got to be kidding,' he spat out.

'Nope. Just consider me the judge. You elucidate your crimes and I'll sentence you.'

'This is so stupid.'

'Yeah, well, the nice thing about me is I'm one of the most lenient judges in the city. If you'd like to take your chances with one of the real ones at the courthouse, then go for it,' I said, pointing to the door.

He sat there for a long time. And I let him. I didn't speak, I didn't fidget and I didn't break eye contact. I had hours to spare and was prepared to wait him out through the evening if I had to.

'OK, I set the fire in Tin Pan Alley with the old rags, I started the one in your garbage can and in the dumpster out in the loading dock.'

I continued to wait.

'And I'm sorry.'

He looked up at me, searching my eyes with his, his pain almost palpable.

'God, Kate, what do you want me to say? I was hurting. I was hurting so bad I didn't know what to do. I couldn't go home to Dad because he's hurting worse than I am. And then I lit the fire pit at home for Dad when my nieces and nephews were over, and the flames just drew me. The heat, the crack-ling, the flames jumping up into the sky. It was intoxicating. I went for two days and couldn't stop thinking about it. So I set those rags on fire and I watched the flames. And all I wanted to do was watch the fire, but it got really big, and then the alarms went off and the Fire Department was here and it was out of control. But it was so exciting. And for that hour or so, while I was watching everything out of the office window, I didn't think about Mom or home or anything. It was glorious.'

'And how did you feel afterwards?'

'I felt worse!' he screamed at me. 'Why do you think I lit another one? And I've been burning everything I could find at home in the fire pit out back. It distracts me.'

'Well, it's over.'

He looked up at me and tears welled out of his eyes. But he held it together.

'What are you going to do to me?' he asked.

'Well, to start with, your ass is mine. I'm putting you on probation for a year and you are going to do everything I tell you.'

'OK. Like what?'

'Well, after extensive research at the Calhoun library in the psychology department . . .'

He rolled his eyes.

'I'm just kidding. I have a friend, his name is Ricardo Carlos. He is a psychologist and he runs the grief program at the Rockyview Hospital. You're enrolled. Here's his card and if he doesn't hear from you by noon on Monday, I'll be looking for you.'

'OK.'

'Ricardo is going to call me and let me know if you're attending the sessions or not, just so you know.'

'OK.'

'And when he says you're ready, you're going to do some community service. I'm thinking something like the boys' and girls' clubs, something like that.'

He didn't look pleased but he nodded his agreement.

'And for the next year I want to know where you are at all times. You thought your mamma was tough when you were a little sixteen-year-old? You ain't seen nothing. And if you slip, if you miss a single appointment, if there is a single suspicious fire anywhere in this city and you are unaccounted for, I will turn you in so fast you won't know what happened to you.'

'Fine.'

'And if I decide that you need to do something else, you'll do it. And if you act strangely, I'll drug-test you or lie-detector you or anything else I deem necessary to find out what is going on in your life.'

'Fine.'

I stood up and walked to the door, pulling the doorstop out. Graham stood up and grabbed his backpack, slinging it over his shoulder. I turned to him, before he could escape.

'And there's one more thing.'

'What?'

I pulled him to me in a big hug and held him tightly.

'I want you to know that I'm here for you. I love you,

188

Graham. If you need to cry or scream or get drunk or anything, I want you to come to me. I loved your mom too and I miss her and we can get through this together. We've gotten through a lot of other stuff that way.'

He laid his head on my shoulder and I felt warm tears dampen my shirt. After a few minutes, he straightened up and pulled away, but gently, not in anger any longer.

'Graham, do you really need to go to the Stampede grounds today or would you be willing to come to my new place and have a little talk with Cam and me?'

'You're not going to tell Cam about this, are you?' he asked, fear creeping back into his eyes.

'I have to, Graham. Keeping secrets from Cam almost destroyed our relationship and I won't do it any more. But he'll be OK with it. I promise. But if you feel up to it, we need your help. My dad's got himself in a bit of trouble.'

He took a deep breath and steeled himself. 'OK, I guess I need to face up to things sooner or later. Putting it off isn't going to do me any good, is it?'

I smiled and took his hand, partly for moral support but partly because I didn't want him to run away from me.

I let myself in at the fire hall and the sound of a pounding hammer told me Cam was home somewhere. I pulled Graham inside and locked the door behind me.

'Cam,' I called down the corridor. 'We're home.'

The hammering stopped and Cam poked his head out of the kitchen. 'I'm in here.'

I led Graham into the kitchen and sat him down at the table, taking three beers out of the fridge for us.

'What are you doing in here?' I asked. 'I thought these rooms were finished?'

'Just hanging some shelves,' he explained, giving me a kiss.

'I've brought Graham home with me. I told him Dad was in a bit of trouble but I haven't gotten any more specific than that just yet.'

'Why not?'

'Well, there's something, Graham – I mean *we* need to tell you first. Come and have a beer with us?'

Cam left his shelf on the floor and limped across the kitchen.

'I'll just take that from you,' I said, pulling the hammer from his grasp and setting it in the far corner of the room.

He sat down and opened a beer. 'Am I sensing there might be something coming up that I'm not going to like?'

'Uh, yeah, maybe,' I admitted. 'Look, you know Graham's been having a hard time since his mom died.'

'Yeah?'

'Kate, I'll do this,' Graham said, taking a big drink of his own beer for a little courage. 'Cam, I've been overwhelmed with the emotion and responsibility that has suddenly happened in my life and I've done a really stupid thing.'

'What?'

Graham paused, taking a deep breath. 'I'm the one that's been lighting the fires at the Plex.'

'You're what?'

'I don't know what's wrong with me, but I can't help myself. Kate found out and I thank God she did because—'

Cam had grown scarily silent and I interrupted Graham. 'Cam, are you listening to what he's saying?'

'I heard what he said,' Cam said angrily. 'Beyond starting fires, I don't know if there's anything else I need to hear.'

'Cam, honey . . .'

He stood up, knocking his beer over on the new table.

'Graham, do you realize someone burned down our loft yesterday? Do you realize we lost just about everything we own and we could have lost our lives?'

Graham hung his head and I grabbed a towel off the kitchen counter to wipe up the spilled beer.

'Cam, sit down,' I said firmly. He stared at me for a minute but finally complied. 'OK, we are totally freaked about our building burning down and all of that. Understood. If I didn't have this other shit going on I would probably beat Graham senseless myself. And Graham took a bad situation and handled it terribly by doing an incredibly stupid thing, for which I am going to make him pay for a very long time.'

'What about the condo fires?' Cam asked.

'What do you mean?' Graham said.

'Cam, those are different kind of fires. Graham's just been starting the little ones around places he knows.'

'You think I could start fires like that? Cause all that damage?

190

Kill people?' Graham asked, his voice rising as he stood up prepared to run.

'Graham, sit down. Cam, calm down. They are different types of fires,' I repeated myself. 'Now can the three of us agree that that's where we stand right now and remember that we have a common goal?'

They both nodded reluctantly.

'Can we all agree to get past that for a few minutes? Just as a personal favour since my dad is probably a murdering arsonist who's going to go to jail for life and the police want me to help them put him there?'

'What?' Graham asked.

'It's not true,' Cam insisted, taking my hand in his. 'The police think he might be involved in this in some way. Katie's just confused and upset and doesn't know what she's saying right now when it comes to her dad.'

'It doesn't matter. He's getting out of the hospital and is going to be released from police custody. What are we going to do?'

'Kate, why didn't you tell me about this?' Graham asked.

'Because I really thought you had enough going on already,' I apologized.

'But I can help. You have to let me help.'

'OK,' I said. 'Cam wants you to keep an eye on me. He's worried because he can't move right now as fast as he normally does.'

'I can do that,' Graham said. 'That's the least I can do. Please.'

We both looked over at Cam.

'I want you to know that this isn't over,' Cam said. 'But Kate's right, we can't deal with everything all at once. So let's get this thing with her dad straightened out and then you and I are going to have a talk.'

'Cam, I've dealt with Graham already.'

'Katie, I don't care what you've done. Graham has to deal with me too,' he said and then stared at Graham awaiting his response.

'I understand,' Graham said. 'I'm willing to be accountable to you as well as Kate.'

'OK. Then what are we doing about your dad?' Cam asked.

'I don't know. When is he getting out? Has anyone heard for sure?'

'Not a thing,' Cam said.

I grabbed the phone and dialled Detective Lincoln.

'Hi, Ken, it's Kate.'

'Hi, Kate, I was wondering when I was going to hear from you.'

'Yeah?'

'Your dad's been asking about you.'

'That's why I'm calling too.'

'Well, he's doing OK. The hospital is releasing him tomorrow morning and his lawyer has gotten him released on his own recognizance. Something about circumstantial evidence.'

'I thought he was getting out today?'

'Nope, apparently the oxygen level in his blood is still a little low, so they want to keep him one more night.'

'Where's he going to go when he gets out?'

'That's what he was asking, since he hasn't seen you for a couple of days.'

'Yeah, well . . .'

'I told him we weren't allowing any visitors. Even you.'

'Thanks, Ken.'

'Can he come back to your place?'

'He has to, doesn't he? I mean, if we want to get this all sorted out.'

'Yes, he does. It's the only way we're going to find out what's going on, Kate, if you can do it.'

'I can do it, Ken. He's my dad and I want to give him a chance.'

'OK, I'll arrange for an officer to drive him over tomorrow morning after he's released.'

'OK. Thanks, Ken.'

'I know this is going to be hard on you, Kate. But it's the right thing to do.'

'Yeah, well, I really can't figure out in what universe it's right for me to help you incriminate my father.'

We spent the rest of the afternoon explaining to Graham what we knew and what we suspected; and then sent him home. And then I spent another hour explaining to Cam what I knew about Graham. After that we were both exhausted and put a movie into the DVD player and stretched out on our new couch to watch it. It was comfortable in the family room, despite boxes and tools piled everywhere, and I found myself drifting off a few times and then jerking awake. After several times Cam clicked off the TV.

'You want to sleep on the couch or go upstairs to bed?' he asked, shaking me awake.

'My beautiful bedroom, please,' I mumbled.

We shut down the lights and both stumbled up the stairs, stripped unceremoniously and fell into bed.

'Are you as tired as I am?' I asked him.

'Worse,' he said.

'Do you think we'll ever not be tired again?'

'Probably, but not for a really long time.'

'Oh,' I sighed.

'So can I ask you a personal question?'

'I should think so,' I said. 'Not that I can believe there is anything left that you don't know about me.'

'How long have you had a thing for vampires?'

'What?'

'I didn't know you were such a fan.'

'Cam, I have no idea what you're talking about.'

'You know the bookcases in our old bedroom?' he asked. 'When I was packing up the boxes to bring over here, I found something hidden behind your text books.'

'Oh?'

'You have all seven seasons of *Buffy the Vampire Slayer* on DVD.'

'What?'

'Katie, don't lie to me. I found them hidden behind your university textbooks.'

'Oh.'

'Are you ashamed?'

'Well, I thought you'd think it was silly.'

'I do,' he said. 'But I watched a little bit of it this afternoon and that Buffy is hot.'

'I'm now going to get teased about this for years, aren't I?'

'Oh yeah.'

'Good night, Cam,' I said, rolling over and pulling the covers with me.

'You want to play vampire?' he asked, rolling over and breathing heavily on my neck.

'Don't make me get the garlic.'

193

Sunday

Iwoke up early – Dad's return home played heavily on my mind. I had a quick shower and dressed quietly, before heading down to the kitchen and getting the coffee on. I mixed up some eggs in a bowl, and pulled out some English muffins and Canadian bacon. I couldn't cook a lot but I could manage scrambled eggs with some bacon and Cheddar cheese, thanks to Cam's tutelage and incredible patience. I shredded some cheese, chopped up the bacon into incredibly uneven clumps and whisked the eggs up with a little butter and milk. I set the frying pan on the gas range, which still scared me, and put some butter in, all ready to go when Cam woke up. I poured myself a coffee and heard him on the stairs so I poured another cup and sat down at the table. He limped in, looking exhausted, but offered me a smile and a kiss.

'Morning,' I smiled back, inhaling the warm scent of soap he carried fresh from the shower. His hair was still damp at the back of his neck and I pulled him back down and kissed him again. Finally I let him go and he sat heavily in his chair, pulling his coffee cup in front of him.

'You're pretty perky this morning,' he said.

'It's all an act. I'm exhausted and I'm stressed out.'

'That's better. I was starting to feel a little inadequate. Are you cooking?'

'Yeah, I figured since you're working so hard I could treat you. Just don't get all excited, it's nothing fancy.'

'I'm excited by the idea of it,' he said, winking at me.

'Now, don't go off into your little Suzy Homemaker fantasy, it is me after all.'

'Yeah, OK.'

I gingerly turned on the burner and jumped as the flame grew bigger. Oh well, as long as I was scared of the stove, Cam would continue to do most of the cooking for us. Not a bad solution overall, if you asked me. I scrambled eggs and toasted and buttered the English muffins and then split everything onto two plates and brought them over to the table. I went back for the coffee pot and brought it back too.

'It's weird having all this space,' I said pouring more coffee. 'I'm used to being able to sit at the table and reach over for the coffee pot.'

'This is definitely going to take some getting used to. So what time's your dad getting here?'

'I don't know. Ken wasn't sure when I talked to him. I would imagine the doctors will do morning rounds and sign him out.'

'Shouldn't we go and pick him up or something?'

'Ken said he'd arrange a ride for him,' I said. 'I think he wanted to make sure he came straight home back to us and didn't disappear somewhere.'

Cam obviously wasn't in the mood to get into an argument about my dad so we finished breakfast in silence and then he washed the frying pan while I loaded the dishwasher. When we were done, I poured another coffee and we sat at the table and waited. I couldn't stand the silence so I turned on the radio and hoped that Don, Joanne and the Coach's morning show would lighten our mood a little. A few minutes later the door-bell rang. I jumped up, startled, and then walked slowly to the front door. We still had the institutional glass doors, but Cam had hung some blinds to give us some privacy. I lifted one of the slats and peaked out, seeing Dad standing there, overnight bag in hand. I dropped the blind and unlocked the door, opening it and stepping aside to let him in.

'Morning, Katie girl,' he said.

'Morning, Daddy. There's coffee in the kitchen.'

'Thank you, sweetie,' he said, kissing my cheek and then going down the hallway.

I took a step outside and saw Ken in his car. I wanted to thank him for personally looking after my Dad and I waved to him. He waved back, but then he pulled out onto the street and sped away. I closed and locked the door up again and turned for the kitchen. Dad was sitting at the table beside Cam, his overnight bag thrown into the corner. I took my seat and looked across the table at him.

'How are you feeling?' I asked.

'Not too bad for an old guy,' he laughed. 'It's not the first time I breathed in too much smoke. I just hope it's the last time.'

I smiled weakly at him and sipped my coffee.

'Katie girl, I think we need to talk,' he said.

'Daddy, you just got home from the hospital, you should rest, we can talk later.'

'I don't think so. Last time I saw you was when they were loading me into an ambulance. What happened to you?'

'Well, you were actually handcuffed to the stretcher when they were loading you in the ambulance,' I reminded him. 'I had just about lost you and Cam in a fire that I found out the police were accusing you of setting.'

'And you couldn't come and visit and ask me about it?'

'They wouldn't let me visit,' I tried.

'Yeah, Detective Lincoln tried to load that line of crap on me too,' Dad said.

'I was a little confused about it all, Dad. I didn't know what to say to you.' I heard the volume of my voice growing but couldn't seem to control myself.

'Well, I would have liked the chance to defend myself,' he said, his voice reflecting the passion in my voice. 'That is if a man has to defend himself to his own daughter.'

'They said you were the arsonist.'

'And you believed them?'

'Wait,' Cam interrupted loudly, to match the volume of our voices. 'This is getting us nowhere.'

'Well, what do you suggest?' Dad and I both asked, turning on him at the same time.

'God spare me,' Cam laughed. 'Two of a kind.'

'Cam!' I warned him.

'OK. Sherm, are you the arsonist?' Cam asked.

'Absolutely not,' Dad said. And I studied his face for the slightest hint of a lie.

'Good. And Katie, do you think your dad is guilty?' Cam asked me, and all eyes were staring at me with the same intensity I had just showed him.

'No,' I sighed, deciding that I really believed it.

'Good,' Cam said. 'So we have a good sound starting point here.'

'I'm sorry, Dad.'

'And I'm sorry too, Katie.'

'I was just so scared to find both of you in that apartment and then almost lose you both. I really wasn't thinking straight. I just started thinking about your fishing lodge and where you were getting all the money from and the fact that you were sneaking into the city and not telling me. It just didn't add up.'

'I understand,' he smiled at me.

'And, Dad, it still doesn't add up.'

'Katie,' Cam warned.

'It's OK,' Dad said. 'I came into a little money. I've been doing some contracting. You know, it's boring to be retired.'

'Well, why didn't you tell me?'

'Katie, I am a grown-up. There's lots of things you don't know about my life. Do you tell me everything?'

'Uh, well that's different,' I laughed. 'Just don't ask me how because I haven't come up with that part of the argument yet.'

'OK, truce,' Dad said, holding out his hand for me to shake. I took it and shook firmly.

'Truce,' I agreed.

'All right, then. Now, do you have more of this coffee? This is the first real cup of coffee I've had since they took me to that damned hospital.'

'I've got this one,' Cam said, fussing at the counter as he ground some beans and started a fresh pot.

'So, Dad, if you're not an arsonist, what is this Sims guy doing? He's really interested in you.'

'Sims?' Dad said, truly looking confused. And then my stomach finally settled and I really did believe him. 'I don't know who you're talking about.'

'Oh, just this guy,' I said. 'About five feet ten inches, kind of paunchy, blondish hair with a little gray in it. He has a funny looking mole on his forehead . . .'

I stopped when Dad pushed his chair away from the table and stood up.

'When was he looking for me?' Dad asked harshly.

'The first day I came down here to check out the fire hall. He was outside when I left, writing down the licence-plate number from Cam's car. I asked him what he was doing and he said he was a police detective.'

'That man is not a police detective,' Dad said.

'I know. I checked with Detective Lincoln and he told me he wasn't.'

Dad turned and stormed down the hallway.

'Where are you going?' I called after him.

'Away,' he hollered back.

I looked at Cam and we both raced after him. Dad was already in one of the offices off the main hallway, which was going to be our spare bedroom. Cam had a sofa bed set up and we had moved what we could salvage of Dad's stuff into the room. He already had his suitcase on the bed and was tossing stuff into it.

'What the hell is the matter?' I asked. 'I thought we were getting along really nicely there for a minute.'

'Oh, Katie girl, I'm not mad at you,' Dad said, though he didn't stop his packing. 'I just have to get far away from you.'

'Nothing like sending mixed messages,' I said, frustrated.

'Sherm,' Cam tried, 'just tell us what's going on. Maybe we can help.'

'No, there is nothing you can do to help. You have to trust me about that.'

'Dad,' I said, grabbing his arm and trying to get his attention. 'Daddy, please tell me what's wrong.'

'Katie, this Sims, he is an incredibly dangerous man. And I don't want him to know anything about you.' Dad turned to Cam. 'Cam, right now, today, you have to get an alarm system in here. Put extra locks on. Get a guard dog. You have to protect my little girl. He already knows where you live . . .'

'Dad, what are you involved in?'

'Nothing. Nothing you need to know about. I'm just sorry I brought any of this around you. I never thought that would happen.'

'Dad?'

'See, I should have stayed retired. I'm too old to do this. I'm not smart enough to do this. I've put you in real danger here.'

'Dad!'

'Katie, I want you to walk me to the door and have a big fight with me. Scream out into the street that you're throwing me out and you never want to see me again. And sound like you mean it.'

'Dad!'

'There's no arguing with me here,' he insisted. 'I'm leaving. It's me he wants, not you. So I'll head straight to the airport and get out of the city. He'll follow me. And then the worst that's happened is that he knows where you live.'

'Dad!' I finally screamed. 'He knows more than that.'

'What are you talking about?'

'He knows a lot about me,' I said. 'I've met with him several times.'

'Oh, Katie,' Dad said, sinking heavily onto the bed.

'Dad, who is he?'

'Oh, MK, why did you do that? Why did you meet with him?'

'Well, Dad, to be honest, it wasn't really my choice at first. He was following me. Asking me questions about you.'

'OK, OK, well if I get to the airport, I'm pretty sure he'll follow me out of the city.'

'You can't do that,' I said, sitting beside him on the bed. Cam took his suitcase off the bed and sat on the other side of him, not sure whether to hold him up or hold him back.

'And why can't I do that, MK?'

'Because Detective Lincoln and I are working together to try and track down this Sims guy. If nothing else, he's been impersonating a police officer.'

'Mother Mary, I asked you to protect my Katie and look what you've gone and let her do,' Dad said, his eyes heavenward.

'Dad, you have to tell us what's going on!'

'I can't. Katie, it's too dangerous.' He looked around desperately. 'All right, maybe we can get you two out of the city. Maybe we can send you on a cruise with your mother or something. Get you somewhere safe.'

'We're not leaving you,' I said.

'I second that motion,' Cam said. 'You need to tell us what's going on and we need to figure out what we can do to help.'

Dad looked up and around, seeing the determination in our eyes, and then looked back down at the floor.

'Well, I think you'd better call Detective Lincoln and then make sure there's a big fresh pot of coffee on. We're going to need some help.'

*　　*　　*

199

An hour later we were gathered around the kitchen table. Suddenly, I was happy for the big table and all the space. We'd only been living here a couple of days and we'd had more people over than in a month at our old place. I had wanted to sit out on the patio, where our old patio furniture was set up and waiting, but Dad didn't feel comfortable out in the open, so we sat around the table, windows closed tightly against prying ears. Dad and Cam had switched to beer and I forgave them for starting this slightly early. Ken had some fresh-squeezed juice and I was working on my second pot of coffee. We all sat expectantly, waiting for Dad to start, and he just kept nervously pulling on his beer.

'OK, Dad,' I said. 'Please, I can't stand this for another minute.'

He took one last look around at us all, trying to figure a last-minute way out of this, if I knew my dad.

'Look, Dad, Ken has a gun and I swear to God I'll make him use it if you don't start talking right now.'

'All right, Katie girl, just take a breath and cool down.'

'You want me to cool down after everything . . .'

'Katie,' Cam said quietly, taking my hand in his.

'Go ahead,' I said.

'Well, I told you, retirement was boring.'

'And that's probably the last true thing you've told us,' I muttered under my breath. Cam squeezed my hand in warning.

'If you're finished?' he asked, but didn't wait for an answer. 'Well, retirement was boring, so I started calling up some of my old buddies and inviting them out for fishing weekends to see what they were up to. Well, I finally met up with another captain I used to work with and he was working for an insurance company, investigating fire scenes. I thought that sounded kind of interesting and he gave my name to the insurance folks and we met up and I started doing some work for them. You know, at first it was just local stuff, they'd call me, I'd drive over and check things out. And you know what, I was actually pretty good at it. I was thinking I should have maybe been working for the arson unit when I was still active in the Fire Department.'

'That's very interesting, Dad,' I started.

'Kate, why don't you let me handle the questions?' Detective

Lincoln asked. 'Sherm, how does that relate to where we are right now?'

'I'm getting there,' he said. 'You kids are just so impatient. So, like I said, I was pretty good at it. So then they started sending me out to the bigger fires, and I started catching some pretty good arsons. You know, things that some of the other investigators had missed. It was pretty thrilling. And if we got a conviction and the owner was responsible, we didn't have to pay out and I got a ten per cent bonus on the insurance payment. Well, a couple of those bonuses and I upgraded that little cabin on the ocean to my cool fishing lodge. And suddenly I'm not so bored. Even when I'm at home.'

'So you're working *for* the insurance company?' Ken asked.

'Yeah, you see these big arsons are all at big condominium developments in various stages of construction. And we always find a dead body in the ashes. And I always found the cause of the fire. Some of them were pretty tricky, like a nail that might have been accidentally pounded into an electrical circuit, but I found them.'

'That sounds pretty cool,' I said, getting hooked on the story.

'But what I couldn't find was the arsonist. He didn't leave any clues as to who he was, or at least any clues that survived the fire.'

'So you're investigating these fires?' I asked. 'Not starting them?'

'Well, I was, Katie girl,' he admitted. 'But actually I set a couple.'

'What?' we all asked.

'They were very well controlled and they were arranged with all parties involved knowing what was happening. You have to understand, this guy has done millions of dollars of damage and he's killed at least five people across Canada. And we don't have a clue who he is or even why he's doing it.'

'You killed someone?' Cam asked.

'No,' I smiled. 'He's faking them out. There weren't really dead bodies in the fires you set, it was just reported that way.'

'Good girl, Katie.'

'So you're trying to take some business and attention away from the arsonist. You're hoping you'll draw him out.'

'That's right,' he said. 'And I got even luckier. I haven't

drawn out the arsonist yet, but I drew out the guy that we think is contracting him.'

'Sims?' I asked.

'Sims,' he nodded. 'Although he told me to call him something else. I haven't even managed to get fingerprints or anything to track him with yet.'

'I did,' I smiled proudly.

'What?' Dad and Cam asked together this time.

Dad turned to Ken. 'Did she give them to you? Did you process them yet?'

'I haven't,' Ken admitted. 'I didn't think this guy was anything serious to worry about. Sometimes Kate gets a little worked up about things and blows them up out of proportion.'

'She's not exaggerating this time,' Dad said. 'You need to run those prints. It's the best lead we've had in ages.'

'I'll call in from the car and get a rush put on it,' Ken assured him. 'But I need to verify your story. I'll need your contact at the insurance company.'

Dad wrote the information down on a napkin and slid it over to Ken. 'Sorry I don't have an official card. I didn't want to risk anyone going through my stuff and finding out I was working undercover.'

'At least now I know where you get it from,' Cam said, finishing his beer.

I just smiled, enjoying my victory.

'So, what are we going to do about this big mess that we've got ourselves into?' Dad asked.

'Well, I think we have to follow through,' Ken said. 'Kate told this guy she would call with information and I think we have to do that. But at least knowing what we know now, we can control the situation. We can work together to find out where to send him and have a whole bunch of people waiting to meet him there.'

'This guy's pretty savvy,' Dad said. 'I've always thought he had Mob ties.'

'That's OK, we've got some smart guys working for us too,' Ken said. 'And we've got the element of surprise. I'm going to get back to the station and talk to some detectives I know.'

'And run those prints,' Dad reminded him.

'Yes, and run those prints. And then I'll be in touch later.'

After a few more pleasantries we saw Ken out the door as he headed back downtown to talk to his boss. I had already called Graham and asked him to run the show today, as we three promised Ken to stick close to home until he got back to us. We locked up tightly and Cam called a security company and made an appointment to get a security system installed, which Dad kindly offered to pay for, still feeling guilty that he had brought this trouble on us.

'Well, what should we do for the rest of the day?' Cam asked.

'Cards?' I asked. 'Movies?'

'Let's pound some nails,' Dad said. 'I feel like getting a little frustration out of my system.'

'We're ready to hang some drywall in the office,' Cam said. 'If you're game?'

'I'll hand you the nails,' I offered.

'Deal,' Cam said. 'And fetch the beer?'

'And fetch the beer.'

'That's my Katie girl,' Dad laughed.

'Daddy,' I said, stopping him as he turned to go down the hall.

'What is it?'

'Thank you for not being a cold-blooded serial killer.'

He laughed at me, but pulled me into a big bear hug, holding me tightly and rubbing my back. 'You're welcome, sweetheart.'

We hung drywall and pounded nails until well after the sun set. Exhausted, Cam put together some hamburgers and Dad barbecued them for us. I hauled some lawn chairs up to the roof along with copious amounts of beer, and the men followed with the food. We sat in silence, eating and drinking and watching the fireworks. It was the last night of the Stampede and the fireworks were spectacular, going on twice as long as they would on a normal night. There was a cool breeze blowing away the heat of the day, and keeping the mosquitoes to a minimum. I could have happily spent the night right here. But after the fireworks were over, we cleaned up and headed to bed, exhausted. Stampede was over for another year, and I had hardly known it was here. Boy, had my life changed from a few years ago.

Monday

Isat in my office at the Plex. I wasn't really working because there wasn't really anything to do right now. But I was supposed to look like I was. We were just going to go about our normal lives and as soon as Ken and the Calgary Police and the insurance bureau were ready and coordinated, we were going to try and get the mysterious Mr Sims. For now, we had to convince anyone who might be watching that life was just going on as normal. So I sat there, pretending I was busy, and daydreaming about what my life was supposed to be like right now. The door opening at the end of the hallway shocked me back to reality and I turned and saw Graham hurrying toward the office.

'Sorry I'm late,' he said, tossing his backpack into the corner after he'd rescued his juice bottle from it.

'You've got a good excuse, right?'

'Actually, I do. I called that guy you wanted me to call at the grief program, Ricardo Carlos, and set up an appointment with him.'

'Thank you.'

'Well, I knew you'd ask, I figured I'd just get it out of the way.'

'So what are we going to do around here this week?' I asked.

'Well, there aren't any shows until the Dance Festival next week, right?'

'Right.'

'I guess we can clean out the bar fridges, restock all the glasses, stuff like that.'

'It's not a bad idea,' I said. 'I've got way too much nervous energy right now. I think a little physical work would be a good thing. Just don't tell Cam I said that physical work was a good thing.'

'I promise. Is he back at work yet?'

'He's got at least another week off. Although he's getting much better at getting around in the brace.'

'The way he's working, with another week he should have the renovations almost done at the fire hall.'

'I know, he and Dad are just going like crazy there. It's kind of a mixed blessing.'

'Well, shall we get started?'

'Sure, why don't you start in the upstairs bar and I'll take the Rodeo Lounge. We can meet at the main bar and do that one together when we've finished the first two.'

'Do you think I should really be upstairs while you're downstairs?'

'What? You mean like those horror movies where the girls go into the dark basement despite knowing there's a serial killer down there?'

'Well, sort of.'

'I'll be fine,' I said. 'The lobby doors are locked, the place is deserted and security is patrolling. Nothing is going to happen.'

'That's what they say in those movies too.'

'Besides, Frank is probably around somewhere doing locks,' I said. I pushed my chair back from the desk and stood up. 'It's OK, Graham. Besides, if anyone comes around, I'll scream loud enough that you'll hear me three blocks away.'

'OK, but for the record I did protest. Because if you turn up dead you know Cam will be coming after me.'

I grabbed a piece of paper and a pen and scribbled on it, then I passed it over to Graham.

'There,' I said. 'You're protected.'

'"Graham tried valiantly to protect me, signed Kate",' he read. 'Yeah, that'll help.'

I wandered down the hall and found a bucket and some cleaning supplies. I filled the bucket with lots of bleach and some steaming hot water and dragged everything into the Rodeo Lounge, our private members-only room. I opened the fridges and took out all the bottles, piling them on top of the counter, then I pulled on some rubber gloves, set the bucket on the floor and got my head right inside the fridge, so I could get right back into the corners, a spot that obviously had been missed a

205

few times. But generally I was pretty pleased, my staff had been keeping everything nice and tidy. I finished with the fridge and restocked it. Then I put all the glassware into several bus pans and carried them to the back room. Graham and I would load them all up on a cart and take them to the central kitchen area, where the Plex staff could take care of them. We'd just refill from the clean stock that was always waiting there for us. I piled the linens into the laundry baskets too, and then went back to scrub down the table and countertops with my fresh bucket of water. I turned the corner into my room and almost dropped the bucket when I saw Sims sitting on one of the bar stools, an open beer in front of him.

'Fuck,' I said, setting the bucket down before I spilled it.

'Nice place,' he smiled, raising his beer to me.

'That's five bucks for that.'

'Why don't you close the door behind you,' he said. 'Quietly. And then let's just have a little talk.'

'Do you know how clichéd this is?'

'I'm sorry, I didn't know there were rules to this sort of thing.'

I reached into the bar and pulled out a beer for myself too, unscrewing the cap and taking a big drink.

'Yeah, apparently there are rules. So, I start by saying how did you get in here?'

'OK, well the locks on your doors are flimsy at best, but in order for them to provide any protection, you actually have to lock them.'

'The doors were unlocked?'

'Yeah, my good fortune,' he laughed. 'What else?'

'Well, there's what do you want, what are you going to do to me, that kind of thing.'

'And that's it?'

'Well, I might be encouraged to beg for my life if required.'

'OK, let's just expedite this, then. You won't have to beg for your life yet, so we can skip that. I'm here because you were supposed to call me and let me know what was going on.'

'Nothing is going on yet, that's why I didn't call you.'

'Did you pass my message on to your dad?'

'Yeah, he knows you're here.'

'So, you don't think that would have been something you

could have called me and told me about?' he asked. 'See, if you just leave me hanging, I think that maybe you're not taking me seriously enough.'

'Oh, I was taking you seriously,' I assured him.

'Or I think maybe you've called the police or something you shouldn't do.'

'No, no, no worries about that. I'm a smart girl. I've just been waiting for the right time to make it all happen.'

He set his beer down and reached across the bar, grabbing a handful of my hair and pulling me roughly across to him.

'OK, well we're going to start with my rules now. My rules are don't fuck with me. I've been trying to be nice to you but obviously that's not working because you're not taking me seriously enough.'

'OK, OK,' I said, my hand covering his, trying to break his grip. 'I'm taking you seriously. I have been all along, I swear.'

'Well, here's the deal. I want to meet with your dad tonight.'

'I'll have to call him and make sure it's OK,' I offered, but he just pulled harder and suddenly my face was very close to his.

'Did you hear what I said?' he asked. 'I said don't fuck with me. I don't want your dad to know. You're just going to get him somewhere and then I'll be there as a little surprise, you might say. The correct response for you is to tell me where.'

'Grounds Zero, the coffee shop downstairs?'

'Not this building, you know too many people here.'

'OK, OK,' I said, trying to think fast and not knowing what kind of place I should be coming up with. This was supposed to be Detective Lincoln's part of the job. 'Earl's on Fourth Street.'

'That's better,' he said, letting me go and taking a final chug from his beer. 'I'll be waiting on the patio. If he's not there by eight o'clock, I'll be coming by the fire hall to see what's taking so long, you understand?'

'I understand.'

'Good,' he smiled, standing up. 'Thanks for the beer.'

He let himself up and as soon as I heard him climbing down the stairs I raced up the stairs to Graham.

'Kate?' he asked, seeing me race across the lobby. 'Did something happen? Oh, shit, something did happen, didn't it?'

207

'Yes,' I said, out of breath as I finally got to him and wrapped my arms around him.

'You're trembling,' he said. 'Are you OK? Cam's going to kill me.'

'I'm really glad your first question was if I was OK,' I laughed. 'Because otherwise I might have to kill you.'

'What happened?' he asked.

'Sims was here,' I said. 'I need to get a hold of my dad.'

'Don't you mean Detective Lincoln?'

'My dad first,' I insisted.

'What happened to that new leaf you turned over? The one where you were going to stay out of things and let Detective Lincoln handle it all?'

'It's my dad he's after. I have to give him a heads up. And we need to call security. I intend to have a go at Lazlo this time because one of his fucking guards left our door open.'

'It could have been Frank that left it open,' Graham said. 'I saw him around here earlier.'

'I don't care who it was. Lazlo is responsible. And you know what, Graham?' I asked, a smile coming over my face. 'Even though it meant getting threatened, I am really going to enjoy having a go at Lazlo for a change, instead of him taking a round out of me.'

'Kate, you need help. I can recommend a good therapist.'

Dad and Detective Lincoln both wanted me in immediate police custody for safekeeping, or at least home behind our new security system. But I decided to stay with Graham and finish our cleaning for the day. I was pretty sure Sims wouldn't be bothering me again unless I couldn't get Dad to show up at the restaurant. And they both had things to do too: Dad had to get some stuff cleared with the company he was working for before he met with Sims and Detective Lincoln had to get some people into the restaurant to look after my dad. Without either Dad or Sims finding out. Yeah, I was much better off being here and cleaning out bar fridges. Plus, I had a call in to our esteemed head of security requesting that I see him as soon as possible. I didn't want to miss that one for the world.

So we finished up the bars together, replacing all the linens, all the glassware, I even polished the mirrors and the chrome.

My theatre was looking good and ready for the onslaught we would have when the new season began. But still no sign of Lazlo. I wondered if he was avoiding me like I had tried to avoid him at times. But I just couldn't imagine him doing that. I dumped the buckets of water and rinsed them out while Graham locked up the bar fridges and then we headed back up to the office.

'It's almost four o'clock, Kate,' Graham pointed out. 'I think we should get you home, shouldn't we?'

'Probably,' I said. 'I wouldn't mind cleaning up before I have to take Dad out to the restaurant tonight.'

'Are they coming to pick you up?'

'No, I'll just grab a cab, I think. Cam can't drive and I think Dad's safer at the fire hall.'

'You worried about Sims?'

'No, I'm worried about his driving,' I laughed.

'Well, I'll walk you down to the stage door and hang around until you get in a cab,' Graham said. 'And then if you're not going to need me tonight, I might call a girl about a date.'

'Krista?'

'Krista.'

'You treat her right, Graham.'

'Her brother has already warned me. Her family keeps a pretty close eye on her.'

'Good, she's a beautiful girl and I'd be worried about guys like you.'

'She warned me that her brother would probably drop by. She's on to them too. She's not as naive as everyone thinks she is.'

'Well, be nice anyway. I promised her mom I'd watch out for her too.'

We both jumped when the door at the end of the hallway opened and we saw Lazlo striding down the hallway toward us.

'Kate, Graham,' he greeted us both, nodding curtly. I noticed he remained standing in the doorway and didn't take the empty chair beside Graham.

'Have a seat,' I said, pointing to the empty chair.

'Kate, I'm a busy man today. We're doing a fire-safety sweep this week, considering all that's been going on. How about if we just get to the point here?'

'All right,' I said. 'The point is I'd like to discuss how your

209

lax security procedures almost got me killed today.'

'I don't know what you're talking about.'

'One of your guys unlocked the front door to my theatre this morning and let's just say a very unsavoury character got in and threatened me.'

'That's it?'

'What do you mean, that's it?' I asked. 'I specifically had everything locked up tight around here because I know there's this guy who's been following my dad . . .'

'What is it about you and your family that you have to get yourself mixed up in everything that is going on around you?'

'Excuse me?'

'Well, Kate, if you just focused on things that were your own concern and left everything else to us experts . . .'

'You experts? You have got to be kidding me.'

'Look, I'm in a hurry but I'll put in a report about your unlocked door,' he said, before turning away. And then he stopped and turned back for a moment. 'And Kate, you know you could have filed this with Nick instead of bothering me.'

I was so shocked I could only sit there while I watched him stride down my hallway and leave the theatre.

'So, do you feel better now?' Graham asked.

At home I had greeted the men, grabbed a glass of wine and then headed upstairs for a shower. Dad was busy with the barbecue and some steaks and Cam was putting together a salad. I dropped my clothes all over our beautiful new bedroom and turned the shower on as hot as I could stand it. I stood under the dual shower heads and let them beat down upon me. The door opened and Cam came in, sitting on the closed toilet seat and stretching his leg out in front of him.

'Everything OK?' I asked.

'I was just going to ask you the same thing,' he said. 'You've been up here a long time.'

'Yeah, well, I was honestly considering never coming out.'

'We have a pretty good hot-water tank, but I think eventually it will run out.'

'Cam, I'm so worried about him.'

'He can handle himself, Katie.'

'I don't care what anyone else says. He's a sixty-year-old

210

man. He can't run as fast as he used to run or fight as hard as he used to fight.'

'But he's probably about three times as smart as he used to be.'

'I don't know if three times is enough. He's acting like this is nothing. A day at the park.'

'I think he's taking it seriously, Katie, but he probably doesn't want to worry you.'

'Well, it's too late for that,' I said, shutting off the water and stepping out onto the bathmat. Cam pulled a towel off the rack and wrapped it around me, pulling me close to him. 'This towel is warm.'

'The towel racks are all heated. I thought it would be nice for winter.'

'Wow, you've thought of everything.'

'I tried.'

'Want to try something else?' I asked, letting the towel drop to the ground.

'Not with your dad outside that window barbecuing our dinner,' Cam said. 'I got him to like me once, but I don't know if I could do it again after something like that.'

'You are a spoilsport,' I said, picking the towel back up and wrapping it back around me.

'Get dressed and come down and have some dinner. It could be a late night tonight and we should probably have a decent supper.'

'I'll be down in a minute, then,' I said kissing him on the cheek and sending him on his way.

I dried off, put my hair into a ponytail and put on some mascara and lipstick. Then I grabbed a black T-shirt and some khaki capris and called myself done. The aroma of the barbecue from downstairs was sending out its siren call to me and my stomach started rumbling. I had never been one of those people who lost their appetite in times of trouble. I pushed my way out onto the patio and was happy to see Dad was just pulling steaks off the barbecue and piling them onto a plate.

'Oh, this looks good,' I said, sitting down and loading my plate up with corn on the cob and a baked potato.

'Nice to see you too, Katie girl,' Dad said, putting a steak down in front of me and taking a seat.

'I've already talked to you today. Besides, you know what I'm like with stress, I like to eat.'

'There is nothing to be stressed about,' Dad said. 'You're simply going to walk me down to Earl's for a beer and then leave me there with Sims. We're going to talk, and hopefully Detective Lincoln will then take him into custody.'

'Just like that?' I asked.

'Just like that.'

'It never works just like that,' I said. 'Pass me the sour cream.'

After dinner, Cam and I cleaned up while Dad had a shower and changed. I kept nervously checking my watch and was surprised at how quickly the time was passing. Finally, at about quarter to seven, Dad stood in the kitchen, dressed casually, a jacket tossed over his arm.

'You ready?' he asked.

'I'm ready.'

'Do you two really have to go alone?' Cam asked.

'Sorry, Hopalong, you're more a hindrance than a help right now.'

He pulled me in a bear hug and kissed me and then shook Dad's hand.

'I'll be home before you know it,' I assured Cam, and then we were out the door and down the street.

'So where is this place?' Dad asked as we started down the street.

'Just up on Fourth Street. It's only five blocks.'

He took my hand in his, something he hadn't done since I was a little girl.

'You've picked such a nice area to live in.'

'Well, I didn't really pick it,' I laughed.

'Well, I think Cam picked it with you in mind, not just for him.'

'Yeah, he did really well. But don't tell him I said that. I need him to sweat for a while longer.'

'I'm proud of you, Katie girl. You grew up well.'

'Thank you, Daddy. I'm really proud of what you're doing too, you know. It's just so scary.'

'And going into burning buildings wasn't scary?'

'Dad, when you were a fireman, I was a little kid. I just thought it was exciting. You had the big truck and the hoses and I got to bring all my friends to the fire hall. I honestly didn't relate to the fact that you actually went into dangerous situations and risked your life.'

'Yeah, I guess you were young. That's a pretty house over there.'

'We looked at that one.'

'What was wrong with it?'

'The rooms were small, the basement was unfinished and it was listed at five hundred and twenty-five thousand dollars.'

'For that little house?'

'Yep.'

'How many square feet?'

'Nine hundred and fifty.'

'Things have sure changed in Calgary since I lived here. What did you pay for yours, then?'

'We've got a $389,000 mortgage on that place.'

'Can you afford it?'

'I seriously doubt it but Cam seems to think so.'

'Wow, that's a hard way to start out a life together.'

'I try not to think about it,' I laughed. 'I actually fainted at the bank when we were signing the papers.'

'I can't say I blame you.'

We came to Twenty-Fourth and I led Dad down to Fourth Street. We stood on the corner, waiting for the light to change, both staring over at the restaurant, the patio half filled with people, all blissfully unaware of the danger surrounding them. The light turned and we crossed the street.

'OK, Katie girl, this is where we part. You go and pretend to make your phone call and I'll go inside and be surprised to see Sims.'

I leaned up and kissed him on the cheek.

'I love you, Daddy,' I said. He turned quickly and I watched him walk into the restaurant. I turned to go and bumped into someone standing right behind me.

'Oh, I'm sorry, I . . . Sims?' I said, recognition coming slowly. 'You're supposed to be in there waiting. I already sent Dad inside.'

'You thought I trusted you?' He laughed at me.

213

'I don't know what you're talking about.'

He took my arm. 'Why don't we just wait over here for your dad to come back out.'

I tried to pull away from him. 'Let go of me.'

He put his hand in his pocket and poked something into my ribs.

'A gun?' I asked.

'Let's just wait over here,' he said, pulling me close to the hedge that surrounded the parking lot.

We waited a couple of minutes and then Dad came out of the restaurant. He looked up and down the street and then saw us.

'What are you doing, Sims? Let my daughter go.'

'I think we all need to go for a walk,' Sims said and started to pull me down the street.

'Kate, did you know he was going to be here?' Dad asked, trying to keep up our pretence.

'You can stop playing games,' Sims said. 'I know you knew I was going to be here. There's at least three cops in there pretending to be waiters.'

'I didn't tell them anything,' I told him. 'Detective Lincoln must be following me.'

'Look, don't get all upset about things,' Sims said. 'I don't really care if you were trying to set me up or not. I wanted to talk to your dad in private and I got that. So I guess I'm happy. Of course I'll be way less happy if you happen to be wearing a wire or something.'

'A what?' I asked.

'A listening device,' Dad explained.

'Oh, well, I'm not.'

'Would you say so if you were?'

'Probably not.'

He led us across the street and down to the river bank. 'Open your shirt.'

'What?' I asked.

'She's not wearing a wire,' Dad said.

'You too, Carpenter, open your shirt.'

Dad unbuttoned his shirt and Sims checked him out until he was satisfied all was clear.

'Now you,' he ordered.

'How about if I just leave instead?' I asked, turning to head for the safety of the restaurant and try and find one of those police officers.

But he had other ideas as he grabbed my arm and roughly pulled me back, throwing me against a tree. Dad stepped forward but Sims' gun came up to my head and Dad stopped immediately. Sims held the gun against my head with one hand and patted me down with the other. I bit my tongue, trying to keep all my witty remarks inside my head and not piss him off enough to pull the trigger. Finally, he was satisfied and he moved me over to a park bench, right on the edge of the water. He sat down and pulled me down beside him, his arm going over my shoulder. Dad sat down on the bench beside us and stared out at the river. I could see his hands shaking and his jaw clenching and I knew he was fighting to keep his cool.

'So what do you want, Sims?'

'I need a job done.'

'I was assuming that's why you wanted to see me. Why'd you have to go through my daughter instead of the usual way?'

'Well, I was just getting a bad feeling about you, Carpenter. I didn't know if you were really on the up and up.'

'And why's that?'

'Because the last guy you were supposed to burn up for me was spotted on the streets of Montreal last week.'

'That gambling guy?'

'Yeah. Interesting, huh?'

'Shit, you mean I grabbed the wrong guy?'

'I guess you did.'

'Well, why didn't you just call me and tell me?'

'I'm telling you now. And I've decided I'm going to be a nice guy and give you one more chance to prove yourself.'

'I don't need your charity,' Dad almost spat at him. 'If you don't like the job I'm doing, there's lots of other people I could work for.'

'I want you to finish the job I've paid you for.'

'I told you I thought I had the right guy.'

'Well, you fucked up, Carpenter. So, can you make things right?'

'It'll take me a couple of weeks. I'll have to fly out to Montreal and find the guy . . .'

'Actually, I've saved you the work. I had some friends bring him here. See, there's another job that got screwed up that I need you to finish for me.'

'What job is that?' Dad asked.

'Your daughter's apartment building.'

'I didn't do that one.'

'I know. I thought I'd try another contractor.'

'Well, I guess that'll show you who the professional is.'

'You burned down my apartment?' I hissed at him.

'Not personally.'

'Sims doesn't like to get his hands dirty,' Dad explained.

'You almost killed my boyfriend and my father.'

'That was the whole point,' he said. 'Is she always this slow?'

'She's just a little emotionally involved here,' Dad said. 'Which is why I think you should just let her go and we can talk business.'

'No, I want you to remember me sitting here and holding a gun to your daughter's head. Just in case you decide to do anything funny, like help this guy get back to Montreal again.'

'That is not going to happen,' Dad assured him.

'Good. Because I want my gambler friend dead and I want that condo burned to the ground.'

'It's going to cost you,' Dad said.

'To fix your fuck-up?'

'No, to fix yours. You didn't contract that building to me in the first place. I'll charge you half my regular fee. Otherwise, the best I can do is kill your gambler friend.'

'I'm not giving you another dime.'

'Then we're done,' Dad said, standing up.

'Daddy?'

'Yeah, Daddy, aren't you concerned about your little girl?' he asked.

'Half,' Dad said, still standing, looking like he meant it.

'Fine,' Sims said, standing up too. 'It'll be transferred first thing tomorrow morning.'

'I'll take care of it as soon as the transfer is confirmed.'

'I'll be in touch,' Sims said, and then took off down the walking path.

I looked at Dad and then burst into tears.

'Katie girl?' he asked.

But I turned and raced for home. I threw open the door and

raced upstairs to the bedroom. I heard Cam hobbling up the stairs behind me and then he limped into the bedroom and pulled me into his arms.

'What's wrong?' he asked, rubbing my back. 'Are you OK? Where's your dad?'

'He's OK,' I sobbed.

'What happened, sweetie?'

'I just got a little scared,' I said, not really wanting him to know about the gun-to-the-head thing. 'I'll be OK.'

We heard the door open downstairs and Cam turned to go, tripping on his brace and landing on the bed.

'I am so sick and tired of this damned thing,' he said, pulling the Velcro fasteners and tossing it aside.

'Cam, please don't do that.'

'It's OK, he said getting up. 'My physiotherapist has got it taped. I can get around a lot better than you think right now.'

He hurried down the stairs to see who had come in the door I had forgotten to lock behind me, and I raced down behind him, not trusting that he was as steady on his feet as he said he was. Cam stopped halfway down the hallway and I stopped on the bottom step when we both realized it was just Dad.

'Katie girl?' he asked, not sure what kind of reaction he was going to get.

'Daddy,' I cried, and raced into his arms.

'You're OK?' he asked.

'I'm OK. I'm sorry, Dad, I was just a little freaked out.'

'You should be freaked out. Sims isn't the nicest man in the world.'

'What happened out there?' Cam asked.

'Nothing,' we both said at the same time.

'Oh yeah, two Carpenters tell you the same thing at the same time and you're supposed to believe them.'

'Dad, you wouldn't have really left me there, right?'

'Oh God, Katie girl, never. But I know Sims a little better than he thinks, and I was pretty sure about how far I could push him.'

'Push him?' Cam asked.

'Let's have a drink,' Dad suggested. 'I'm guessing Detective Lincoln will be here shortly, I'd like to have at least one beer in me before I have to tell this story in front of Cam.'

217

Tuesday

Cam had tossed and turned half the night but managed not to say too much about the situation I had gotten myself into. He finally gave up at about six in the morning, put on his robe and tiptoed downstairs. I smelled the coffee brewing but I was exhausted from the evening before and I pulled the covers back up over my head and didn't hear anything for another couple of hours. When I woke again I felt a little guilty, so I put my robe on too and made my way downstairs.

'Wow,' I said, looking at the spread on the table. 'Have a little energy to burn this morning?'

Cam had baked muffins and biscuits, and had a steaming roast pan of egg burritos with a big jar of homemade salsa sitting beside it. And the bread machine was busy churning away some dough on the side counter.

'Have a seat,' he said, pouring a coffee for me and sitting it in front of me. Then he grabbed a plate and served me up a burrito and a biscuit.

'Thanks,' I said, taking a bite.

'You ready for seconds, Sherm?' Cam asked, and Dad pushed his plate over to be refilled.

'Did you sleep well, MK?' Dad asked.

'Like the dead,' I said.

'Perhaps you could find another way to put that,' Cam suggested.

I smiled and shoved another forkful of food into my mouth. I heard a beep and noticed there was a small PalmPilot-type device sitting on the table beside Dad.

'What's that?' I asked.

Dad picked it up and pushed some buttons, checking the screen.

'It's the next generation of miniature communication devices,' he explained. 'It's like a BlackBerry tripled. I have a friend who knows a guy . . .'

'So what's it beeping for?' Cam asked.

'To confirm that my payment has been transferred into my offshore account. And I've just emailed Detective Lincoln to let him know.'

'So when are you going to do this?'

'Tonight. Sims wants it done fast and I'm ready to go.'

'Then I want to go over to the apartment this morning.'

'Don't be silly. Detective Lincoln is getting the building cleaned out and secured. We want to make sure we don't accidentally hurt someone.'

'What about this guy he wants you to kill?'

'We're going to sneak him out the back way. We've done it before.'

'Well, I'm going to the apartment. I just want to have one last look around and make sure we haven't left anything there.'

'Katie, it's just stuff,' Cam said. 'We can replace it.'

'I'm serious,' I said. 'That's six years of my life. I just want one last look around.'

'No,' Cam said.

'I agree with him wholeheartedly on this one,' Dad added.

'If Dad won't take me, I'll call Ryan or Detective Lincoln. Someone will let me in there.'

'Fine,' Dad said, and pushed a few more buttons on his device. 'I've let the detective know we'll be there at about ten this morning. After that, the building is secure and no one goes in. Understand?'

'Yes, Daddy,' I said. 'I understand perfectly.'

Cam and Dad both rolled their eyes at me, but I ignored them and turned back to breakfast.

After breakfast I cleaned up the kitchen, which was never a bad job after Cam cooked because he was a clean-as-you-go kind of guy, and I let Cam go up and have a shower first. Dad got himself cleaned up and then busied himself sending a bunch of other emails and I headed up for a shower.

'We shouldn't be too long,' I said to Cam, while I brushed my teeth and he shaved. I loved having all this counter space.

'I know you won't be,' he said. 'Because I'm coming with you.'

'No, you don't have to do that.'

'I know I don't have to but I'm not letting you head out alone again after last night.'

'Cam, you're still a gimp, you'll just slow us down.'

'Katie, you have two choices. Either I come with you or you don't go.'

'You wouldn't really stop me?'

'Try me,' he said, in the quiet voice that suggested this was not the topic to pick a fight about.

'Fine. But you're staying in the car.'

'We'll see.'

'Cam, the elevators aren't working. You're not climbing nineteen flights of stairs. I don't even know if I can do it.'

'We'll see,' he said, and then headed for the closet to get dressed.

We drove in silence. But Cam did look a little calmer, now that he was back behind the wheel of his beloved car. I sat beside him, staring straight forward and chewing some nicotine gum harshly. Dad was in the back seat, pretending he didn't notice anything amiss. We finally pulled up across the street from the old apartment building and Cam parked the car and turned off the ignition.

'Are we going to have a fight?' Dad asked.

'No, I don't think we are,' I said, noticing Cam was not making a move to open his door.

'I'll just wait here for you two,' he said.

'All right, let's get this over with,' Dad said, climbing out of the back.

'I love you,' I said, leaning over and giving Cam a quick kiss before I followed Dad across the street and into the building.

We climbed the stairs in silence, knowing we would need every last bit of oxygen to make our way to the top. I was huffing and puffing after five flights and by the fifteenth floor my legs were about to give out from under me. Somehow, I convinced myself I could make four more flights of stairs, since Dad seemed to be keeping pace with me and I didn't want to look bad. I made my way into the hallway and leaned against the wall, gulping in some air and waiting for my legs to stop shaking. Dad was breathing heavily too but he continued down the hall to my apartment.

'Katie girl, I think you should take up a regular exercise program.'

'As I recall, you had some troubles with the stairs last time you were here.'

'And I had serious smoke inhalation too. I work out. I'm in great shape for a man half my age.'

I followed him down the hall, still hurting.

'I could take you to the gym tomorrow and help you work out a program,' Dad called back to me.

'Shut up, old man,' I grumbled under my breath.

'I have excellent hearing too, by the way,' he laughed, holding open the door for me.

I gave him a dirty look and headed into the apartment. It was a mess, with smoke damage and water damage and I was pretty sure anything that was left here was pretty much ruined. I guess this had all been a mistake. But I opened up the cupboards and had a bit of a look, just so this wasn't a totally wasted trip. And then Dad's little computer beeped again. He pulled it out of his pocket and looked at the screen.

'That's strange,' he said.

'What?'

'I can't tell who this is from.'

'What does it say?' I asked.

'Ladybug, ladybug, fly away home . . .'

'Oh my God.'

'What?'

'Dad, don't you remember the nursery rhyme? What's the second line?'

'Your house is on fire and your children alone,' he finally said, understanding dawning on his face.

'It's the message Sims sent me when you and Cam were caught in the fire here the first time.'

'That bastard set me up?' Dad asked, anger clouding his features.

'Do you smell something?'

'Oh crap, it's gas.'

'Daddy?'

'We gotta get outta here, Katie girl.'

'I'm with you on that one,' I agreed.

I picked up my backpack and reached for the light switch.

'Don't touch it. Any spark could set this off. We have to get out of here now.'

For the second time I was racing down the nineteen flights of stairs in my former home. But at least this time I hadn't been breathing in smoke and trying to carry a semiconscious man down with me. It was much easier this way. I turned the corner on the last flight, hearing Dad a flight above me, breathing a little heavy. He had stopped on ten to send a 911 email message and told me to keep going.

'You OK, Daddy?' I called.

'I'm fine,' he said.

'OK, you're almost th—'

'Katie?' he called down to me.

'Oh my God.'

'Katie girl, what is it?'

'Daddy, you need to get down here fast.'

I heard his pace on the stairs quicken and he turned the corner, almost knocking me over in the process.

'What is it?' he asked, but then noticed what I was looking at. 'Oh shit.'

'Is that what I think it is?' I asked.

There were wires and what looked like PlayDoh wrapped in duct tape. But what had really caught my eye was the digital readout that was counting down rapidly to zero.

'Run, Katie girl,' Dad instructed me, pushing me through the fire doors and toward the main entrance.

'Daddy?'

'Run!' he said and I did, with him right behind me. And I did.

The smell of gas spurred me as I raced for the front door, trying to get there before it happened. I knew I couldn't do it, with my leg and all, but I tried anyway. I was still a good three or four yards away when it happened. And at first I didn't even realize what had happened. There was a huge noise and all the oxygen seemed to be sucked out of my lungs. And then I was flying. And while I sailed through the air, I realized that the building had exploded. And as I gasped in a final lungful of air, and I smelled the acrid aroma of gas, I knew that it was all over. The last thing I remember was hitting the ground.

The next thing I remembered was someone shaking my shoulder. In an annoying manner. I had a horrible headache and I didn't want to open my eyes. But they kept at it and kept calling my name, so reluctantly I slowly opened my eyes a crack.

'Sam, Ryan?' I asked. 'I'm not dead?'

'You're not dead,' Ryan reassured me. 'Though you should be. I was just crossing the street when I saw you flying through the air.'

I tried to sit up but Ryan held me against the asphalt.

'Just stay there for a few minutes and don't move. You went a long way and hit the ground hard. I'd like someone to check out your head and neck before you try moving around too much.'

'God, it would be easier if you were an accountant,' I tried a joke.

Sirens were filling the air, smoke was billowing across the street and my memory of what happened slowly came back. I turned my head despite Ryan's warnings and saw what was left of the building across the street, flames licking the clouds that hung lazily in the sky. And as my memory came back a sudden ball of fear formed in the pit of my stomach as I realized why I had been running for the door. I pushed myself up off the ground, deflecting Ryan's protective grasp, and took a couple of wobbly steps toward where that door had been. Ryan grabbed me and this time held on like he meant business. Sam took hold of the other side of me for good measure.

'Let me go!' I demanded.

But they didn't. We all just stood there and stared at the rubble that used to be a building. Tears burned my eyes and started running down my face as that feeling in the pit of my stomach slowly built, like a fuse working its way toward a detonator. And when it finally got there, my mouth opened and the explosion burst forth.

'Katie,' I screamed, my voice unrecognizable. Anguish tearing my heart into thousands of pieces. 'Katie!'

And then I couldn't stand and my legs came out from under me. Ryan held on to me and slowly lowered me to the ground.

'You're OK, Cam,' Sam said, putting her arm around my shoulder and pulling me close to her as the sobs escaped my body. 'You're going to be OK.'

*   *   *

223

I sat on the couch in the fire hall. It wasn't a home any more and I couldn't think of it that way. I could barely think at all. There was a noise in my head, a buzzing noise, blocking out all sound and filling my ears. In a way it was welcome: it drowned out all the voices that kept telling me how sorry they were. I wasn't sorry. I was angry. I was so angry I couldn't even speak. Someone put a Scotch in my hand and my hand automatically brought it up to my mouth. The burning amber liquid shot into my brain and, for a moment, I felt my head clear. I took another larger sip and my brain started functioning again. Not on its normal level, mind you, but in some basic instinctual type of fashion. I stood up, worried my legs might not hold me, but I was feeling some adrenaline running now and they felt stronger than earlier today. I set the Scotch on the table and took a few steps to the kitchen where Sam and Ryan sat at the table.

'Cam?' Sam asked, starting to stand up.

'Where's Ken?'

'He said he'd be by tomorrow,' Ryan explained.

'Why the fuck isn't he here? He needs to be fucking investigating what happened.'

'He'll be here,' Sam reassured me, a hand on my shoulder. But I pushed it off, much more roughly than I had intended.

'I want to talk to Detective Lincoln.'

'Tomorrow, Cam,' Sam said firmly, using her mother voice. 'He'll be here tomorrow and we'll figure out what's going on.'

I was about to explain in no uncertain terms why that was simply not acceptable when the doorbell rang. Ryan stood up to get it, but I pushed him back into his chair and walked down the hallway. I opened the door and then tried to slam it when I saw who was standing there. But she managed to wedge herself in and I couldn't get the door closed without doing her some serious harm.

'Get the fuck out of my house.'

'I'm alone,' she said. 'No camera crew, nothing up my sleeve.'

'You think I'm in a joking mood right now?'

'I'm sorry, it was inappropriate. Look, I'm going to take two steps backwards and you can look out and see I'm alone. Please don't lock me out until you've heard what I had to say.'

She stepped back and I hesitated. I really wanted to slam the door and never see her face again. But I didn't. I pushed the door open and looked up and down the street, making sure she was here alone.

'Satisfied?' she asked.

'What do you want, Geneva?'

'Can I come in?'

'No.'

'OK, OK. Look, I know right now you'd probably rather be anywhere but here talking to me. But I have a proposition for you.'

'What?'

'I can help you find out who did that building.'

'How?'

'I'm an investigative reporter, remember? An award-winning one.'

'Well, I'm pretty sure the police will be taking care of the investigating.'

'So where are they?'

I didn't know what to say to that one.

'Cam, don't you want to find out who killed Kate?'

More than anything in the world, I thought, because then I was going to kill them.

'Can I come in now?' she asked.

'No, there are people here. You know where that little foot-bridge is to Lindsay Park? By Holy Cross Lane?'

'I can find it.'

'There's a bench just down the pathway from that bridge. Meet me there in thirty minutes.'

'You'll really be there?'

'Thirty minutes,' I said, and then closed and locked the door.

I stood at the door for a minute, trying to get my brain working, and trying to formulate some sort of plan. I had to get rid of Sam and Ryan. If they figured out I was trying to find out who did this, they would do everything in their power to stop me. But I was unstoppable right now. It felt like it was the only purpose in my life right now and I was not going to rest until the killer was dead. After that, I didn't care what happened to me. I had nothing left to live for, so the thought of spending the rest of my life in jail didn't really bother me. I grabbed my Scotch glass from the family room and washed it out, replacing it with a strong cup of coffee. I could hear Sam and Ryan on the patio, Ryan was whispering and it sounded like Sam was crying. I had forgotten she would be sad, that she would be mourning Katie too, as would Ryan, and for a second I wanted to go and wrap my arms around her and hold her while we both cried together. But then I realized that if I did that, I would lose my purpose. I had to stay alone and strong and keep this hatred rolling around in the pit of my stomach so I could accomplish what I needed to do.

I poked my head through the patio door.

'Hey.'

'Cam?' Sam asked, dabbing at her eyes.

'I'm just going to go upstairs to bed. You guys should probably go home to your little girl now, she probably needs you more than I do.'

'Cam, we've been talking and one of us will be happy to stay here with you tonight,' Ryan said.

'I don't want you to be alone,' Sam said. 'You shouldn't be alone.'

'I need to be alone,' I said. 'I need to work a few things out in my mind. But I'll see you tomorrow, I promise.'

They shared one of those looks, the looks that said nothing to the rest of the room but spoke volumes between the couple who had been together for years and could practically read each other's mind. But then they got up and each gave me a hug before heading for their car. And then I was alone. I watched them pull away and then closed the blinds. I did a quick check of the place, turned off the coffee pot and checked the doors and windows were locked before I headed out for the river.

I cut in behind the convent and connected with the river pathway. I wanted to make sure I got a good view of Geneva before she saw me. I didn't trust that girl at all. The pathways were busy with people, some wandering, some walking dogs, some jogging or rollerblading, all of which kept me from looking obvious as I hung close to the edge and tried to fade into the shadows of the tree line. I pulled a cigarette from my pack, the one I had bought a couple of hours ago, and lit it, leaning against a tree and smoking it while I watched Geneva squirm uncomfortably on the park bench, looking up and down the pathways for me to appear when she wasn't checking her watch.

226

I finished my cigarette, liking the idea of her waiting for me, and then stubbed it out into the ground and walked over to where she was sitting. I sat down on the park bench beside her and lit another cigarette.

'Those things will give you cancer,' she said.

'I know.'

'You working on a death wish right now?'

'Sure am. Just not mine.'

'So, Cam, I guess you're interested on investigating this arson with me?'

'Well, I'm interested in finding who did it,' I admitted. 'I still haven't decided about working with you yet.'

'You know, there are some saying your father-in-law did it, and killed himself and his own daughter in his last botched job.'

'You don't believe that?'

'And I guess you don't either?'

'I guess not.'

'So you're here with me.'

'I figured I'd listen to what you have to say. Is there a law against that?'

'There's a law against what you want to do to the arsonist.'

'Are you going to try and stop me?'

'Hell, no, I'm probably going to try to film it.'

'Fine.'

'So where do we go from here?'

'How about if you tell me what you want from me? Beside some good film footage.'

'I want you to get me into the places I can't go. You've got your friend the fireman, you've got an all-access pass to the Plex, and I'm sure Detective Lincoln is more than happy to accommodate your every wish right now.'

'So where do you want to go?'

'I want to go to the fire scenes. I want to see where the fires were lit.'

'You think you can find something that the Arson Squad can't?'

'Yes, I do. Cam, I've been following these fires all across Canada. I know that the arsonist always leaves a clue, I've found them. As a matter of fact, he called me about two weeks ago. He's seen the press I can give him and I think he likes it. This is always when they start to make mistakes, when they get blinded by the celebrity.'

'And tell me why you even care. You didn't like any of us much before this.'

'You're right,' she admitted. 'If my investigation can uncover the arsonist, I will win every major journalism award this year and I will have every network fighting over me. We each have goals, Cam, those are mine. Are yours any more honourable?'

'Nope.'

'OK, then I think we make a pretty fitting pair.'

'So what do you want to do?'

'I want to get into your old building. It's the most recent and I think I can find the clue that he left me. I have to get in there before they condemn the building.'

'It's been less than twenty-four hours. We're not getting in there unless we break in.'

'OK,' she said. 'How do you want to do that?'

For a minute I just stared at her, wondering if she had any scruples or any morals. And then I realized she really was no different than me. She had a goal and she was going to reach it no matter what. And nothing and nobody was going to stand in her way.

'Meet me in the back alley at eleven tonight,' I said, not really sure what I was going to do but thinking that was late enough that most of the prying eyes would be asleep for the night.

'I'll be there.'

'And I don't want a big media circus there either tonight,' I said. 'Just you and me.'

'I'll bring a handheld video camera,' she promised. 'No crew.'

I stood up and walked away, taking another indirect route back to the fire hall, just in case she had anyone set up to follow my movements once I left her company. I never looked back once. I didn't have to. I knew she would be there tonight. I could almost smell the anticipation on her.

It was quiet out for a Tuesday night. There seemed to be half the traffic this city would normally have and most of the lights in the surrounding apartments were dimmed. I wasn't sure if it

228

was an omen for success or failure, but frankly I didn't care. I stood in the back alley, half hidden behind the dumpster in case the security guard came by on his rounds. I expected that when I got here my knees might be shaking, or my heart racing, or even that I would be overwhelmed with sadness and unable to move. But I wasn't. I felt nothing. I was disconnected from this place that was my home less than a month ago, and the life I had lived here, that had ended here earlier today. I stood there, my mind empty, scanning my limited horizon for the appearance of my accomplice. And there she was, at the end of the alley and walking hurriedly toward my wave. She was dressed all in black, as was sensible for a midnight raid, but still very stylish, I noticed. Figure-hugging knit sweater, black leather shoes that were stylish despite the rubber soles that silenced her approach and tight black leather pants. She had on a tiny backpack that I almost expected to hold camouflage make-up by Estée Lauder, and a small digital video camera in her hand.

'I'm glad you're here,' she said. 'I wasn't totally sure you would be.'

'I'm here.'

'So, what's the plan?'

'I thought I'd try my key,' I said, pulling it out of my pocket. 'If this door is blocked, we have six floors of the parkade we can try.'

'Good plan,' she laughed, pulling the key from my hand and hurrying forward. She put it in the lock and the door opened right away. We let ourselves in quickly, closing it tightly behind us.

'OK,' I said, after making sure the door was closed tightly. 'What do you want to see?'

'The exit signs,' she whispered. 'It's always in one of the exit signs.'

'Which one?'

'I don't know.'

'There's nineteen floors in this building, are you telling me we have to check every exit sign on every floor?'

'Maybe we'll get lucky,' she smiled and then turned on the camera. 'It's Tuesday night at eleven fifteen . . .'

She continued her whispered narration and headed toward the main lobby. I stood and just looked around. Nothing looked familiar. The walls were scarred with the detritus of the explosion. There were big pieces missing, and others painted black with smoke and soot, as if by a mad water-colourist. It didn't even look like the home I remembered. I picked my way through the rubble in the lobby and followed Geneva over to the north stairwell.

'Do you have a plan?' I asked her.

She had pulled a screwdriver out of her backpack and was trying to wedge the exit sign apart. I took it from her hand and popped it open, revealing nothing but a light bulb. She pulled the screwdriver back quickly and held on tightly to it.

'I have done this before, you know. I'm not one of those helpless girls you're used to dealing with.'

My hand itched to form a fist and hit her with it. But I breathed deeply and maintained control. I still needed her right now, conscious and on my side.

'What is your plan?' I asked again.

'I'll take this stairwell, you take the south one. It'll go twice as fast if we're both looking.'

'Fine,' I said, not arguing. Five minutes later I was on the second floor when I heard her racing up the stairs behind me.

'I found it,' she said, holding something tightly fisted in her right hand.

I dropped the glass cover I had in my hand, not caring that it smashed into pieces on the floor. Geneva opened her hand and revealed a little round piece of metal, about the size of a quarter.

'That's just one of those metal punch-out things, from a junction box. Like an electrician would use,' I said.

'Uh-huh. Same thing I found at every scene.'

'Geneva, these are construction sites, you'll probably find hundreds of those.'

'In the emergency-exit signs?' she asked. 'It's what he's leaving for us to find and I'm the first person that's found it. Now I just have to find a list of electricians that are new in town and cross-reference them with my list from past cities.'

'I know an electrician that's new in town,' I said. 'Frank. Frank Kotkas.'

'How do you know him?' she asked, putting her finding away in her backpack.

'He's been contracted at the Plex to replace the locks with the new electronic key-card system. We used to play baseball together when we were kids.'

'Well, that's as good a place as any to start,' she said. 'Let's go.'

'Go where?'

'To find him.'

'Nope,' I said. 'I'm finished sneaking around for one night.'

'Cam, I thought you were in this with me,' she whined, batting her lashes and flipping her hair.

'Tomorrow,' I said. 'Let me check on his schedule. And when it's safe, we'll go check out his locker at the Plex. And you bring your lists of electricians from other cities . . .'

'You don't think he's using the same name?'

'Maybe not. But maybe we'll find a name that gives us a hint or a clue or something that might point to Frank.'

'Why can't we just go now?' she tried one last time.

'Tomorrow, I'll call you after I get a hold of his schedule. If you do anything before that, I'll have you arrested.'

I didn't wait for an answer and headed for home. There was a bottle of Scotch sitting on the kitchen counter that I suddenly wanted more than anything else in the world.

Wednesday

'Wake up, you souse,' I heard through the fog in my head. And then felt a slap on my face and I flailed my arms out to try and protect myself.

'Go away,' I screamed, immediately sorry I had, as my head screamed back at me.

The covers were pulled off me and I felt myself being pushed off the bed. I tried to stop myself but I hit the floor before I fully realized what was happening. Immediately after I hit the floor I was showered with a rush of ice-cold water. My eyes finally flew open and I blinked rapidly, trying to catch my breath and understand why I was being awakened so violently from my peaceful, dreamless slumber. As I kept blinking and my eyes slowly came into focus, I saw Detective Ken Lincoln standing above me, hands on his hips, looking thoroughly disgusted.

'What the fuck are you doing here?' I asked, holding my head against the pain that followed the sound of my voice.

'Looking for you.' He picked the two empty bottles of Scotch up off the floor beside the bed and set them on the dresser.

'They weren't both full when I started,' I said, trying to pull myself into a sitting position.

'You think this is the best way to handle things?' he asked.

'I think I'd like to know how you got in here?'

'Kate's keys,' he said.

I pulled myself into an upright position quickly at the sound of her name, and made my way into the bathroom. I avoided looking in the mirror, not wanting to see my own reflection, and pulled out a handful of aspirin, swallowing them dry and wishing they would start working immediately. I grabbed a towel and wiped the water off my face and chest, pulling off my soaked T-shirt and tossing it on the floor beside the laundry basket.

'I think you should leave,' I finally told Ken.

'Cam, we need to talk.'

'I don't want to talk. I want you to get the fuck out of my house.'

'Cam . . .'

I grabbed his arm and pulled him out of the bedroom, down the stairs and to the front door, which I opened and held for him.

'Don't do this, Cam,' he said. 'We have to talk, it's very important.'

I pushed him roughly through the door and tried to close it, but he had his body still partly inside.

'Don't make me hit you, Ken,' I begged him.

'Don't make me arrest you, Cam.'

'I don't want to talk to you,' I said. 'Not right now.'

'Cam, I have to talk to you.'

'Where were you yesterday, huh? I thought you were our friend and I didn't see you around here yesterday.'

'There were things I had to do. Look, Cam, I can explain it all, but not out here. We have to go inside.'

'Fuck you,' I said, pushing him outside the door and then closing and locking it.

I stood there for a minute, feeling the emotions trying to break through, and overwhelmed by the sense of them. I took a deep breath, formed my hand into a fist and pounded it into the cinder-block wall. Then I hurried upstairs for the shower. I had things I had to do today.

I ran the hot-water tank dry, standing in the shower for so long, and then still stood under the cold water for another few minutes before I finally started to feel human again. I took more aspirin and a big glass of juice to try and get my blood sugar up. Although I wasn't sure if that was a big problem after all the alcohol I had put into my system last night. I made a quick call to the Plex and got the information I needed. Then I dialled my second call.

'Geneva, it's me,' I said into her voicemail. 'Meet me at the stage door at the Plex at noon. And try not to look quite so obvious.'

I stood outside the stage door waiting for Geneva to arrive, so we could go down and rifle through the lockers of people that I had called my friends just a few short days ago. Geneva finally appeared, walking down the street, not a camera truck in sight. I was surprised she had been so willing to give up her spot-light, until I noticed the little hand-held video camera was slung over her shoulder. She had tried her best to look normal, to fit in, wearing jeans and a nondescript white T-shirt. But she couldn't turn off her smile, or the sparkle in her eyes. And I had noticed her red hair still swung freely across her shoulders. Kate would have pulled hers back into a ponytail to try and appear a little more incognito. But a beautiful woman couldn't stop being a beautiful woman. I should know, I had lived with one for the past year.

'Are we ready?' Geneva asked.

I nodded and led her into the building. There was a security guard on the desk who was fairly new and didn't seem to know that condolences were the order of the day. Rather, he smiled as I signed in, and then buzzed open the door for me. I held it while Geneva passed through, and then headed down the stairs, with her following closely from behind. I crossed the floor in the second basement and opened the door to our locker room. It was empty and no one was due in or out for the next hour at least. The locker on the far left had a strip of masking tape on it, marked Frank Kotkas, in a black permanent marker. I grabbed the lock and looked at the back; he still had the combination taped on the back, trusting that none of us really wanted to steal his things. I flipped the lock open quickly and opened the locker. I stood there, not really able to bring myself to going through his personal belongings. Geneva, sensing my inner turmoil, pushed me roughly out of her way and emptied the locker.

'We can't do this,' I said.

'Cam, go get yourself a coffee and give me five minutes.'

I stared at her, knowing she was right. We had come this far and there was no turning back now. I left her alone and went to my office. I came back with a couple of coffees in Styrofoam cups and handed one to her. She had searched everything and already had it back in the locker, pretty close to the way we'd found it.

'I take it you've done this before?' I asked, handing her a cup.

She sat on the floor and took it from me, taking a sip and smiling up at me. 'Journalism is a dirty business.'

'Well, finish that up and let's get out of here,' I instructed her, standing by the door and watching for signs of anyone approaching us.

'You haven't asked the million-dollar question,' she said, still sitting on the floor in front of the locker.

'What million-dollar question?' I asked.

'Geneva, did you find anything?'

'Well, Geneva, did you find anything?' I asked, sarcasm dripping from my voice.

'Yes, Cam, I did.'

'You did?' I asked surprised and hurrying over to her. 'What did you find?'

'I found this,' she said, setting up a bottle of lighter fluid on the floor.

'So, maybe he's a smoker.'

'And this and this,' she said, adding some matches and two more cans of lighter fluid to the line-up.

'Well, that is a little excessive,' I admitted.

'And this.'

She held up a T-shirt and then another, identical and with a very distinctive logo.

'What're those?'

'T-shirts. Don't you recognize them?'

'Should I?'

'This is the exact same T-shirt that was soaked with lighter fluid and started the fire in the dumpster outside the stage door here.'

'Really?' I was shocked.

'And these,' she said, bringing out a handful of the same metal plugs we had found at the loft last night.

'Wow,' I said, more shocked than I could say.

'I was right. It's Frank.'

'It's Frank?' I repeated.

'All right. When is he on duty? I need to get a camera crew together and confront him. You can have the police here to arrest him. It'll be great.' She tucked all the items into her backpack and closed up Frank's locker.

'We can't do that.'

'And why not?'

'That's not enough evidence,' I stammered. 'We have to catch him in action.'

'In action?'

'Setting another fire.'

'But that could be weeks or even months from now. I need to get this wrapped up now.'

'Maybe, if he thinks you're on to him, he'll get pressured and do his next job sooner and then try and get out of town.'

'I don't know . . .'

'Imagine the shot, Geneva, imagine it. An abandoned condo construction site, a man trussed and tied and waiting to become the city's next murder victim, and you and your crew get Frank on camera trying to light the fire. And as soon as he's off the site, you'll have your footage, the police will arrest him and the Fire Department can save the day.'

I was trying my best to channel Kate. She could talk people into almost anything. I didn't know if it was working, but I held my breath and waited. And then I saw her eyes light up as she visualized the scene, the camera angles, and how she would look against that backdrop. And I knew I had her.

'Well, if he behaves anything like the last time, he'll be calling me tonight, twenty-four hours after the fire. I'll tease him with something, make him think I'm on to him, and then we'll just have to follow him until it happens.'

'OK. Let's get out of here before we get caught,' I said, closing up Frank's locker and pulling her up off the floor.

'What's the hurry, big guy?' she asked, as I hurried her up the stairs.

'I've got somebody I've got to meet,' I said. 'Don't want me to be late and raise suspicion, do you?'

I pushed her through the stage door and out onto the street, in case we ran into anyone I knew who would want to get into a long and complicated conversation, something I really wanted to avoid right now.

'I suppose you're right,' she said. 'You know, I'm really amazed at your control. I figured the minute you knew who it was, you'd kill him.'

'Well, I'm showing amazing self-control right now.'

'Well, I'll stick to the Frank detail right now,' she said, as a E-News TV van pulled up for her. 'I'll call you if I find anything out.'

I waved goodbye but found I couldn't say another word. I strode across the street and got into my car, and raced down to Graham's house. I got there without the benefit of traffic tickets or police escorts and parked half on the driveway, half on the grass, not even bothering to close the door as I raced to his front door. I rang the doorbell several times and then started pounding on the door. Graham's dad opened the door and I raced past him and saw Graham sitting on the couch in the living room.

'Cam,' he sobbed, his face tear-stained.

I threw myself across the living room and tackled him, forcing him down on the couch and holding my face inches from him.

'I want you to tell me the truth,' I said.

'Swear to God,' Graham said. 'Anything.'

'Swear on your mother's grave.'

'I swear,' he said. 'What's wrong?'

'Did you start the fire in the dumpster at the Plex?' My hands were on his collar and they were shaking.

'I told you I did.'

'By yourself?' I pushed him. 'No help from anyone? No one coercing you into it?'

'I did it all by myself. I told you I was frustrated and I'm really sorry it ever happened.'

'Tell me about it.'

'What do you mean?'

'Tell me how you did it.'

'I stole a T-shirt from Mom's drawer. It was from one of those volunteer things she did. Cam, what's wrong?'

'Tell me how you did it!'

'I soaked the T-shirt in lighter fluid and I buried it in the dumpster. I lit a cigarette and dropped it in. I didn't want it to start right away. I didn't even know if it would start. But it worked.'

I let him up and fell to the floor beside him. Graham's dad stood in the doorway watching us.

'What's wrong, son?' Nathan asked me.

'Everything's wrong,' I said. 'Everything is wrong.'

Nathan walked across to the bar and pulled out three beers. He handed one to each of us and uncapped the other one for himself.

'Why don't you tell me about it, Cam. We're your friends. Maybe we can help you figure this all out.'

'I think I know who did it. I think I know who killed Katie.'

And then I felt those emotions again. Only there was nothing around that I could safely hit and force the pain back deep inside me. And it exploded. Graham slid to the floor beside me and wrapped his arms around my shoulder. He knew first hand what it was like and somehow that was strangely comforting.

I was back at the Plex, talking quietly to Nick. I had emptied out my locker and filled out the paperwork for an extended leave. I was changing from medical time to personal leave and there was a whole other set of paperwork required for that.

Nick had whispered his condolences through eyes blinking back tears, and then we had quickly changed the subject to the impending hockey season and how the Flames were going to do this year. We both turned when I heard the basement door open and we saw Frank coming up the stairs. I took a deep breath and tried to summon the right emotions, the fake emotions, the ones I was supposed to use to make this work. But they weren't there, nothing was. I strode over to the door.

'Cam, I've just heard what happened and I'm so sorry . . .'

He didn't get to finish his sentence because I couldn't find it in myself to stick to the original plan. Instead, I had let the frustration I was feeling take over and I hit Frank with everything I had in me, and he was on the floor, blood dripping from his nose. Feeling slightly satisfied, at least for the moment, I turned and headed out the stage door and back to the fire hall. That would have to do.

I poured myself a stiff drink and turned on the television, settling myself on the couch because the bedroom was too empty to spend too much time in. And there, on the news, was the image of me hitting Frank, him falling to the floor, and then me hurrying out of the building. I should have known Geneva and her latest sycophant wouldn't be too far away. She smiled as she reported live from the scene, happy with her footage. You could almost see her quiver with excitement as she wondered out loud what would happen next at this troubled arts complex. I flicked the TV off and waited for the telephone to ring. I knew it would and I wasn't disappointed.

Thursday

I woke up stiff from sleeping on the couch and still in the clothes I had fallen asleep in. There were several empty beer bottles lining the coffee table and I realized I probably shouldn't have had that many, since I wanted to try and keep my wits about me today. Geneva had called and told me the arsonist had called her and told her that he had one more job to do in this city and then he was gone. He had challenged her as the famous investigative journalist to try to catch him. She told me she was going to do some snooping today and get back to me this afternoon, after she'd nailed down the site where he would be setting the fire. She sounded so sure of herself that I didn't even bother questioning her.

I picked up the beer bottles and generally tidied up the place. It was partly out of habit and partly to keep myself busy. I left a message on Ryan's voicemail and then left another message on Ken's voicemail and then got into the shower, so I wouldn't have to actually talk to any of them if they called me back.

I still hadn't heard from Geneva by the time I was finished up in the shower, so I went downstairs and gathered some drywall, thinking I might try and get some hung in the guest bedroom. I was sure pounding nails would make me feel better, since hitting things really seemed to be working for me. The phone rang and I listened as the answering machine picked up.

'Cam,' the voice said. 'Cam, pick up.'

But I couldn't. It was Katie's mom.

'Cam, I need to talk to you,' she said. 'Please if you're there pick up.'

There was a pause while she willed me to cross over to the phone and answer her.

'Then if you're really not there, call me back the very minute you get home. Cam, I really need to talk to you soon. It's very important.'

'Yes, I'm sure it is,' I screamed to the empty walls. 'You would like to know why I let your daughter get killed. Well, Aggie, I'll talk to you about that when I've taken care of the killer.'

I threw the hammer across the room, narrowly missing the window but putting a huge dent into the cinder-block wall. And then the phone rang again and Geneva's sultry voice came on the answering machine. I let the tape pick up her message as well, still not feeling like I had enough control to talk to anyone.

'OK, Cam, I'm pretty sure I know where it's going to be. I want you to meet me at the Vale Point condo project at exactly six thirty tonight. Don't be early, because I've got the timing of the security guard's schedule and I don't want you to screw this up. Call me if you have any problems getting there, otherwise I'll see you tonight.'

I smiled to myself. There was almost an end in sight, a moment when this would all be over and I could just lose myself in this pain I kept fighting.

I kept busy all day, pounding nails, framing, work that helped with the anxiety and frustration. Though I was pretty sure whoever looked at this workmanship later would not be very impressed. But it wasn't about accuracy for me today, just about anger. At five o'clock I couldn't stand it any more and I got myself cleaned up and got in the car. I wouldn't get there too early, but I just couldn't sit here for another minute.

The Vale Point development was in the far north-west of the city, past Country Hills and you could get a good view of the street lights of Airdrie when the sun went down, so close were the two cities to encroaching upon each other. I parked a couple of blocks away and sat in the car for several minutes, screwing up my courage. Then I got out of the car and worked my way slowly toward the construction site. There was fencing up but nothing insurmountable. The sign warned of security guards patrolling regularly, but I didn't see any sign of another human being nearby. I tiptoed across the loose earth, trying not to disturb anything that could make noise and give away my presence. I poked my head through the window opening of one of the buildings and saw signs that our arsonist had been there, several buckets of turpentine being piled up, a gasoline can and an empty coffee pot all sitting under the circuit box. But there was no sign of anyone around.

'Cam?' I heard my name whispered.

I tried not to jump, but my heart started racing as I turned around and saw Geneva tiptoeing her way across the construction site toward me.

'I thought I told you not to be early,' she whispered angrily.

'You did, but traffic was light.'

'You could have ruined everything. Do you know how hard this was for me to set up on such short notice?'

'I'm sure it was,' I said, but I turned back to the building, playing the game with her. 'But look, he's been here. His tools of the trade are piled up and waiting.'

When I turned back, I saw something out of the corner of my eye, something falling toward my head. I tried to get my arm up and protect myself, but it was too late. And almost as soon as I felt the pain explode in my head, I felt the world grow dark.

I woke up, my head still pounding, and grateful not to be dead. Which surprised me. That I was grateful, that was. But then I remembered I had unfinished business here. I didn't care if I died, but I was going to take the arsonist with me. I noticed that the cans of turpentine and the gasoline were now set up, the timer on the coffee pot set and the circuit box open. Someone had been busy while I had been unconscious. I heard a moan next to me and turned, half expecting to see Geneva trussed up like I was.

'Cam?' she said.

Instead of beside me, Geneva's voice had come from above.

'Cam, are you awake?' I felt the pointed toe of a shoe poking into my shoulder.

'Geneva?'

'Good, glad to see I didn't cause too much damage. How many fingers am I holding up?'

'Geneva?'

'Or maybe I did cause some damage? Are you in there, Cam?'

'I don't understand.'

I heard another moan beside me and turned to see Frank, tied up and struggling against his ropes. His mouth was taped shut with duct tape.

'Oh my God, it *was* you?' I asked.

'Yes, it was me.'

'So this whole investigative journalism this is your cover? Isn't that a lot of work?'

'Actually, my dear man, the arson is what got me here. I was stuck in armpit Saskatchewan doing human-interest stories. Do you know how many farmers say they've grown potatoes that look like the Virgin Mary? And then one day, when there was a cave-in at the potash mine, I thought that was my ticket out.

A big story that could go on for days, national coverage. And they flew in a reporter from Regina to cover it. I was out, just like that.'

'I'm sorry,' I said. I know Katie always told me she tried to keep these people talking until she could figure out what to do, and that was my goal now.

'But then I set a fire and funny enough I made sure that me and my news crew just happened by at exactly the right time. There was nothing the network could do, I was there and I covered the story and it got picked up nationally.'

'And that's how you came to Calgary?'

'Don't be stupid,' she spat out at me. 'One story does not make me a nationally sought-after commodity. But I set another and another. Not too fast and not too many. But I started getting fewer human-interest assignments and more hard news. And then the most interesting thing happened. One day, I was minding my own business and this man came up to me and suggested he would like something burned down. And he wanted a body disposed of in the fire. And he offered me a huge amount of money to do it for him. Well, that story got me moved to Regina and it was only a few more after that before the big cities started sending out offers.'

'So here we all are?'

'Here we all are,' she said. 'Although some of us will no longer be here in a few short minutes. I hear it's not a horrible death, though. Apparently the smoke gets you first and you'll be dead before the fire ever hits you.'

'Well, that's comforting.'

'You know, it's too bad really. I was hoping I could get this done before you arrived, and that maybe you and I would have a bit of a future together. At least a few good rolls in the hay, so to speak. You've always seemed very athletic.'

'Yeah, well I guess they can take the girl out of the small town, but they can't take the trashy slut out of the girl.'

She looked at me for a moment and then slapped my face.

'Well, thanks for that. At least now I have no regrets about killing you,' she said.

'Anything I can do to help,' I said. Now that she was far enough away, I was able to try and get my Swiss Army knife out of my back pocket.

242

She crossed back over to the circuit box and inspected her work for the last time, while I opened the blade on my knife and worked at the bonds that held my wrists. I was sloppy in my mechanisms and cut into my wrist a couple of times, but I didn't give up. I had to get free before she was finished or that really was the end. I felt the last piece of fibre finally give way just as Geneva turned around. She realized that I was free the same instant I realized she was about to set the fuse. I lunged for her as she tried to reach into her pocket for what looked like a gun. I hit her hard and she fell to the ground, with me on top of her. The gun flew across the floor and landed at Frank's feet. All I could think of was pulling that trigger and watching the blood flow out of her, speaking Katie's name over and over again until her veins were empty and her heart could no longer beat. I left her on the ground, the wind knocked out of her, and picked up the gun. I aimed it at her, trying to decide where the most painful spot would be, the spot that would cause the greatest suffering and the slowest death possible. Geneva, seeing me holding the gun on her, slowly stood up and that award-winning smile slowly reappeared on her face.

'Cam, you don't want to do this,' she said.

'Oh, you're so wrong there,' I said. 'I really want to do this.'

'I don't think you can. I don't think you have it in you.'

'Maybe I didn't two days ago, but I assure you I'm a changed man. I am perfectly capable of doing this now and enjoying every minute of it.'

'Cam, have you ever thought about how far we could go if we were in this together?'

'Geneva, you can't even begin to measure up to the woman you took from me. Don't even try.'

'OK, how about this, you'll be no better than me if you pull that trigger.'

'I can live with that,' I said, taking my final aim.

'But I can't,' another voice said. 'I can't live with that.'

What, so now I was going to start hallucinating?

'Put the gun down,' the voice told me. 'You've caught her and she's going to jail. It's over.'

I turned slowly, expecting to see an angel, floating in the clouds, sent from above, golden halo, trying to save my soul from the eternal-damnation track I had it on right now. But it was no angel. My Katie stood there. In jeans and a T-shirt, her dad standing right behind her.

'Cam, if you've ever loved me, you'll give me that gun,' she said, holding out her hand and taking a step toward me.

And as always, I was pretty much putty in her hands. Katie only had to ask for something and I would try everything in my power to give it to her. I held the gun out and she took it, tentatively, and passed it quickly to her dad, who unloaded it and put it in his jacket pocket. Then Katie crossed the rest of the way and wrapped her arms around me. She was real, I could feel her as my arms encircled her. I could feel her breath on my neck and feel her heart beating against my chest.

'I'm so sorry, Cam,' she cried.

'Katie?' I choked out, still not really understanding what was happening.

'Thank you,' Geneva called to her, over my shoulder. 'Thank you for saving my life.'

Katie pulled away from me but I was reluctant to let her go.

'There's just one little thing I have to do,' she said, undoing herself from me and crossing over to Geneva.

'Thank you,' Geneva said again, and I noticed her knees were shaking.

'Geneva, I want you to know I didn't stop Cam from shooting you for you. Frankly, I would have been more than happy to load the bullets for him myself. I just didn't want him to have to live with that every day for the rest of his life. So I guess I only have one thing to say to you.'

And then my dead girlfriend hauled back and hit Geneva with every ounce of strength she could muster. And Geneva fell to the ground, staring up, trying to figure out how she had got down there. If this were a cartoon, there would be stars and birds circling her head.

'And the only thing that makes me happier than that,' Katie continued, 'is the fact that you're going to have to wear an ugly orange jumpsuit for the next twenty-five years. No more suede or leather, no expensive highlights in that pretty hair, and the paparazzi will be taking pictures of you with your roots showing and plastering them all over the front pages of the newspapers all across this country. Now that's what I call justice.'

And then she turned and took my hand, leading me out of the

building. On our way out, I noticed that Detective Lincoln was there, along with half of the City of Calgary Police and Fire Departments. And then I saw a spotlight go on and a camera was filming Geneva, who still lay on the ground, but now was on her stomach as two police officers searched and handcuffed her.

'This is Leslie Horton from Global TV, here at the Vale Point Condominium development, where the arsonist that has been terrorizing Western Canada has just been caught . . .'

We both snickered at that, but kept on walking to the car. I had to get Katie home. I had to make sure she was real and wasn't going to disappear on me again.

Friday

The barbecue was going and there were countless steaks marinating in our amazingly gigantic subzero refrigerator. This was Dad's last night in town, and Ken Lincoln and his wife were here, along with my friends and co-workers, all anxious to find out why I wasn't dead. I was just happy they were glad to see me and none of them was ready to kill me . . . again.

I refilled my glass from the pitcher of margaritas that sat on the patio table while Cam started taking orders for the steaks. Sam had managed the baked potatoes and desserts, and I had opened a few bags of salads. Cam had thrown some raisins and walnuts over the top, to make it seem like I had actually done more than open a bag.

'So, when Dad and I saw the bomb, we knew someone was on to him,' I said.

'And I knew we couldn't get out of there in time,' Dad added. 'The timer was set to a very short period of time. They wanted us dead.'

'So how'd you save yourself?' Ryan asked.

'We were racing for the door,' I said. 'And then Dad pushed

me into the garbage room and up into the dumpster.'

'I figured that was our best chance,' he said. 'We had the concrete wall and reinforced steel door between us and the blast, plus the steel of the dumpster and the garbage might even cushion some of the blast.'

'And I'm still trying to scrub it out of my hair. I have never smelled an aroma like that in my life.'

'But it worked,' Dad said. 'And then when the coast was clear, we called Detective Lincoln and hatched our plan.'

'Yeah, imagine two Carpenters coming up with a plan,' Detective Lincoln laughed. 'And I thought my life was difficult before.'

'Well, it worked,' I said. 'And no one was hurt, right?'

'Almost,' Cam said. 'I do have a big goose egg on the back of my head.'

'Kate, I understand you not telling us,' Graham said. 'But what about poor Cam?'

'I tried to tell him,' I defended myself. 'But Mr Caminski is about the most stubborn man on the planet and he wouldn't listen to anyone.'

'What do you mean?' Sam asked.

'Well, I sent Detective Lincoln to talk to him and he tried twice, but Cam either ignored the phone or threw him out of here. And thank you, Ken, for not charging my boyfriend with assaulting a police officer.'

'You're welcome,' Ken said. 'But please remember that's normally not one I like to let slide.'

'Point taken,' Cam said.

'I even had my mother call him,' I said. 'But Cam was too busy either getting drunk or trying to find my killer. And I guess I can't really get mad at him for that, can I?'

I raised my glass to him and he blew me a kiss. And suddenly I was sorry we had invited everyone over, because all I could think about was taking him upstairs to bed in our new home.

'Well, cheers that Kate's alive,' Graham said, raising his glass, and everyone joined in.

'Graham, I am especially sorry to put you through that after what you've been through in the last couple of months,' I told him.

'It's OK, Kate,' he said, 'I'm working through it. And I

understand that you had to do it. For the greater good and all.'

'Graham, your good will always be the most important thing to me. You know that, right?'

'I know that. I just forgot it for a minute or two there.'

'Well, since we're getting all mushy here, I guess we have some news too,' Sam said.

She looked over to Ryan, who smiled and took her hand.

'We're pregnant!' he said, beaming.

Everyone let out a cheer and Cam and I were the loudest.

'And it's a girl,' Sam said. 'At least according to the early ultrasounds.'

'Another girl,' I smiled.

'And with Graham and Nathan's permission, we thought we might name her Rose.'

I had tears in my eyes, and I looked over to see the same in Graham's and his dad's eyes as well. Nathan took his son's hand and squeezed it and then turned to Sam and Ryan.

'We would be honoured with your choice,' he said, wiping the corner of his eyes with his shirt sleeves.

'Damn, I need another beer,' Cam said, wiping at his eye too. 'You know, us guys aren't supposed to have all this emotional stuff thrown at us in one day. How do you expect us to handle it?'

'More beer,' I laughed, popping a fresh one for him.

'Is that how you handle it?' he asked.

'And making wild passionate love with your girlfriend the minute all these people leave,' I whispered into his ear.

'Well, that I think I can handle,' he laughed, taking a big drink of beer. 'OK, everyone, time to get out. It's late and I'm sure you've all got homes to get to.'

'Cam!'

'Fine, but everyone is getting their steak done rare!'

When everyone was finally fed, I fixed a plate for Cam and myself and we sat down at the table, next to Dad, who was deep in conversation with Detective Lincoln.

'What are we being so serious about?' I asked.

'Sims,' Dad said.

'What about him?'

'We lost him, Kate,' Ken told me. 'We followed him up to the airport and then lost him.'

'Should we be worried?' I asked.

'I don't think so,' Ken said. 'He's too well known here. And Geneva has been more than happy to tell us everything she knows about him.'

'He's gone into hiding, Katie girl,' Dad assured me. 'And I'll find him eventually. But for now, I'm happy if he's hiding.'

'OK, well I suppose that if you're happy I can be happy.'

'Good. Katie girl, there's something else I'd like you to know. And you can't argue with me because I've already done it.'

'Oh, God, what now?' I asked.

'Well, I make ten per cent of what the insurance company would normally have to pay out on a job like this. And because there's such a large number of fires involved here, they've offered me a very generous settlement.'

'Good, then I don't have to worry about you and that silly fishing lodge.'

'Well, see, that's the thing, Katie girl, I don't want to have to worry about you either. I've deposited ten per cent of my ten per cent into your bank and asked your banker to pay off your mortgage with it.'

'Daddy?' I asked, shocked and at a loss for words.

'We can't let you do that,' Cam stepped in for me.

'Well, see I knew you'd say that, so that's why I went ahead and did it without asking.'

'Daddy . . .'

'Look, your mother and I started out in debt and it was hard. I want to be able to take this opportunity and help you kids to start out free and clear. You can travel, or you can renovate or you can work on some grandchildren for me. But whatever you choose to do, you can do it with a freedom that we didn't have, because you won't have a huge mortgage to pay off.'

'Oh my God, Daddy, that is the most amazing thing anyone has ever done for me.'

'No, actually your mother pushing that gigantic head of yours out when she gave birth to you was the most amazing thing anyone has ever done for you. This is just an old man with more money than he knows what to do with. And now I'll have to do something equally self-sacrificing for your brother too. People are going to start to think I'm a nice guy.'

'I promise,' I said, the tears overflowing my eyes. 'I promise I won't tell anyone you're a nice guy.'

Epilogue

I sat on my patio and looked at my view. It's not the view I'm used to, not the one I've looked at for the last six years of my life. Instead of looking to my right and around a wall to see what weather is blowing in, I can look at it straight on. The wind is harsher up here, blowing in unbidden and unfettered by any high-rise towers. But it is sweeter too, as it blows across the neighbourhood gardens, picking up the scent of sweet peas and honeysuckle. Behind me is a wooden arbour, set up to allow some privacy from the neighbours. There was nothing growing there yet, but I was promised some honeysuckle of my own before the season was out, providing the unique prairie flavour that Cam had grown up with. I stood staring, trying to memorize my new place in the world, watching the sun slowly set over the horizon, casting a pink glow as its rays reflected off the snow-capped peaks that were just beyond my vision.

I heard a noise behind me, coming up the stairs. Cam was not his usual quiet stealthy self while still struggling with his leg brace, which he had been sentenced to for another two weeks. I fought the urge to turn and make sure he was OK, as I knew he was growing weary of being dependent. Instead, I let him walk up behind me, wrap his arms around my waist and pull me close to him.

'It's going to get chilly in about ten more minutes,' he said. 'Do you want a sweater?'

'No, you're warm enough for both of us,' I said, realizing my tank top and shorts weren't going to take me through the evening. We were at a pretty high elevation, being almost in the Rockies after all, and evenings got cool.

We just stood there, locked in each other's embrace, watching the sky go from pink to golden to a deep indigo as the sun set lower and the stars started to appear.

'I've got the barbecue warming up,' he said.

'We have got to start eating earlier, like normal people do.'

'Well, when we lead a life like normal people do, maybe that will happen.'

'You're such a smart ass.'

'Dinner in about half an hour?' he asked.

'That'll give me time to make a salad.'

'Make a what?'

'Well, I am a homeowner now, I feel like I should contribute a little here and there. I think I'm ready to do a salad, don't you?'

'I'd be honoured if you made the salad.'

'Just don't expect too much from me too soon.'

'No worries there.'

'You know, Cam, I didn't think you could really do it, but you did.'

'Do what?'

'You brought me home.' I blinked quickly, before he could see how watery my eyes were getting all of a sudden. 'Come on, let's go make dinner.'

I led the way down the stairs, moving slowly in case he needed help, but he was getting pretty good at being Hopalong. We walked through the destruction that was our second floor, still awaiting a main bathroom and guest-room completion, although I had my beautiful bedroom to go hide in when the construction got to be too much to bear. I led him down the next flight of stairs and marvelled that he had managed to finish the kitchen and family room with my dad's help. And a few other friends. We even had furniture in now, a beautiful oak dining table that could seat sixteen if all the leaves were put in, big leather couches and oversized armchairs in the family room, just as pretty in our place as they had been in the store window where I had been dreaming about them for months now. The floors were covered with cork flooring and the walls had been drywalled and plastered, painted in rich earthen tones. And then there was my present to Cam, his Sunday-afternoon dream come true, a 54-inch plasma TV, mounted on one wall of the family room, complete with 120-watt surround sound.

He loved it for his Sunday-afternoon football games, which I promised to give him this entire season of without complaining even once, but I sure loved my movies on it too. So we had another year of construction ahead of us and three rooms we could retreat to when we couldn't stand the smell of sawdust. And there was the garage, which proudly held Cam's bright white Hemi Barracuda, surrounded by his tool chests and exhausted to the outside. Sometimes I caught him just standing in that room and staring, like he couldn't believe it was all his. But then I did that too sometimes.

Cam went out to check the barbecue and I pulled out some appropriate vegetables from our super gigantic subzero fridge. I set things up on the stainless-steel counter, selected a knife that I felt secure that I wouldn't chop off a finger with, and set to work. I selected one of the bottles of homemade salad dressing that Sam had dropped off, and tossed everything in the salad bowl and waited for Cam to return with the steaks. The phone rang and part of me felt like ignoring it, a big part. But the other part of me picked up the receiver.

'Kate and Cam's love nest,' I greeted the caller.

'Kate?'

'Yes?'

'Kate, it's Ken Lincoln.'

'Oh, Ken, Detective, I'm sorry. Just being a smart-ass again,' I tried to explain, my cheeks feeling warm as they changed to red.

'It's OK, Kate, I remember what it was like when we got our first place,' he laughed.

'Ken, I swear, I haven't stumbled across a dead body or interfered in any ongoing police investigations for several days. So what can I do for you?'

'We need to talk,' Ken said. 'I just wanted to let you know I'll be over in about ten minutes and wanted to make sure you were home.'

'Is everything OK?' I asked.

'Well, Kate, I think it's better we discuss that when I get there, if you don't mind.'

'Ken, you're worrying me.'

'Well, once again, Kate, if you had told me what you were planning on doing, we wouldn't be having this problem now.'

'Ken, am I going to jail?' I asked, his tone of voice making me a little nervous.

'Well, you might be wishing for jail when I'm finished with you,' he said, and then the phone line went dead.